For the grandchildren of Wendell & Stephanie Dietz:
William, Andrew, Laura, Andres, Daniela, Anthony,
Samuel...and the single great grandchild, Jonathan

CHAPTER 1

Gary—

Gary, Indiana.

"Gary, Indiana! Gary, Indiana! Gary, Indiana!"

My orders are simple: assimilate primes, nihilists, undesirables. Where assimilate means poison darts shot out of my eyeballs. Suck vacuum, recalcitrants!

Blaze on dying Earth, dying people! Your hordes shall be assimilated. And the children will lead—

Ian Scanlan had to write a 500-word essay for the nuns by tomorrow. He tried to shift his attention from the constant space battle in his head. He scratched out the doodles he'd scribbled, went on to the next page in the notebook. He read too much science fiction. He kept too many notebooks.

(Kids liked devices. So did Ian. Ian liked pens and paper.)

The essay had to be about the future, what he hoped for. He kept twitching, stealing glances out the front window. What does that even mean? Stealing a glance? He was alone in the new place, his dad wouldn't be home for hours. He sat in the living room before the big front window, like another piece of furniture. Plenty to see, to steal out the window—

The Terrace, a consolidated community, near what had been Gary, Indiana, was an unpaved hellhole of approximately 1000 prefabs. Do the math! Twenty rows of fifty each. Ten sets of rows facing each other. Ian had three, white to gray, rectangular boxes across the street in front of him, all with big front windows. They were thick, plastic windows. Two had curtains. His dad called theirs drapes. The third unit, directly opposite theirs, had no drapes. He had their drapes open all the way. So when the antiquated gas pickup pulled up and parked in front of that unit opposite theirs, he saw everything.

He saw this big dood get out of the pickup and hustle to the front door. He knocked or pounded on the front door— Ian couldn't tell. No one came to the door. The big man walked away from the front door, paced along the unit's length, peeking in the window. Didn't seem to be anything going on inside the unit. Ian'd need binoculars or x-ray vision to be sure. Then from the side of the unit, the end of the house opposite the front door, a girl stepped out. She was small, skinny, very pale, with bare feet, and long white hair. The man hurried to her, got down on his knees to embrace her. Her white T-shirt and white pants were enveloped by the big man. He had on a gray work shirt, jeans, boots.

She couldn't have been more than eight or ten. Ian had seen her once before, since they moved in. The unit was one of those kids' houses that had been springing up in consolidated towns across the country. Too often, parents couldn't support their kids. Governments had limited funds—no money. They weren't really halfway houses, or foster homes. A bunch of kids would get together, find a kid eighteen or over, and set up housekeeping. There weren't nearly the problems, like sex crimes or drug abuse, common to the bankrupt government programs. The kids took care of themselves, getting to charter school or training center as

required, on time. What was left of the government supplied
the houses with cots, commodities, maybe a couple
antediluvian tablets. But the Net was too expensive, anyway.
Plenty of crappy reruns available. Everybody watched
reruns, the CK, or common knowledge of the times, plus
there were free education sites.

Maybe it was her father, come for a visit. Ian noticed
that the girl's thin arms were not hugging him back. The
man's head seemed as big as her body. The man dropped
back, releasing her. They talked for a while, both speaking.
The man fell forward, like he was bowing. His big head
drifted down to kiss her small white feet. She stepped away,
headed back around, behind her unit. The man got back on
his feet. He returned to his pickup and took off in a puff of
gray exhaust.

So much for that adventure. It was like a silent
movie—

**Danger, Will Robinson! Locked and loaded, the
assassin of pants sprang to his prance! He couldn't
read his writing. Assassin of penmanship!**

Out the front door, he charged. This was his chance!
He paused to make sure he'd thumbed the lock.

Outside tasted like ammonia. At least, not
pneumonia. He ran across the cinder road, over to the side of
the unit, then around to the so-called backyard. All the units
had backyards, strips of bony weeds and toxic tailings,
where only humans grew. Their own private Disneyland,
where they could get stung, bit, punctured, infected. The girl
was there, standing by the back door with two other kids.
One was a girl about the same age, with the same pale skin
and long white hair, wearing the same whites, barefoot, and
this girl stood halfway in and halfway out, her shoulder
holding out the door. Sisters? The third kid was a boy, older,
long curly brown hair, in regular clothes—jeans, T-shirt,
sneakers. They watched Ian approach. It looked as though
they were coming out or going in. How could he tell?

"You okay?" Ian called.

The girl he'd watched through the window said, "K-L-M-N-O-P: pee comes out of my knee, in a tree, sets me free. What's a tree? Free, free, free!"

"You're a rapper."

"DLA, flatfoot. Duh, Sherlock, PI all the way. Inquiring minds want to magnum: magnify. I see you. I see shoofly, one of those microscope drones I poop out. You're ugly."

"I know what DLA is. Who doesn't? I saw that guy. Wanted to make sure you were okay. I'm Ian."

"Rescue me."

The boy said to Ian, "She's funny funny Fun. That's her moniker. You're the new kid cross the street. Don't lie: you needed an excuse to come over, or you're blazed for a little girl."

Ian said, "This is a kids' house."

The second girl shivered a little, then said, "Who's a little girl?" She tsk-ed loudly, and the other kids were about to laugh. She went on: "Homework's on. We run a tight ship. Keep the pirates' schedule. You can come in if you want a steaming hot cup of Joe. I'm Moon."

Fun gasped. "Joe Blow! Make it flow: just got back from a dinosaur show." She looked from one to the other of her comrades. Then she looked at Ian and said, "Ignore them, they don't know what stratum we're on. Right, chiclets, worm skins, pork lips?"

Ian wasn't sure how to respond. He stood there, statuary, then he became a bush.

Fun moved her hands up and over her face and head without touching herself. She intoned, "Sweetness is all. If you come in, you have to practice. It's like a commitment. These days comet mints, strangers on the fritz. Fringe, hinge, magic binge. Are you friend? I'm grizzly bear. Sorry I said you were ugly."

Ian stared down. He checked out the girls' dirty little feet.

The other girl, Moon, said, "You can come in if you're ugly, but don't look at my feet. Okay? Feet are entrances to the world soul."

The boy said, "No one is ugly. You're alive, we're alive— no random. Random all, protocol. I'm Pop."

The girls laughed together. Together, they sang, "Lit bit, bit from bite. Turn on the light! Clap on!" They clapped.

Ian said, "What are you guys up to?"

Pop said fast, "No good! Like likee like. You?"

They went into their unit. Ian saw what they were doing. The wretched kids were full of history. They had tubs of eels. Three kinds of hot sauce. They liked paper. They flew. They drew. The walls of the place were covered with their art. There was no hope for any of them. They only had a few moments each day. They had tubs of oats and groats. They knew how to manipulate folklore, mythology, revolution. They made tea. Ian went home, glad to have met their mess.

Resuming his position in front of the window, Ian tried to think about his essay. The move, his dad and mom, barged in. He looked over his notebook. He stole more glances out the window. Right now, outside was nothing—

Outside used to mean nature. Now, outside meant poison. Everything was poison. Even the dust was poison. Poison weather, poison water. Then it would pour and flood for forty days. Just don't get any onya! Wildlife was newlife. Poison life! Ian didn't want to go outside. The kids across the street depended on outside—the trains, the cargo. That's what he'd learned about homework. That's what he worried about. Now that he had mints. He hadn't realized the DLA was across the street! At least in Colorado, where they'd lived on the front range, he could go outside, but this was the Midwest Technical Corridor. The future was reorganized. Something had to happen. There were too many homeless. Too much hunger. Basically, the Midwest was now divided into corridors consolidating power, food, housing.

New manufacturing and infrastructure centers were located in each corridor. This was the 22nd century. This was his home. What could he write about? Twenty-two:2-2. His time. Now and later.

He didn't want to write about his mom, because he'd already worn out the novelty of her minor celebrity. Besides, it had gotten out, too, that his parents were separated and probably getting a divorce. Awkward at a Catholic school. In Colorado he'd gone to a free school.

In the 21st Century American public education had basically gone to charter schools. When it was clear that didn't work, a remarkable thing had happened: unemployed teachers organized free schools. These teachers, and their comrades, the nurses, had saved the nation's basic services in education and medicine. They provided a survival net to the collapsing nation. The free schools were student and staff run. They were nonprofit sanctuaries willing to give education a go.

Catholic schools were run as they'd always been: strict discipline, rigorous academics. Which was why his parents were delighted to find one near the Terrace. Ian excelled in academics, so he had that part covered. He wasn't a troublemaker, he wasn't class clown. But this essay, if he were to be honest, would expose his true point of view. They'd say he wasn't a team player. Hope? How hope? Who hope?

Maybe he should spark up his dad's old pad. Maybe he could find some inspiration there. Or he could turn on the 3-D TV. What a joke! 3-D reruns! He was expecting a call from his mom. She knew his cell was dead, so she'd promised to call the land line.

The pad lacked the new filters and zoltans which were standard today. Its online interface was dominated by political sites, which paid their way to come first. 22nd Century net completely at the mercy of trolls. And the style of politics? The new, so-called Despair Revolution. That's all anyone had to say anymore: America was dead. There were a bunch of states holding on, then a bunch that had gone under. Every man for himself! Every man proclaiming the new America of the real Americans! With the real Constitution! Finally, everyone was a conspirator, a hero, a traitor, a coward.

TV was palliative. But 3-D caused headaches, which conspirators claimed turned to brain cancer. A Pandora's box of reruns, one hundred and fifty years of reruns, that basically formed the bank of CK—common knowledge. Hundred-year-old cartoons were hard to beat. Since Hollywood had collapsed—no money, there were few new programs. The big new show everyone watched was Billionaire Club, but Ian hated it.

His mom was doing important work—water work. She was an aquifer specialist, and the new drilling she was supervising could be a real breakthrough. Problem was, she traveled so much, so was away from home a lot. Also, she pretty much hated Ian's father. Which meant he had to stay with his dad. That was the illogic logic—parental units' style....

His mom was an adventurer, out in the abandoned areas, looking for water. Huge parts of Texas and Oklahoma and New Mexico were ghostlands. Looters, squatters, coyotes didn't last long without water. His mom was in New Mexico, he thought. Clovis, New Mexico? Well, east of there. Maybe in Texas. Following the aquifer, the receding underground water. The precious water was still there, just deeper, harder to get to, buried in silt and clay and sand. His mom had all the latest tech. Devices that were cutting edge developments in imaging in to the Earth. She was moving around the area, mapping out the water. How deep it was. Precisely! Accurate maps would allow pinpointing of spots to drill. That's what the phone call was about—which drill site had panned out. So much was riding on finding water, bringing water back to the region. Back to the Earth.

Ian wrote his essay:

"What's Wrong with People

"By the year 2100, the future was bad. People joked that the Dark Ages had nothing on the 21st century. That's because the 21st century was when everything fell apart, even the planet. By the time 2100 hit, it was too late. We were dregs already. No guilt, no blame, just an awareness for our generation that no one could explain away. Because plague comes in all shapes and colors. Who knows who will blow next? And spark a massacre? Nobody ever said how manic people got in the Dark Ages. I mean compared to us now. Because we are manic! We are worried, hustling, stretching every last resource. We are straitjacketed by our legacy. The legacy of leftovers. We are civilization's crumbs. And the people from the coasts are coming north, and inland, and no wall can stem the flow. There's nothing anybody can do. They're heading for the Great Lakes, because, even though it's hotter for sure, agriculture is still viable there. There's still water there. Water turns out to be the central kernel: water runs industry, agriculture, life itself. In the 21st century, people didn't realize that capitalism ran on water too. What was bad by 2100 was there was nothing to take capitalism's place. Except the least common denominator: survival. Make do. Endure. Now nations host bankruptcy parties. Mass suicides are common. As are despair killings. Vast experiments in consolidated housing for climate refugees. Business, medicine, agriculture, on triage. If it wasn't for the nurses and teachers, nothing would get done. Maybe the people of the Dark Ages were just as manic as we are. Because no one wants to just sit around waiting for darkness. These are the challenges of my time. They do not allow much in the way for later. Now and later. Something new is required that *has not been thought yet. That is what I hope for."*

The land line rang. Ian jumped to his feet, positioned himself, took the phone. "Hello."

"Ian!"

"Hi, Mom."

"How are you?"

"I'm fine. School is fine. Dad is fine. The house is fine."

"They said they'd get you into much better accommodations. Closer to your school and closer to Dad's school. You have to be patient. Are you okay?"

"I'm good. Come on, what did you guys find out?"

Ian quit writing. It was too long and boring—everybody had heard these dystopias before, either read the book, or seen the movie. People were sick of them. It wasn't an essay. It was a giddy short story with essay embedded. Complete with show off words. Ian didn't even know what *palliative* meant. He couldn't read it out loud in class. But that's what he got; that's what he'd come up with.

He left it on his small desk in his bedroom, slammed through the doorway, slapping his hands right and left against the trim, and entered the hallway, which, still so new, made him imagine he was living in Creep Motel. Behind this door, a cannibal; behind this door, a razorfish; behind that door, a tubular corn man completely made of golden plump corn. New house. Dad house. Indiana house. He missed Colorado. His dad insisted the Midwest had its charms, so give it a chance—

A new home, which was an old house, with siding painted turquoise, and a gray shingle roof, a simple ranch-style with sliding glass doors to the backyard porch and lawn. For some reason, the realtor had been mad for those sliding glass doors, eagerly demonstrating them over and over again, as though they were the latest in high-tech furnishing. Ian went outside, left the sliding glass door open. It wasn't too bad outside, maybe in the 50s or 60s, so for early spring pretty nice, and with a vibrant blue sky. The high country back in Colorado would still be snowed in. Christmas in Colorado! Used to be a dream come true— last Christmas in Colorado was the worst Christmas imaginable. The worst of his life.

Open sesame, and like magic the sliding glass door had whooshed aside!

Ian stepped into knee-high grass, weeds, and bushes. Ian couldn't tell which were volunteers and which were ornamentals, which had actually been planted there on purpose. It was such a mess of green, there was no way he could get the lawnmower through it. His dad had shown him the mower—pointed at it, but did not touch it, in the new house's connected garage. In old reruns, dads kept their tools on peg boards in the garage, maybe with a workbench for building bird houses. In Ian's family, no one had skills. At least those kinds of skills. His dad claimed it was because they were theorists. He was a mathematician. That wasn't fair to his mom, who was a hydrologist, and had been known to rip apart a faulty water pump at a moment's notice. His dad wanted him to 'tidy up' the yard, so he'd get a sense of being part of the new homestead. Ian wasn't buying that, but what could he do? He didn't know anyone around here. Or even at his new school.

His dad gave him a ride to school the next day. It was right on the way to his dad's school, the area's community college. His dad was glad to get the gig, as he had had to get away from Colorado, and this opportunity presented itself first. Why Ian had to go to the Catholic school, St. Bartholomew's, was unclear. Ian was certain it meant his dad was coming down on him, wanting to keep a firm grip on him, because his dad knew that he would be the one responsible for Ian. They didn't talk on the way to school. His dad didn't bring up the backyard or the lawnmower or anything like that.

Ian didn't have to wear a uniform to school, like the girls did. But he had to wear regular pants, not jeans. His dad called them slacks. And he had to wear a button-down shirt, with no pop-culture insignias on it. Ian was adjusting to the new school. Or, at least, trying to convince himself that he was. It did seem that the Catholic school had a more rigorous curriculum. There was more expected of the students than he was used to. But as long as he kept at it, with his strong writing skills, he should be okay. He'd felt like he had to tell the nuns that he was an atheist. His dad didn't mind. In fact, Ian told the nuns this when he and his dad went for their sign-up session.

When they got to English and their writing assignments, the kids were called up front, one by one, in alphabetical order, to deliver their essays. Ian was amazed at what devout believers they were: Catholic kids were all about sin and heaven and hell. Commandments. Sacraments. It could've been one of his dystopian novels! But Ian didn't want to make fun, he had to get along with these kids. With his last name beginning with an S, he had some time to go before it would be his turn. He kept his eyes ahead, avoiding the kids on either side of him, in their old-fashioned desks. The girls in their school uniform dresses seemed prim and proper, and the dresses went below their knees. He could see their legs and feet, in little white socks with penny loafers, he thought they were called. He hadn't talked to a single girl in class. He hadn't talked to a single boy either. It was all pretty new so far. His teacher, Sister Mary Boykin, finally called on Ian.

Ian stood, his hands went around his waist to make sure his shirt was tucked in properly, then he took his essay up to the front of the class. He nodded to Sister who was sitting behind her desk, and turned to face the class. Some of the boys made goofy faces or grinned wickedly. The girls looked at him with sly, deadpan, reserved features. Ian began to read his essay—

Ian realized he had to tread carefully, so he had marked with light pencil marks those words or sentences that might be dropped, without destroying the total effect of the short piece. Pretty quickly, the snickers began. The snickers turned into real, out loud laughs. But the nun said nothing, so Ian went on. Ian was getting into it, reading with gusto, when a girl at the back, a big tall girl stuck in the last seat of the far row, burst out:

"Sister, I don't want to hear this. It's disgusting. I don't understand why you would allow it. This boy watches too much TV, so he's saturated with pop culture lies and despair. Of course the world looks like this when you only know the pop culture. It's odious! It pretends it has real power, cutting through history and politics, offering a lesson. But all it really offers is odium, which can only be quelled by Dionysian excess."

The kids started to clap. A couple boys hooted. Sister glanced around her room, nodding to boys and girls, then smiling to the big girl in the back. Ian took a good look at this girl in the back: she had to be six-foot-tall, which for a thirteen-year-old was pretty tall, and she was as they said big boned, with messy red hair, which looked like it had never been brushed. Her uniform hung from her as though worn out, washed too many times, stretched to its limit. She had pale skin, maybe some freckles around her nose, some freckles on her arms, freckles on her legs. The girls were not allowed to wear makeup. Ian wasn't quite sure about that, whether it was a good thing. But he liked the way she had attacked him: because it played right into Ian's quick reply:

"Thank you! It's true, I probably watch too much TV and read too many dystopian novels. But the only alternative seems to be magic, making a leap of faith. You sound like you know, I accept your belief or else. Hey, don't get upset. Is this upsetting? It's not like a person wants to accept despair. It's that despair comes marching in when there's so little left to do. I don't even like social media. I know we're not allowed to have our phones in school here. I'm just saying. I'm just getting to know the rules in this school. I apologize if this was too gross."

Sister mumbled something that Ian didn't catch. Maybe it was a secret prayer that only Catholic kids understood. But he knew his time was up. So just as all the other kids had done, Ian turned to the nun's desk and dropped his essay there. The nun shook her head and picked up the papers of Ian's work and tossed them in the nearby garbage can.

Now what? Ian knew this did not bode well. He knew this would mean a phone call to his dad this very evening. He knew this was not a good fit for a starting out student at a new school. That's how he would logically try to phrase it, as though it had nothing to do with his essay's content. But his parents would think he was *acting out—*their expression. They would be *disappointed* in him. That meant he wasn't pulling his own weight, in this tough period for the family. Ian ran through the lectures he knew to expect. He'd have to buckle under. No choice. Stay with his dad, go to this crazy school.

Bridget Tilson was called next. The big girl stomped up to the front of the room. She handed her essay to Sister Mary. She said, "I memorized it."

She might as well have said 'this is the way to do it'.

She began:

"I love polar bears. I love birds, butterflies, but also worms and slugs and cicadas. These are God's gifts that every day we acknowledge and understand. When we understand nature, we learn to understand His gifts, thus ourselves. Reason is a gift too, perhaps one of the most important there is. Let me give you an example, my heritage is from Ireland, and our DNA turns out to make very pale white people. White skin is good for absorbing UV radiation, which can help in vitamin D production, especially in northern latitudes like Ireland, which don't get as much sun. That's just logical. But if people who have DNA like us, if they move to a place with more direct sunlight, then they'll be getting more radiation. This can lead to cancer. It's just logical. So, when we go out into nature, we have to be careful and wear extra sun block. We have to be logical. We have to use what God has given us, this reason that we were given to help us survive in health and safety. Polar bears, you may have noticed, are white creatures too. I wonder if they get skin cancer? I don't know if birds and butterflies worry about skin cancer or vitamin D. But with reason, we have a way to think about it, then with family and friends we act. We make intelligent choices. So humans need reason and each other. Family. They need family. They need community. Reason and community will take us into the future, will guide us in to the future. Reason and community make us realize that we are more than the sum of our parts. This, too, is a gift from God."

Sister took the pages of Bridget essay and tossed them in the garbage can. She muttered painfully, "Humanism. You left out salvation. Jesus died for our sins, this is the greatest gift, the greatest gift ever to the world, the greatest gift the world will ever have or know."

Ian was fascinated by this entire exchange. His work was trashed because he was a nonbeliever, under the spell of pop culture. Her work was trashed because she *was* a believer, but not exact enough in her beliefs. The rest of the day was blurred notes, doodles—space wars, monsters, then he read from a textbook. Then he sneaked in the novel he was reading by Neal Asher. After the bell, he hung around, to run into her...then he missed his bus—

He decided he would walk home very slowly and not think about her. He adjusted his backpack. It wasn't that far. He couldn't get lost. It wasn't cold or raining. 'It was a cute little town,' he mused, thinking that nugget would assuage his dad. It was at most a couple miles.

School, plans, parents—freak out. Of course he was freaking, that was his job at his age, his dad would cry. That didn't make him feel any better. It wasn't funny. He knew it was up to him now. This tangle of life, this juggle of priorities—how could a young person of the 21st Century, awash in the surfeit of stuff and excess, be true?

He was a book. He was a nerd. He was a writer. Surely, all the books he'd consumed, both classics and genre, must offer some clarity. The story began, introductions were made, suspense, build up, climax, release. Dénouement. Ian loved to follow the logic inside a story that led motivations in its own way. He loved to see intentions play out, especially in the classic stories, like Mark Twain, Chekhov, O'Connor (both of them), then Ray Bradbury and Raymond Chandler and Ursula Le Guin. Intentions were characters, characters were intentions. Story emerged from character. Balzac on his death bed, Ian had read in an online zine, he wasn't exactly sure who Balzac was, had been visited by his characters. He had called out to his favorites in his final moments. Ian loved the inevitability of a story. Right now, he was deep in a Neal Asher novel, his go to writer for space opera—code *monsters.*

Ian wasn't a real nerd. He wasn't into gaming. He thought *Star Trek* and *Star Wars* were dumb. He liked the girl in *Rogue* One, and the new girl, Rei, was okay. He preferred SyFy Channel's *Battlestar Galactica* and *The Expanse.* There was such a flood of junk out there, it was a ridiculous challenge to find new writers to love. He learned so much about writing from a book he loved. If he didn't like a book within twenty pages, there was no way he would finish it. He depended on libraries and used bookstores. He loved Scarlett Thomas, Matt Ruff, Tade Thompson, and Lauren Beukes. He'd read all of their books. Besides, Scarlett Thomas and Lauren Beukes were gorgeous ladies. Not that that mattered—but he had googled them and checked them out. He imagined them talking, being friends. But he kept up with the classics, too. He had to! His parents expected it. He had to read the short story *Araby* by James Joyce at his last school. He googled James Joyce, found out about this book of his, *Portrait of the Artist as a Young Man*. He loved the title, but the librarian said it was an adult book. Apparently, it was about a young writer, with a famous tagline about *exile, loneliness, cunning.*

Stories had to end in a different place from where they started. It was the basic lesson. Maybe the first lesson a writer learned. Proposition, considered Ian: human relations are a story with their own logic, heading to a different place from where they started. Time was the context or setting. Time for kids was incredibly slow. Time for adults was incredibly fast. It followed, then, that how this turned out would take forever for Ian, while his parents thought it rushing by.

Ian recognized the suburban style of the houses around him, because they matched his house, his neighborhood. He felt better. He felt worse. 'Little plastic boxes with little plastic lives', he enunciated in his head. He knew he was grasping for straws: he knew no matter how clever he would be, he was going to get in trouble. He got tired of walking down the street. Right out in the open! Suburbs meant everything was presented upfront by the road, which is why siding must be painted, and why lawns needed to be crisp and proper. He should be skulking. Sometimes there was a bit of sidewalk, but most of the time no sidewalk at all. He'd try the alley that ran between the rows of houses, that was used by the garbage men and the power company and the occasional kid. Alleyways in the suburbs were unpaved roads between fences, garbage cans, sheds, then weeds and trees, in a riot of dead leaves and broken branches and bottles. Alleyways, then, were in-between zones where kids could re-energize. Ian liked the alley right away.

A couple kids in regular clothes, no uniforms, with requisite backpacks, were ahead of him in the alley. He shimmied his pack, to make sure it was still there. He didn't know them, but he thought he might have seen the girl. Maybe they were neighbors? As he got closer, he realized he had seen this girl. Hard to miss! She'd been walking near their house. She was hard to miss with her long white hair and milky white skin. Polar bear, unaware! Ian flushed with it! Was this the girl who had given him the idea for Fun and Moon? The second person with this small white human girl was a boy about Ian's age, with regular pigmentation.

Suddenly, the girl spun around and glared at Ian. She went, "Umm! Spy!" Then: "We're being followed!" cried the girl.

Her face! Her face had a nimbus of energy about it. Ian was bedazzled! He'd never seen a person with a halo.

The boy with her said, "It's that kid who moved in to the Abbey house, you know that place where those nice old people lived."

'They're dead!" proclaimed the girl.

Ian saw how white the girl was: white, like bed sheets white. Ian announced, "You're an albino!"

The girl said, "You are so rude. Look at my eyes—do they look pink to you? I'm supposed to be wearing sunglasses, and a hat, but certain people, who shall remain nameless, forgot to bring them."

"We call her Bunny," said the boy. He took a step forward towards Ian, nodding quickly. He was a good three or four inches taller than Ian, and he must have outweighed him by twenty pounds. "Where do you go to school?"

The girl burst with, "I'm gonna tell mom! You are not supposed to call me that. You promised. You know what my real name is." She paused, looking from who must have been her brother to Ian. "Tell him!"

"My name is Dan. Don't worry about her."

"My name's Ian. We live right over there." He pointed vaguely.

Dan said, "She's my little sister. I'm supposed to be nice. I have to be nice to her. And we're not supposed to call her Bunny. On account of her real name is Funnybunny."

The white, white girl erupted all over Dan, hitting and slapping him. Dan pulled back. Ian stepped away as well.

The little white girls at the Terrace! Ian didn't understand. This seemed weird. Frantically, he rationalized, what do little white girls symbolize?

Finally, Dan squirmed in defeat: "Okay, okay! I get it. Her real name is Princess Plum."

The girl made a retching sound, as though she were turning inside out. But at least she stopped hitting. She grunted out, "Better!"

Dan said, "We got pop tarts. No one's home right now. Are you into gaming?"

The girl said, "You don't game! Mother does not fancy gaming. You look at porn. I caught you so many times. And I'm gonna tell, if you ever call me that name again."

Ian said, "No one's home at my house either. Which— why I have to get home. I promised my dad. We've just moved in."

The girl looked surprised. She pursed her lips and spat a bubble. She said, "We can come over to your house. If you want. Unless you watch porn, too, like this idiot."

Ian said, "Oh no, I never do that." He laughed, and

Dan and he exchanged a quick look. Ian went on, "Where do you guys go to school?"

The girl clarified her inside scoop: "Boys are all alike. Why do you like to watch people doing it? That's why people do it in the dark, behind closed doors! I need a pop tart or I'm going to faint."

Dan said, "We go to the school down on Hazlet Street, Hughes. It's not that far. I'm in eighth grade. She's with the little kids in kindergarten."

She attacked with slaps and pinches to her big brother. This time he grunted and said in a serious voice 'stop it'. Ian kept following them to their house.

Ian was surprised at how similar their house was to his house, the same layout and funk. They lived with their mom, who worked at a bank. Their father had run away to Alaska with another man, the girl explained. She said they had two dads now, and if their mom ever got married again, they'd have three dads. They toasted their pop tarts and munched them sitting on bar stools at a wraparound bar in the kitchen.

Ian said, "I go to the Catholic school. It's the other way. I'm in eighth grade. We came here from Colorado."

Dan said, "Wow! They got recreational weed there, don't they? Indiana is a total shithole. Known for the KKK and high school basketball. We're supposed to have some of the best high school basketball in the country. I don't know. Been here all my life. I'm sick of it. The whole thing, eighth grade, the jock buzz." He laughed like it was a private joke, but went on anyway: "High school, well, at least it's gotta be different, right?"

The little girl said, "Umm, said a bad word!"

Ian burst with, "What should I call you? I keep wanting to call you Bunny, but I don't want to get beat up. What's your real name?"

She grabbed her brother by the arm and dragged him away from the kitchen, up a hallway where Ian couldn't see, the whole time ferociously whispering. They consulted in private for a few more seconds, then they both came out. The boy rolled his eyes at Ian. The girl was triumphant and resumed her seat and munch.

She announced, "Call me Tallulah."

Ian said, "Tallulah? Fancy name."

Tallulah said, "I'm a fancy girl. And it's not just a bunch of princess stuff either, huh, Dan? I'm real smart. Prodigy Grade A. Smarter than Dan."

Dan laughed, then snorted: "Smarter than dirt! Ignore her. Do you game? What are your favorite games?"

Tallulah said, "Ignore me at your own risk."

Ian thought a second, then shrugged his shoulders. "I'm not very good at games. Or sports. I guess I lack that kind of hand/eye coordination. I don't know."

Tallulah clapped her hands and snorted, "You're a nerd! I knew it right away when I spied you. You and I are going to be best friends. You read books, I read books. You like science, I like science. You take notes, I take notes. Right? Isn't that true? Isn't all that true? Dan can come along though, because he's my brother."

Dan said quickly, "The fairies took my sister and exchanged her for this creature."

Tallulah rolled her eyes. "He knows all about that already."

Ian gasped and chuckled nervously. The little girl was exactly right about what he liked and what he did. He liked this pair of kids. But he rarely made friends with jocks. And never with a little girl. He didn't have a sister. Regular girls were hard enough. But she was right: he did know all about fairies stealing children. He wanted Dan to like him. He was not some nerdy loser. Ian said, "Next time, after school, we can go over to my house."

Tallulah said, "We'll bring him along, okay? He can be our bodyguard. Ask him to show you his Legos. He likes to pretend he's too old for Legos—"

Dan said, "Big mouth. Just what I always wanted to be, a bodyguard. I guess I'll have to bring my nunchucks. But, yeah, no basketball practice right now, so I'm babysitting, we could come over—I'm sick of school, I'm sick of sports, I'm sick of girls."

Ian thought that sounded interesting. He would've liked to have heard more on these subjects.

Tallulah said, "Teenagers!" She shook her head.

Ian asked, "Can I ask you guys a question? I guess I just did. How come you guys don't have phones or Blackberries or some kind of platform going, like all the other kids, as soon as they get out of school?"

Dan answered, "That's the longest sentence I ever heard, I mean just when people are hanging out, sitting around. You're right, Lulah: guy's a geek."

Tallulah folded her arms across her chest. She looked either grumpy or stern. She said, "Mommy! It's against her religion." She made a very profound and dramatic roaring, growling sound. "We have an old PC tower."

Dan droned, "Not really a religion. You said you live with your dad? So you probably know all about divorce, too. Eventually, you get the talk from whichever parent you end up living with, in our case our mom. The talk explains that because she has to work so much, and because there's no father on the scene, that means we kids have got to step up to the plate, think outside the box, go the extra mile, and stand up above the crowd. You know, like all those slogans on posters in classrooms."

Tallulah went, "That's the biggest sentence I ever!"

Ian said, "And that's why you don't have a smart phone?"

Dan said, "Where's yours?"

Ian said, "You can't even bring them to the Catholic school."

Tallulah asked, "What's a Catholic?"

Ian hated it when he fidgeted, so he played with the

cinnamon crumbs of his pop tart. He hated to think he would come on all intellectual. Ian said, "I think it means universal."

"Universal what?" asked Dan.

Ian said, "What is your religion? I don't believe in God."

Tallulah went fast, "Atheist!"

Dan said, "Don't!"

Tallulah said, "Our mom is real smart. She's doing it for our good."

Dan said, "Don't you love it when you get the talk about how they're doing things for your own good? Our mom is okay, but she thinks all electric devices are a distraction from school and 'normal' life. Do you know what *normal* means? I think she's trying to duplicate her childhood, when all they had was books and TV."

Tallulah interjected: "For goodness sakes, we have to do chores!"

Dan went on, "It's crazy, too, because she has a cell phone, a really good one. She says it's for work."

Tallulah came in again: "It's for emergencies!"

Dan said, "You should see it when my coach is trying to find me. Land lines suck."

Tallulah said, "Our mom is a lady. She wears makeup. And fancy clothes. She has one hair growing from the beauty mark on her chin. It's got to be two inches long. That's five centimeters long, growing on her chinny chin chin."

Sizzle rain made the main entrance to the Terrace a mess of white mush mud. But it was almost warm, definitely fetid. Ian, Fun, Moon stood in the playground with the broken swing set opposite the entrance. Ian had no idea how he got talked into this. He had never been to the playground.

He had been over to the kids' house again, done the homework. They wanted him to go on an operation, simple breach and seizure, prove his Cheerios. And mints. DLA was everywhere. The Terrace was a node. Everybody played.

The Catholic school was coming down hard on him for his essay. His dad had reported the whole thing to his mom, who couldn't get out of New Mexico for at least a few more weeks. His mom had revealed to Ian that they had made an important discovery, which she didn't want to go into on the phone right now, because she was too disappointed in him, showing off, being an ass. Oh, Mom! Ian had no idea where else to go, but across the street.

Ian and the two girls played playing on the broken swing, which still had good chains, then they kicked the collapsed merry-go-round, then they droned on the ladder to nowhere without its slide. The girls jumped around in the white muck with their bare feet. They were bundled in white shawls. Ian had his white jacket on and a Hello Kitty backpack they insisted he wear. Sickly, pale, little kids, especially little girls, could go anywhere, do anything they wanted. Nobody wanted to look. They had backpacks too.

On the second visit to their house, they had explained that white confused surveillance eyes, whether drones or satellites or CCTV cameras. Plus, if you danced around in a jerky way, and had some LEDs on your head— they couldn't get a clean shot. Invisible! So they were doing their jerky hopping twisting, like any kids having fun, pretty much unnoticeable, unless you paid attention to the way their fingers and hands then feet and toes crunched and spread in key patterns. They had three LEDs on top of their heads.

Fun hung from the broken swing, halfway gliding, halfway dragging herself along. Moon stayed close to him, snapping and popping. She didn't want to talk, she thought Ian should jerk more, you know, like kids do. It would confuse the eyes.

The main entrance of the Terrace had a guard station with two vehicle lanes, one for in, one for out. A caged in cattle chute type passenger way paralleled the lanes. The gray uniformed guards controlled a big gate, that was always open. They checked ID's. The Terrace wasn't walled in, or fenced in. It wasn't a prison after all, Ian's dad kept saying. It was temporary, while they got their bearings here in the Midwest corridor.

The way the layout worked was the Terrace was a couple miles from Gary, out in what had been corn fields. Beyond the entrance was a fuel station and a dollar store. The kids called the dollar store the Trough. The whole area around there had all these old on ramps, exits. It used to be a hub, highways, state and federal, meeting up with local roads. Trucks still bellowed through there. The railroad tracks were down the road.

About a half mile from the Terrace, the Pram station. These were the new trains that levitated, crisscrossing the nation, because they were able to use the corroded, busted up old train tracks without flipping. Serving the trains, from this side of the tracks, humongous metal warehouses that looked like giant metal coffins. In and out goods flowed. When you have very little, distribution is everything.

People from the Terrace were not really supposed to walk among the warehouses or go down to the train tracks. Regular robot buses picked up kids or parents, and regular folks, to take to work or school or training in Gary. They pretty much came on the hour, moving back and forth between stipulated destinations. Schools and training centers and workplaces were all on the other side of the tracks.

To get through the main entrance, you had to have the proper ID. As soon as you signed up to live in the Terrace, you were issued ID's. Ian and his father had their own ID's. The kids from across the street all had several ID's. They told Ian that the guards were pretty sloppy about checking IDs, because there wasn't really much going on in the Terrace—no terrorism, etc. When nearly everybody depended on emergency distribution of supplies, smuggling and larceny were up against impregnable need. Until DLA....

The three kids kept up a jerky, jazzy dance, which Ian had practiced at their house. Electronics were easy to fool, the kids said. Some kids had the knack. Fun and Moon could make street lights go out, walking by them and casting a quick glance. The DLA was a good fit, birds of a feather, and if everything went sour, he'd hitchhike back to Colorado, or grab the train like they were going to teach him.

Now, Moon moved away from the broken swing and signaled to her partner, and Ian, that it was time. She knew because the bus was taking off from the entrance, taking people to their workstations or personnel uplift. The jazzy dance confused the guards, who had no time for kids goofing around. The kids proceeded through the entrance, skipping down the pedestrian pathway, past the gates, past the guards, who never gave them a second look. They headed towards the Trough, weaving around lumbering trucks, big as Triceratops.

No one knew how long gasoline would be available. But vehicles ran on many fuels today. The Trough was right next to the fuel station. The kids paraded Ian in, as though he were their mascot, and they wanted to show him off. The workers at the dollar store greeted them with a hearty welcome, their programmed invitational, because they'd just gotten in a big order of Mexican Slim Jims they were pushing. But the flesh and blood workers connected on the mud and muck and wetness the kids were tromping in and started yelling. The girls knew all about yelling back in rhyme. Ian was learning.

They got chased out of the Trough and hung a quick left, weaseling their way into a warehouse alley, a thin seam between structures, whether for service access or accidental was unclear. Ian worried about drones, which patrolled while coordinated security around the warehouses. He wasn't sure his dancing would work. Not a drone in sight. Moon stood in front of Ian, hunched up, and pressing, almost melting, into a warehouse wall. She looked like some kind of moth creature, that resolved to a white smudge. She came around fast. Her pretty baby face squinched up. Moon whispered to him, "Task, last gasp! Bowwow, Joe blow, target on your noggin toboggan. Think white!"

The warehouses made an inorganic maze. But inside those warehouses, the Beast of Supply, distribution and abundance, a node station for goods along the network, pickup and delivery, then shot every which way, to every corner of the broken nation. The kids avoided lanes with robotic haulers. They saw a few human workers, and those wore special suits with helmets that covered their faces. Ian followed the little girls through alleys smelling too sweet, like candy. He was wishing for a mask. Why was he here? If he was a target, then maybe it was deliberate, and he was a decoy for the kids.

Everything depended on timing. They had to be in and out in minutes, when the next train came in. At arrival, as a courtesy, all the computers had to have a confab, an exchange of pleasantries, with boasts and prevarications. Systems had to debug and debrief. The kids had timed it over and over again, arrival to start of unloading, until they knew that the shortest time it took was seven minutes, while the longest time it took was ten. Mainly, the trains pulled flat cars stacked with containers, which giant container cranes unloaded to haulers or trucks, which distributed them to the proper warehouse—or wherever they might be going. Then, when the train was unloaded, the cranes got busy picking up the filled containers waiting at the dock, to be placed in precise arrangement on the train's flatcars. The warehouses that took in containers, then emptied them, juggled their own dance with the contents, until they were *ready for corridor distribution by truck. Other warehouses received the corridor's productions, mainly agricultural, to be packed for shipment. Then to the trains, the Pram levitation, hauling stuff out, hauling stuff in, the cycle went on and on, containers through the blast zone. The trains were controlled by nice, simple AI's which the girls had teased into submission, and enticement. Ian had seen it at their house. He had learned a lot! This was their favorite AI coming in now.*

They called him Bruno on account of he started by being a bully. But then when he learned about DLA, he would do anything for them. Even tell them the top-secret codes to the containers they might harvest. They'd worked out two basic principles with Bruno: first, the container had to be easily accessible; and, second, the container had to have what they needed. Bruno didn't care. He controlled the manifests and losing a few choice computer components was easily scrubbed. As long as DLA kept him in the loop, he was good. He adored being on the inside of human secrets.

DLA, Dirty Little Angels, were all about art, revolution, evolution, culture change, breakdown, dying, disease, and titillation. Then they were about shame, humiliation, human misery, pathos. Dead girls were tied to this precious moment of the 22nd century eating itself. The dead girls online, or in posters or graffiti or zines, could have been about cannibalism, monsters beyond zombies—they were still technically alive and beautiful. There were white girls, black girls, brown girls. DLA dressed the same, in whites, usually dirty, with bare feet. Usually, with long hair. Not so much an ad scam—nobody made any money. Fun and Moon exchanged the highest tech, the latest electronics for DLA imagery. Photography was so easy now, even a kid could do it. They knew how to plug in, go deep, deep, tribal mind beneath the surface of misery. They were dirty girls, they were dead girls, and no one knew what to do. Everybody and everything were dying, and no one knew what to do. Shouldn't someone be taking care of them? Is this what we have become, our children like strays, feral runaways covered in filth? The government or law enforcement or church leaders sought to eliminate the DLA and their imagery. Bad for morale. The American worker could not afford guilt. Fun and Moon kept their faces fuzzy, and they never did anything nasty. A lot of pictures of skinny legs and dirty feet. Responsible adults, citizens in general, denied they existed.

Moon said, "Train brain."

Fun said, "Ripe now. Bruno crew-oh."

Ian couldn't hear the train. Yes, he knew levitation was soundless, so how did the girls snow know? He followed them, hurrying from an alley, between giant units for hauling, or loading or unloading. When they got to the tracks, several workers in fancy suits were crowding around. The train, controlled by Bruno, pulled in, whooshed by, a beautiful synchronicity that made Ian feel confident. They hung back, waiting for their moment.

The humans got busy elsewhere, and Ian followed the girls up and onto the third train car. The girls knew it was the third one. Each of these cars had a two-tier stack of containers, so eight containers on a car. They climbed fast, using the metal joints and seams for holds. The girls' toes were as flexible and grabby as monkeys'. They ended up on a back container, snuggled in to its corner, where there was a control pad. No one was supposed to know of these emergency access panels. The girls jiggered off the pad's cover, a few metal curly cues on the sides. Underneath it, they peeled open a small control box. They put in the code Bruno had taught them and immediately an adjacent hatch slid open. Just barely...barely big enough. The hatch was not for egress, but for a worker to stick a light and camera in, to glance around and make sure everything was okay. The two girls, like slick white eels, slid through the hatch, disappearing at once, leaving their shawls behind.

This is the scariest moment of my life, thought Ian. *Does this make me a terrorist?*

They didn't have flashlights. The LEDs provided gratuitous light.

So Ian was lookout? Or decoy?

They couldn't have been gone more than a couple minutes, when Ian spotted the twinkle twinkle of the LEDs. Next thing he knew the girls were cramming oddly shaped boxes and containers up through the hatch. They were out! Immediately, they secreted their goods into hidden pockets of their clothes and shawls. Fun loaded Ian's pack.

Fun sang softly, "Flim flam, Pram tram. Grab my bag, hag. Grab my box, dirty socks. Cram it, slam it."

The haul filled their shawl. They closed the hatch, what a batch, tightened down the control box, pad in place, and started their climb back down.

Ian said, "Time flies, toes rose, who knows? Don't lose your toes."

Fun said, "Don't tinkle tinkle tinkle thinkle that."

Moon huffed, "Hocus-pocus focus."

Like lemurs, without thinking, they were down, and running for the nearest warehouse alley. Suddenly, Fun yodeled and crammed to a stop: "Scat rats, scat rats slow, blow circus bowwow."

Ian knew 'bowwow' meant now, so he stopped. They had been running away like civilians. Ian realized they weren't jerky dancing, so he started and the girls did too. No alert sounded. Ian led them to an alley, expecting any second to be zapped by a drone.

At the last visit to the kids' house, before the heist, Pop took Ian aside, man to man, away from the clatter of kids, to murmur, "Some say DLA stands for 'dirty little angels', others say 'dirty little assholes', but you didn't hear that from me."

CHAPTER 2

Wasn't there some old movie his dad liked about a CIA 'reader' who is compromised, but has no field experience? 'Memory is like a story you dip in,' wrote Ian in his notebook.

Proposition: Theory of Deep Reading leads right away to deep writing. A hard code to snatch from the oysters. The deeper you read, more exposure, and the more exposure, the more experience. Time again! Age pretended experience was mandatory. Deep reading, the deepest game there was, was virtual experience. He knew where he had to be, and he was there, because there was only one way to get there.

Assault excavation. Uh tiny laser ejection unit should stabilize and cauterize the offending neurons—

Ian's bedroom tonight was a motel room stage. Sitting up in bed, he looked around, he tried to read, he tried to figure what was happening. Nothing to see. No posters or pictures on the walls. Just his favorite books on a single shelf. He had decided to go all minimal, because he didn't want to get comfortable, like this was home. Home meant where the shouting took place. All this was, was Ian's temporary staging ground.

Ian had gotten home late. His dad was there. Sister had

called him at the community college, where he was heading out to a study session. He was forced to cancel the session so he could get home to Ian, only to find him gone. His dad had called his mom, who decided on the spot, as she was prone to, to fly in this very weekend. *His mom was on the way! He hadn't seen her in—he hadn't talked to her in—*

His dad had said, "We can discuss the situation."

What situation? It was so they could finalize the divorce.

He felt like a runaway. He could run away. He was no runaway. He hated sports. Didn't you have to like sports to run away? All that running....

...stupid! He wanted to write. He had these stories in his head, but they were vague. How did he—The Terrace came naturally. It felt good. He knew it was way too derivative. Way too much explication, awkward backstory. Then he just had to insert words like 'fetid'. Was it showing off? Was it pervy about the DLA? He pondered that. 'Stranger danger' and TV clogged kids' minds with what adults were capable of. He kind of liked Fun and Moon. He liked Tallulah.

His dad was so mad at him he barely said a word. Ian couldn't help but imagine the scenes to come. But his mom and dad hated each other now. It was done. Ian knew it wasn't his fault. Teachers and counselors and experts told him that all the time. They promised him it was true. Bunch of liars! He felt like it was his fault.

His dad said the essay was 'kooky'. 'Kooky'? What did that mean?

Tomorrow, he had to go back to that school and apologize to the nun. He might have to apologize to the class. He was sorry for his very existence!

Then there was that girl. He'd put off thinking about her, about what had happened, but he wanted to remember now—

He'd run into her after school. He was pretending for the bus. She didn't ride the bus, she was walking by. She was by herself, she spotted him, erupted with, "Your ideas stink."

He replied, "At least I have ideas."

"Imply, infer—which is it? What are you saying, Mr. Ironic? Speak clearly."

"You got in trouble, too."

"Don't be obvious."

"That whole thing you did on my essay was a setup."

"That is so twisted. You're trying to make yourself a post-modern hero. But, oh, so, ironically."

"Subterfuge. That's what it was, so when your turn came up, the nun would be softened up."

"I have to admit—I hate to admit, I have to admit, the new boy, a bona fide atheist, has his humanism techniques down. Rhetoric!"

What was rhetoric? He heard the word all the time. But if she hated him, why was she carrying on? Because in movies the girl who hated the hero at first ended up being into him at the end—big time. He missed the bus. That's when he'd decided to walk home.

This big mouth, redhaired girl was clearly a thinker. She had to be a reader, a deep reader, and he'd never known a girl like that. Actually, he'd never known boys like that either. Plus, she was a blasphemer. Rebel at the Catholic school! She probably liked to write. Her favorite novel was *Jane Eyre*. This felt fabulous! But, simultaneously, the divorce, his mom's coming visit, his educational future, crammed the other side of his life balance.

Thursday, he took the bus home. He'd apologized meekly to the sister. But he didn't contact her, the redhaired girl. Friday, he looked, and she looked back, and her look turned to an awful glare. He walked home on Friday, and ran into Dan and Bu—Tallulah in the alley, so invited them over. Tallulah wore shades and hat.

Tallulah was aghast at their house, because it had no 'decorations'.

"You gotta have decorations," she explained, "to give the house that homey feel. This place is a dump. It's like living in a motel."

Dan said, "You've never stayed in a motel."

Tallulah groaned, "Uh-huh! That time we went to Pensacola—"

Ian said, "We just moved in. We haven't had time to decorate. We got pop tarts, the cinnamon kind. Is that okay?"

Tallulah said, "You have to show us your room."

Dan said, "Don't be a brat. You're being rude."

While the kids dropped their stuff on the living room floor, Ian said, "You didn't show me your room."

Tallulah said, "That's because we were getting to know you, and we hadn't decided yet whether you were a serial killer, who would sneak back in to our house in the middle of the night and murder us in our beds."

Ian said, "My room is the worst—"

Tallulah stomped from the living room to the hall where the bedrooms were. "Which one is it?"

Dan said, "Just ignore her. It's Friday, what are you up to tonight?"

Tallulah began to yodel.

Dan yelled, "Stop it right now or we're going home."

Tallulah stomped in place with her arms folded in front of her.

Ian strode over to her and said, "Come on, I'll show you my motel room."

First thing Tallulah did when Ian opened his door was squeal and rush for his bed, where she leapt, landing in its center.

"Where are your stuffed animals?" she cried. "Not even a Chewbacca plushy? I bet you have Darth Vader sheets like Dan does." She, again, leaped forward, tearing down the top blanket of his bed to uncover the sheets. Plain white sheets.

Dan said, "Are you done? Come on! Let's do this." He stayed by the bedroom door, embarrassed but snarky chuckling about it too.

Tallulah said, "One shelf of books." She levitated from his bed to the small chair at his small desk. She started going through the papers on his desk. "Where's your laptop?"

Ian said, "Don't have one. We share the PC in the kitchen. That's homework. Don't mess it up."

Dan said, "Come on. We saw his room."

Now she took a small paperclip she found on his desk and unfolded it. She moved over to the bare wall opposite his bed, with the paperclip and a piece of paper from his desk that was folded in half. She opened the paper, put it up against the wall, then drove the paperclip's unfolded tip through the paper and into the wall. It held. She stepped back to admire her decoration.

Dan said, "Tear it down after we leave."

Ian said, "Nah, she can decorate my room any time."

Tallulah ran over and gave Ian a hug.

Ian showed them the crappy old PC tower they had on their dining room table. They had cinnamon pop tarts and laughed about Dan's stories of teens on Friday night. In a lull in the laughs, Ian blurted, "My mom's coming in this weekend. Plane gets in tonight."

Dan went, "Uh-oh."

Tallulah said, "The plot thickens. What do we know about her?"

Dan tsk-ed, "Shut up! That's not right. Prying."

Tallulah looked like she might cry.

Quickly, Ian said, "No biggie. I hardly see her. I haven't seen her in a while."

Tallulah mumbled softly, "Is she a spy?" She adjusted

her shades and hat.

Dan said, "T!"

Ian said, "She works for a mining company in Colorado."

Tallulah said, "Buried treasure!"

Dan said, "We are out of here. Have a good night."

Ian said, "You, too."

Ian liked the decoration in his bedroom. It was a faded gray copy of the periodic table Sister had given him in science class. He left it up.

The ride to the airport was classic, with rain and pissed off dad. The ten-year-old Camry had a defroster as weak as an exhale, so only flashes of clarity came to the windshield, random as his dad's yelling: "Do you have a handkerchief? Let me borrow your handkerchief! Do you have a handkerchief?" Ian had never carried a handkerchief. His dad went into: "Where is your handkerchief?" This was repeated two times. Then, frantic: "Is there a rag? Do you see a rag?" Ian looked around. Frantic was contagious. He let his hands feel around by his feet on the floor, then under his seat. More screeching ensued: "Look! Find something!" Ian swung around on his knees to face the back of the car. He leaned over to check, grabbing wildly at anything on the floor. No rag! He leaned, he stretched, fell right over the seat, into the back. He cuddled on the floor of the car, staring up at the twinkly rear window.

His father was still yelling, something about responsibility and stepping up to the plate. Ian watched the rain drop prisms on the back window and wondered what the other Ian, the one who climbed over giant containers for loot, would do.

The airport terminal wasn't too busy. They found their

gate. A few single men and women, young people in a group, then some old people, waited with them. They all watched the TV monitor, which showed arriving passengers. Arrivals started coming in, guided down the hallways, until the final walk, broadcast on the monitor. Ian imagined, on TV that final walk down the hall built suspense. When the waiting people spotted their passenger on TV, they squealed with delight. When Ian's father spotted his mother making her way down the passageway, he gasped, "She's so skinny!"

Ian barely knew her, this pretty woman in a hat.

The last leg of the arrival compelled passengers to take steep steps, or the escalator, to the waiting loved ones.

Ian thought, 'what if they're not loved ones, but business associates?' There was nothing his mother could do to ease this visit's mission.

She spotted Ian and her husband on the way down the escalator. She wore a hat, not quite a Crocodile Dundee, but close to it. She could have passed for a middle-aged Laura Croft. She had a carry-on with wheels beside her, plus she wore a good-sized backpack. She waved and smiled. Her eyes looked big and red and wet, so a bit electric or sad.

When she left the escalator, she grabbed her carry-on and hurried over to her two human males, who stood there transfixed, staring at her, watching her every move.

"Hi, hi," she laughed, pushing aside her carry-on, grabbing up Ian, her arms going around him fiercely, muscularly, as she pulled him close. "I've missed you," she said into his head, her lips against his temple, her smell and power against his soul. "You've grown. You look good. Ian, I love you."

She broke away from him and turned to her husband. "Ethan." She nodded, smiling.

He nodded, said, "Taylor."

She went to him and they embraced. Not too long.

His father said, "Ian, get her bag."

Ian stepped up to the plate.

They walked to the parking garage humbly, quietly, in a file: Ethan, Taylor, Ian.

Ian got in the back. Mom, upfront. The rain had stopped.

Behind the wheel, his dad said, "Oh damn. Forgot my wallet. What are the chances of that? I never forget my wallet. I don't have any money for parking."

Taylor laughed but not in a mean way. Ian had forgotten her easy laugh. He'd missed it without even knowing he missed it. That made him feel hopeful and lost at the same time. It sounded so young—youthful, full of energy.

She said, "No worries. It's fine. I got it covered. I'm starved? How about we get takeout on the way back—"

Ethan snapped, "Finish the sentence, Taylor. *On the way back to **your** place.*"

Taylor said softly, "I was going to say, my treat. That's all. Let's have a truce until tomorrow when we can all sit down and talk for real." She turned around to face Ian.

Ian said, "Truce."

Ethan said, "Truce."

They ended up getting KFC, Taylor's favorite, extra crispy. She only ate the skin Ian remembered now, and remembered how Ethan found it disgusting. He remembered her joke in those burgeoning moments before the fight which Ethan also hated: 'my doctor says with my metabolism I need to take in more fat—more cigarettes.'

They got through the chicken dinner at the table in the dining room. Ethan had removed the computer to his room before they left for the airport. Taylor ate a few bites of chicken meat, besides a lot of crispy skin. She'd removed her hat.

Because of the truce, she didn't want to bring up Ian's

school, so she asked Ethan about his. Ethan answered with one-word replies. Ian tried to work in questions about her job and where she'd been, but she kept putting off her response with a smile and a 'later', which tilted her eyebrows up.

Finally, Ian and Ethan cleared the table, while Taylor went to clean up in the bathroom. Her hands were greasy from the chicken. She ate with her hands.

She came back to join them with bare feet, in jeans, with a T-shirt top. They sat at the table. Ethan folded his hands in front of himself, resting them on the table. Ian didn't know what to do with his hands, so held them in his lap.

Taylor said, "Ha! Now that I have your attention, Ian do me a favor and go get my pack. Just my backpack."

Ethan quickly inserted, "Ian, take her other bag back to your room. I thought she could have your bed, and you can take the couch."

"No way," went Taylor. "Couch is fine for me. I'm so tired I could sleep anywhere."

Ian thought, 'don't ask me'. He went and retrieved the backpack. It was heavy.

"Good boy," she said to him, like he was a dog. "Now, you still have that twenty-gallon aquarium I got you for those hermit crabs?"

"Crabs didn't make it, Mom."

She said, "Do you still have it? Does it leak?"

Ian answered, "Sure. It's in my closet. Why should it leak? Don't think it leaks."

"Get it. Prepare yourself for the surprise of a lifetime."

Ian went for the aquarium.

Ethan said, "What's this about? What's going on? Oh, God, you didn't bring him a puppy, did you?"

"Calm down. Of course not—a puppy in an aquarium?"

"No guinea pigs either. No rodents of any kind. Oh, God, you don't have a ferret in your backpack, do you?"

Ian returned with the aquarium. It was a mess of dust and cobwebs but seemed intact. For the crabs, they had put down about three inches of sand. The sand remained, now with funky spots. Ian was about to set it in the middle of the table—

Ethan yelled, "Wait, wait, wait! Let me put down some newspaper first."

"Good thinking, Dad," said Taylor. "Hang on, Ian."

Ethan found some old newspapers in the living room. He spread a few open pages across the table. Ian set down the aquarium.

Taylor said, "Ian, maybe we can clean it up. Paper towels, wet paper towels, some rags. Maybe a spoon to dig out the nasty spots."

Ethan said, "Not one of our good spoons."

Ian was not aware they had good spoons.

Ian and Taylor did their best to get the aquarium to an acceptable shape.

Taylor said, "We'll need a bowl, small, shallow, for water."

Ian said, "I know, not the good bowls."

Ian found the perfect bowl. He and his mother both leaned over the rim, into the aquarium to get things set up. Taylor used the spoon to clear space in the sand for the bowl.

Taylor said, "Good. In the morning we'll get dirt, sticks, some grass."

Ethan said, "Not more hermit crabs, for the love of God—"

"Nope," said Taylor, and up went the smile, which Ian now remembered could be wicked. "Now, I must tell you a tale that will freeze thy young blood and harrow up thy bones."

Ethan said, "Now you know why I prefer mathematics."

Taylor went on, "We were in New Mexico, way out in the eastern part. It's all plains, flat with a lot of dead grass, near where it meets Texas. Totally dried out. Dust. We were out there measuring the aquifers, updating maps—"

Ian interrupted, "I read that material on aquifers you sent."

"Good boy! We knew the aquifers shifted. They change, depths rise and fall as water tables discharge. It's a dynamic. We'd been developing this old shaft, an old mine. We fixed it up, got it running. It had been a bust. Metals in small amounts only. All that work, down over 2000 feet, and all they got was potash. We sent down new shafts. Strictly to get samples. They looked promising. The best shaft was expanded. We took more samples, continued to drill. Started seeing strange stuff, a porous alluvium, which is when we knew we were close to an aquifer. Forces deep, deep underground had snarled things all up. We were seeing something new. Then the drill went through."

Ian asked, "What does that mean?"

Taylor said, "It broke through. The strangest thing, and so deep, no one had expected anything like that."

Ian was off: "Could it be a cave? What happens when the water is gone in the aquifer, does it just sink into itself and collapse? Could some kind of big chamber have opened up, that no one knew about? That no one even knew was there?"

Ethan rolled his eyes and shrugged. "So, what was down there, the lost city of Atlantis? You're like a regular Indiana Jones, except you only do it for profit. I mean what is the motivation to mining? What are you teaching our son about humans affairs?"

Taylor said, "Subsistence. Subsidence." Taylor looked a little sickly. She said, "Geological forces are always adjusting. What we discovered may represent new forces, a deep mantle architecture never seen." She inhaled quickly, puffing herself up so she could go on: "It's impossible to trace all of the benefits and gifts that mining has bestowed on humanity. Ian, good questions."

She swung around in her chair and started tearing open her pack. Open, she dug into it from the top. She pulled out a small plastic bottle with an eye dropper top. She put the bottle on the table. She said, "For chlorine," and dove back into her pack.

Now she dug deeper, feeling around inside the pack. Her hands came back up to tug around the top, opening it wider. Her hands went back into the pack and took hold of something and brought this something out. It was wrapped in newspapers. Like a small cigar box, maybe 3 inches tall and 6 inches long. She brought the package to the tabletop. Ethan and Ian watched her every move.

"Oh, boy, what have we here?" cried Ethan.

"Dad," went Ian, "chill."

Taylor said, "Yeah, Dad, chill." She began unwrapping the newspapers. Several sheets had been folded in a specific pattern, making a thick covering.

Ian said, "If it's alive, it could be out of air."

Taylor said, "Insulation. What if it's anaerobic?"

Ian remembered (vaguely) what that meant—

The newspaper was off, pushed to the side. Ethan made a fuss gathering it up. On the table was a plastic container like people carried lunch in, big enough for a sandwich. It was a foggy white-gray container with a green lid. Ian saw a darker form inside it, maybe a shadow, in a corner. Was that water in there?

"What is it?" asked Ian.

Taylor said, "Open it."

Ian reached for the container, found the lip projection and peeled off the top.

Ethan cried, "Whistling cockroach from Madagascar! I read about them."

"No!" went Ian.

"Shush, everybody," said Taylor. "You're going to scare him." She huddled in closer, hand going in for the critter in the container.

It was a bug.

It was maybe an inch wide and two inches long. Clearly, it was a bug, because it was heavily segmented with little tiny legs underneath its body, which looked armor plated. It sat there on Taylor's palm, then quickly, as though it were floating, it slid up her arm to the inside of her elbow where it stopped. Very fast! Like it was levitating, which was silly because it must've been the action of all those tiny, tiny legs underneath. She smiled. "He tickles. Okay, three guesses. You have three guesses. Ian, pick him up, gently, on the sides, and hold him in your hand."

Ian said, "It's not a whistling cockroach?"

"No. That's one guess."

Ian gingerly moved his hand to the creature on his mother's arm. "Almost like a crab?"

Ethan said, "I knew it! Hermit crab! The *grande* edition!"

"Geez, really? That's a guess."

Ian said, "I got it: baby horseshoe crab." He had the little animal in the palm of his hand now. It wasn't a bug. It wasn't a crab. It had three lobes to its body, each lobe segmented from top to bottom. Bumps in the front, at the top segment, must be the head. The tapering segments were a deep brown color. The most amazing thing was the feel of its little legs, for the most part hidden under its body. "It feels prickly," said Ian.

"I know," said Taylor. "This incredible present for my incredible son is his under one condition."

"For goodness sakes," went Ethan, "what the hell is it? Tell us that first."

Taylor nodded, smiled, said, "Trilobite."

Ian went, "Trilobite!"

"I have its scientific name written down for you."

Ethan said, "Trilobite? Three lobes—got it. But aren't

those things extinct and have been for a long time?"

Ian said, "Hundreds of millions of years."

Taylor said, "The condition: you can't tell anybody you have him. Absolutely no one. You have to promise."

Ethan said, "Why? What does that even mean?"

"I promise," said Ian.

Ethan said, "You took it when you weren't supposed to. You stole it."

"It's complicated," said Taylor.

Ethan rose from his chair in a noisy flush. Ian felt the Trilobite's little legs, which had hardly been moving, suddenly go into—like waves of prickliness. The Trilobite didn't move though, remaining in his palm. Sounds—the vibrations, startled the Trilobite? Why did his mother refer to the Trilobite as he?

Ethan said, "What's next? Homeland Security showing up in hazmat suits, because this thing is covered in million-year-old viruses?"

"No, he's not," said Taylor. "We checked. He's relatively clean."

"Why do you call him he?"

Taylor's hand came over to touch Ian's hand, then slowly her index finger extended to touch the Trilobite, right at the top head segments, in the middle. She gently wiggled her fingertip. "He likes this," she said. Taylor beamed at Ian, and they shared a deep moment of satisfaction and fascination. "These bumps, on either side of the cephalon, this central head part, they could be light receptors."

Ian felt the legs settling in from their tiny shifting. "Like eyes?"

Ethan said, "A trained cockroach? What's next, a service animal bug?"

Taylor smirked. "That's just stupid. Let me finish my story so you'll understand."

Ian said, "What does he eat? Did you name him?"

"*Bug* sounds perfect!" cried Ethan.

Ian and Taylor both exclaimed, "No!"

The Trilobite cringed. At least that's what Ian thought it felt like, then the waves of prickly feet started rippling again.

"Let me tell this. Ian's right, some kind of cave chamber had opened. Maybe it was new. Maybe it was ancient, and no one ever knew it was down there. Initially, from what we could tell, the chamber seemed too big and there was water. Lot of water. Our development of the shaft gave us the capability to send down a drone. Obviously, the shaft's tube and thousands of feet of sheer rock would limit contact with the drone. Our guys programmed it to descend, then to leave the shaft and fly around, recording. Then it'd return to the shaft, back up. The pictures were bad, but we got our first inkling of how big the chamber really was. It was of huge proportions, just tremendous. We adjusted the shaft to handle a capsule that a person could descend in."

This was all too much for Ethan, and he was about to shudder and shake, then screech and stomp. Instead, he melted back into his chair. Ian thought this was the greatest story he had ever heard.

Taylor pushed on: "The air down there seemed okay. We sent in a man. He was eager to go, Ian, I can assure you. He actually walked around, took pictures, got samples. There was a lake in the chamber. Well, everyone was electrified! We notified the higher ups. Multinational mining companies need all the good PR they can get, and our company's discovery in geology is a phenomenal coup."

Ethan said, "I can see where this is going?"

Taylor said, "You'd be wrong. This is a major scientific discovery. It's not about money. It's about deep underground formations no one has ever encountered."

Ethan said, "The cockroach-a-bite comes from that

lake?"

"It does," said Taylor.

"It does," whispered Ian, eyes still glued to the Trilobite in his hand.

Taylor said, "We were going through the samples. Our guy had had the foresight to take samples from the lake bottom. He said the water was very cold and clear. I have the temperature somewhere written down if you're interested. And there's no light down there. Probably very little air until our shaft cut through. We're talking an anaerobic, lightless environment. Anyway, we were going through the lake bottom samples, sorting and straining, when we came on shells. We didn't know what they were at first, or even if they were some kind of fossil. They were from these guys molting, their cast-off shells, from these guys, Trilobites."

Ethan said, "Bacteria! There must be bacteria down there, decomposing bodies."

Taylor said, "Exactly. There must be an entire ecosystem down there—producers, consumers, decomposers. We found seven Trilobites. This was the largest. The small ones, about the size of my fingernail, died unfortunately. Maybe the light, maybe the air. That's when I got your phone call about Ian, and without thinking, when no one was around, I stuck this bad boy in my pocket. It was a spontaneous—"

"You stole it!" said Ethan.

The Trilobite on Ian's palm vibrated. It was a slight, minuscule movement of the legs. He must have literally hundreds of tiny legs, all able to move in consort. The Trilobite began to slide around in little circles in his hand. What could it mean? He could feel the legs' cascading prickle scrolling over his hand. It made him feel special. The circular movement kept to his hand. No explosive getaway, like a bug would do to run off. "What's he doing?" asked Ian.

"Probably finding the best place to insert its proboscis into your flesh to deposit its eggs, which will hatch and gnaw their way out through your innards."

Taylor interrupted before he could go on: "Really, Ethan? Alien parasite jokes?"

"What are you feeding him?" asked Ian. "Does he have to stay in the water?"

Taylor said, "You are the one who will discover his basic characteristics. I want you to keep notes. Put the Trilobite in the aquarium and get him some water. Then you can put him in your room. But first the water—bring me a glass of water. We'll put in a drop from the little bottle to get rid of the chlorine."

"First put him in the aquarium?" checked Ian.

"Of course," said Taylor.

Taylor stood. Ian felt the legs react. He leaned and stood slowly next to his mom, trying not to alarm the Trilobite, then placed the Trilobite, very carefully, in the aquarium. Ian kind of slid him off his hand onto the sandy bottom. The Trilobite sat there unmoving.

Taylor said, "They don't have jaws or a mouth really. At least from what I understand. More like a hole, a stoma, on the bottom, on the other side of the cephalon, where I was tickling him. They're kind of like little vacuum cleaners sucking up the stuff on the bottom and scrubbing off organic matter they discover for food. At least that's how I understood it. Son, you are off on an amazing adventure."

"I'll get the water," said Ian, and hurried to the sink. He called back, "What's he doing? What's he doing now?"

Ethan said, "If he dies, he'll stink up your room with million-year-old skank."

"Stop it!" went Taylor.

Ian returned with a glass of water.

Taylor said, "You do it," nodding to the small bottle with eyedropper.

Ian did it, let the water swirl for a minute, then poured it into the bowl in the aquarium. Ethan said, "Probably should have done that after taking the tank back to your room."

Taylor said, "Fine. There's only one solution then: big strapping fellow like you, you heft this sucker back to the boy's room."

"Thanks, Dad!" cried Ian.

Ethan bubbled, burbled, sighed, and stood. He said, "I can't wait until we talk tomorrow."

On the next visit to the kids' house, Ian got to see the setup. Three kids were there, each working assiduously. Two of them Ian did not know. Each kid had his or her own duties, and each got his or her duties done. Ian felt like a fifth wheel, then he realized he was their sixth wheel. No one laughed but they didn't ask him to leave. He had gone out with the little girls. They said he had had a good run. Ian asked where the girls were. They said they were in the setup. Then they dropped the bomb. Or dumped the bomb. Or sprayed it around the Terrace in a gagging syrupy splash: security had his picture.

Terrace security was lackadaisical at best... but still—

Ian said he wanted to talk to Fun and Moon. Pop, who'd been taking him around, showing him what Turd and Romper were doing, led the way.

Turd was a big guy at fifteen or sixteen. He didn't know which, and besides no one celebrated birthdays anymore. What would they give as gifts? Half a roll of toilet paper? No, Turd had learned electrics at Training, but was a maker at heart. He even had a certificate in nanotechnology, but Fun and Moon frowned on nanites. Turd was the eyes, the visual artist of the group, who'd turned the walls to luxurious vistas. That's what Ian thought of them, beautiful vistas, places no one had been, places everyone wanted to go. He supervised photo shots, took care of details, for DLA. He worked in all media. One wall in their house was a portal to the diamond dimension. Sparklies! One wall had a fire tornado.

Romper was a female with shaved head, probably around thirteen or fourteen. She also was an artist, but of words. Sounds. She was their voice. She helped with their rap, coming up with easy rhymes which were impenetrable. She, too, was a maker. Ian thought she looked like Tank Girl, a character from a 20th Century comic. He tried not to stare. Her big black boots.

Pop took Ian to a door in the hallway that was closed. Pop knocked once, opened the door with a flourish. He went dramatically: "Duh-duh!"

The setup was electronica extrema. Servers and towers, monitors big and small. Stacks of circuit boards, pads, plug-ins. All in a weave of cables. The room glowed in monster monitor electronica. Two stations in the middle of the room had keyboards and joysticks. On the two lawn chairs positioned there, Fun and Moon in their whites, their long white hair pulled back with scrunchies. They were low in their seats so they could stretch their legs out, with their bare feet up against the largest monitors' screens. They weren't touching a keyboard or a joystick. Their hands rested across their stomachs. The monitors cascaded with code and intercepts, a downpour of green and blue symbols.

Pop said, "Check it out! Contact!"

Fun said, "Through the feet is bestus restus festivus."

"Code with your feet," said Ian.

Pop popped: "Don't be shrewd mood! They're just doing that. They knew you were here."

Moon was staring at Ian, like she had a secret on him, or he had a secret she wanted, or she wanted to talk to him privately. Ian looked back, smiling questioningly.

"All ants in your pants, you want answers. Antlers will

be anthered." Moon smiled back at him, pulling in her legs, swiveling around in her lawn chair with wheels.

Ian said, "They have my picture."

Fun retracted from her monitor, like a little erector set set in reverse. She was too cute to be an android. She squalled, "We took care of it! Your care is fair, in the DLA lair. Figure it, swigger it, here it comes: you owe us."

Moon quipped, "You flow us. You muss us."

Ian stepped back, moving towards the door. He wasn't sure what was going on, which was pretty common when he was over here, but this time it seemed to be pointing to something he'd better be sharp about.

Pop held up his hand, "Easy, greasy, chock full of measly."

Ian said, "If my parents find out. My mom made an important discovery in the aquifers out West. I can't mess things up for her. My dad will freak."

Moon went, "Teatime! Tea, me, tea, me. Tea, plea."

Fun said, "Tea!"

Turd and Romper peeked in from the door, hanging back in the hallway. Turd said, "Tea party?"

Romper said, "You're farty."

They all left the room, closing the door behind them, walking down the hallway to the kitchen area. Lawn chairs, picnic table. Turd and Romper got the kettle going. They scampered through shelves and drawers, pulling out items, until they got it right. Pop put out mugs around the table. Romper had the teabags so went around to drop one into each mug. They sat.

Ian said, "What do you mean owe, flow?"

Fun said, "We do something for you, you do something for us."

Moon said, "Why do we live with bibs and fibs—"

"Dibs!" cried Fun. "It's like a balance sheet, one vector goes up, the other vector goes down."

Turd said, "What's a vector?"

Moon said, "No know know how, where there's a fling string going in on the one-way direct arrow monte."

Turd returned to the stove, checked the kettle, leaned back on the counter nearby. He folded his arms in front of himself. "Sure," he said. "A string is a vector in the delta."

Romper leaned forward, head and arms on the table. Muscular white arms, a long neck. She waited while they caught their breath, then, "What if we gave a favor and no one came? Rumple, crinkle, scaredy-cat?"

"No way," went Pop.

Ian figured he was scaredy cat extreme, with all options ending up in one of the new reform school orphanage hellholes where uncontrollable—undesirables ended up. They didn't serve gruel there, they injected it direct into your pie hole. He couldn't upset his new comrades. He had acted with them. They had done something together. But to extricate himself now was everything.

He said, "The only reason I got spotted was because I was helping you."

Fun said, "We told you: do the due, dance the pants, wear the lights, see the sites, hold on tight."

Turd used a hot pad to carry the steaming kettle to the table to fill their cups. Each cup held a teabag, government issue, commodities tea. Fun leaned forward over the table like Romper, both of their heads low, opposite Ian.

Fun said, "One last thing much it."

Pop said, "One thing returns the balance. You have to do it? Of course not! Of course you do! Ultimate—"

Moon said, "Penultimate." Her chair was back a few feet from the table, and she was crunched up in her seat, with her legs pulled up on the chair with her sad, moony face on her knees.

Pop said, "We are going to insert a heist, and we need your zeitgeist."

All the kids clapped, except for Ian, then they all slurped on their hot tea.

Pop finished with, "We are going to heist the world and destroy the world which will save the world. So we can go on making art."

Ian returned his cup to the table. The tea was harsh, bitter, black. And he was desperate. The last thing in the world he wanted to do was another action with these guys. But if not, if he didn't do it, what would he be, how would he live in the Terrace? He said, "What if—what if I had an idea, that was so good, so powerful, such a great concept for DLA, that we are talking major breakthrough?"

Romper emitted, "Do tell, do spell, do smell."

Fun said, "Breakthrough breakdown break clown."

Moon said, "It's later than you stink."

Pop said, "Like a trade? But what about the heist? We need you. Your face."

Ian said, "Heist sounds so—"

Romper tsk-ed: "Heist mice, clear ice, porridge splice."

Pop said, "What? What's your idea?"

Ian explained as though his life depended on it: "You'll love this! Look, everybody knows DLA basics now, what's been seen and done. Now's the time to spice it up. No, not like that. I mean, add to the horrors, the cringe, the gross out. The fringe factor. What we do, we make giant, lobed cockroaches, brown colored, not gross ones but ones that look weird, extraterrestrial, maybe even smart, and we have like fishing line to hold them on, and we tie these monster bugs to the girls, and move them up and down their bodies remotely."

Moon slurped on her tea. She started bending and flexing, like she was being animated. She slapped her hand down hard on the table. "I like it!"

Turd said, "That packing material we saved, seriously it should work."

Fun sat up straight, said, "And the heist mice?"

Romper said, "What about real live bugs? We could train them. We should use live bugs, hugs, mugs?"

Moon said, "Let's do this first."

CHAPTER 3

Monday at school Ian kept it on Hessler. Otherwise, he'd end up binge obsessing about his mother and father, and the bomb that was Saturday's talk. He hadn't even gone to the airport to drop her off yesterday, claiming he had too much homework. She had dug out of her pack the genus and species names on Saturday, *Hesslerides bufo*, from which they made his name, Hessler. Ian had never imagined a bug as a pet. The hermit crabs didn't have a lot of personality. Hessler did, no other way to say it. They'd gotten use to each other very quickly. Ian loved stretching out on his bed, Hessler over his heart, pillow under his head, up enough to see the undulating ripples of the legs. Ian was keeping his observations in a notebook.

In math, Ian raised his hand without thinking. His whole plan to lay low, under the radar, unnoticed by the nuns, his entire scenario was threatened. Sister, at the board, pointed to him. He was ahead of the class, who were just beginning algebra. He said, "The equals sign is like a balance, like a teeter totter: a kid jumps off one end, a kid on the other side better jump off too."

"Class, does that make sense? Ian has offered a good analogy, I think."

"Thank you, Sister."

"That's the basic concept for sure, whatever you do on one side, you do on the other. The equals sign is like the fulcrum. What about something like this." She went to the board and wrote out three equations in three variables. "Three variables, three equations."

Ian looked over the three equations. The class was not here yet, so what was Sister doing? He plowed ahead, "Since you can only solve for two variables at a time, you gotta express the third variable in terms of the others. It's not that hard."

"Show us." Sister held out her hand with the chalk.

Ian went up to the board and scribbled through the steps. At the end, he wrote: "A = B, B = C, A = C."

Bridget smirked from the back, "Show off!"

"Shhh!" went sister.

Ian returned to his seat. Will

Ian got through the day, furiously drawing Trilobites. Soon, all over his notebooks, he had miniatures, giants. He put them along borders, over page numbers, as punctuation. It would be fun to get home and be with Hessler. When they were cleaning up, packing their backpacks, Ian got up to use the pencil sharpener one more time. It was screwed into the wall by the class sink and its small work area. Right next to where Bridget sat.

She saw the whole thing unfolding. She was ready, sniggering already, squishing up her face, ugly as her mood.

Ian floated by her and she growled, "Odious one."

Ian kept going. Ignoring the world was impossible! He sharpened his pencil, began his return, went into his bit. She was turned, sideways in her seat, one long leg folded up, shoe on seat, the other long leg stretched out. Uniform skirt carefully positioned, etc.

After the math performance, then factoring in move, divorce, Trilobite, Ian felt an odd exuberance, an itchiness under his skin that could only be relieved by doing something. As though he suddenly had to be unafraid. No hesitation. He went into his bit with a bam bam, fancy footwork before Bridget, muttering in a rapper voice, "Obadiah!"

Bridget gasped, "You don't know what odious means."

He had every intention of looking in the class dictionary before the end of school, but suddenly everything had returned to the odious routine. It was the total embarrassment universe, where he could barely stand and walk at the same time. So he spaced. He stopped for a drink from the water fountain on his way out, after the bell rang, which waylaid him, got him wandering in circles, puttering around. He wasn't going to run into her! He missed his bus. That was upsetting. He wanted to get home and check on his bug.

He walked home stilted, as though his legs were unbendable, so he had to go back and forth in a rude wobble. His father hated when he did that. His mother would say, he's just a boy. He headed home, let divorce proceedings burgeon forth—

Friday night, Ian had gotten up on the hour to check on the Trilobite, shining his flashlight into the aquarium to see if he was okay, noting every wiggle and waggle in his handy-dandy, new geology field notebook his mom had given him. Saturday morning, Ian and his mom went out back into the overgrown yard and gathered rocks, some with moss, then a handful of twigs, a handful of grass and leaves, and a handful of dirt—good black soil. Now the aquarium was a terrarium, and it looked complete, cozy. Ian asked his mom if he should make some kind of top cover, like a lid. His dad insisted it was absolutely necessary. His mom replied he couldn't climb glass. She knew because she'd kept him in a glass jar at first, before she'd left. And he'd never managed to climb out. His dad huffed and puffed, while making scrambled eggs and toast for breakfast. Ian knew he was warming up—

Ian kept asking his mom about the Trilobite and the underground lake. She seemed hesitant in her answers or remarks, or else she too was simply prepping.

His dad said something like, we sign the papers today, right now, and we're divorced. Kaput. Zilch. Over and out. And you will have to stay with me until your mother gets her work schedule worked out. It's just for a few months, his mother claimed. Ian can go back and forth for visits. In Colorado, Ian asked. His mother didn't know. His dad said something like, your company is going to milk this. Then she interrupted to say it was an important discovery. Press conferences were planned. She had to get back. This was big, she said, like discovering a precious gem deep in the Earth, a once-in-a-lifetime discovery, from a half mile under the Earth. Trilobites are going to change everything! Dad said something wicked about the masses and a prehistoric bug, the whole time laughing like it was the funniest thing. His mother started talking about progress. Dad asked, at what cost? For whom? Change is not always for the better, Ian said, then regretted saying that because his mom went into the whole capitalism thing, that, like Churchill said about democracy, capitalism was an easily corrupted, flawed system, but still it was better than all the other systems. Dad got on his high horse and said we don't have a capitalist system, because capitalism is based on equal opportunity and equal pay for equal work, and everyone knows that's bullshit. Screams and hiccoughs ended breakfast. Then the signing, then....

"Toodles," cried Tallulah, running towards Ian when she spotted him enter the alley behind the houses. Was she a fairy princess in sunglasses and hat? That was insane. But this small person walking towards him had an unmistakable glow. "We were waiting for you," scolded Tallulah when she got close. Did little boys get that glow?

Dan had stayed where he was, watching, looking bored

and disgusted at once. He was wearing jeans and a sports jersey. He commented, "I thought you said you had a rock in your shoe."

Tallulah was in pink today, and she and Ian joined Dan, and they walked up the alley with the girl between them, taking it easy, looking as though they had a kid in a bunny costume between them. Ian dared not think it.

Tallulah said, "Spill the beans, SpongeBob!" She was keyed up, too attentive, like she could attack. "I can tell you want to. I can tell."

Dan tsk-ed, "Leave him alone! Shut up. Did you have a good weekend?"

Ian started to say, "Great weekend—" but Tallulah jumped in, explaining: "His mom came for a visit. You know what that means. Presents! She's a supersecret spy, and they're going to have to send him to assassin school, and we barely got to know him. Sad. Are you like *Inspector Gadget*?"

Dan ignored her. "Want to come over to our place? I don't think we have pop tarts."

"We're going to his house," said Tallulah. "For the surprise."

Dan said, "What surprise?" He fidgeted, glanced back and forth between them, caught the drift. He shrugged, said, "Friday night, bunch of people went out to this pond. Out on the highway. We were supposed to go skinny dipping, boys and girls. But it was too cold, so—"

Tallulah exploded with: "Yuck!"

"Shut up," went Dan. "See, there were two cars, these two guys had their licenses and got their parents' cars. They're brothers to two kids in my class. On the team."

"You are being rude and mean," went Tallulah. "Hanging around with old people—"

"So on the way home, all of us crammed in the cars, and Britney Grouper had to sit on my lap. All the way home. She's in ninth grade."

"We are so impressed," said Tallulah. "And you got a uh-uh."

"Shut up or I'll kill you."

Ian interrupted the escalating fight. "Come on, come over to my place. It's okay. My dad doesn't get home till late. We got pop tarts. And I got a super special surprise to show you. Maybe. If you stop fighting."

"I told you!" triumphed Tallulah. "They're secret spice spies!"

"You guys are sure mad at each other."

She closed her eyes and shook her head tragically: "He treats me like dirt."

"You treat me like dirt."

They got to Ian's house, dumped their packs, ended up in the kitchen. Ian got the pop tarts going. "Cinnamon," he said.

Dan and Tallulah sat at the table, an informal truce percolating.

"Where's the computer?" asked Dan.

"Ha! First, what's the secret, Philip J. Fry? Dan, doesn't Ian remind you of Fry from *Futurama*?"

Dan giggled. "You're like Lisa Simpson."

"You're like Butt Joe of the Butt People," announced Tallulah.

Laughing, Dan gurgled, "That's pretty good, for a funny bunny."

Tallulah stood, glanced over at Ian's expression, came around slowly to sit again. "I'm making a list. In my mind. That cannot be erased. No matter what. You ignore me. You want to kill me. Shut up three times. One funny bunny."

"Maybe today's not a good day—" Ian began and Tallulah pulled an imaginary zipper across her lips with thin white fingers.

Ian studied her pallor. But she was here. She was real. Her face looking at him, her eyes startlingly blue, full of life. This person! Brother Dan caught his eye, rolled his eyes, and the toaster dinged. They ate in silence, then had water, as there was nothing else to drink in the house.

Finally, Tallulah couldn't take it any longer and burst with: "If you're gonna live in a motel, then get yourself some Kool-Aid to mix in with the crappy motel water. I know! After I finish my pop tart, I have to go look for the top-secret, and you tell me when I'm getting warmer. Like a scavenger hunt."

Dan said, "She did pretty good there—what? Two minutes quiet?"

Ian said, "Can you guys keep a secret? I promised my mom I wouldn't tell anyone. So you have to swear."

Tallulah finished her pop tart and pushed back in her chair, making a sign of the cross at the same time. She held her hands together in front of herself. She appeared to be praying. She lowered her hands and got up to walk over to where Ian was sitting. She put an arm around him and pulled in close. Her face right in Ian's face. Her hair was so fine and white. Her skin seemed transparent, cloudy, as though he could see clouds softly moving underneath. She whispered, "Give. Tell."

"You don't want to search?" asked Dan.

Ian sat back, away from Tallulah, and stood. "It's in my bedroom. But you got to swear. No goofing around about it."

"I swear," said Tallulah, holding her left hand over her heart.

"Promise," said Dan.

Ian led them to his bedroom. Tallulah gasped when she saw the periodic table still up on the wall. The terrarium was on his small desk. They went to work, hurrying to it, looking, searching. Nothing. No Trilobite.

"Is it a snake?" asked Tallulah. "You got a spitting cobra! You have a spitting cobra, I'm leaving."

Dan said, "Shut up. It get out? What is it? Gerbils? A

ferret? You gotta keep those guys caged up. I had a buddy who had one. Stink up the place too."

Tallulah declared, "No smell, lamebrain."

"Shut up."

Ian was bending into the terrarium, gently shuffling his hand through leaves and dirt and rocks and twigs. The water was getting muddy. He couldn't find him anywhere! He had to change the water.

Dan went 'woof' and jostled Ian's shoulder, making him and Tallulah jump.

"Don't!" cried Tallulah. "Boy can't find his new pet. Be supportive."

Ian retreated from the terrarium, baffled.

The three of them kept looking. They bent their heads in. Their eyes went back and forth scanning. No one saw a thing. At the exact same moment, the three of them saw movement in the sand—

—in the sand, of an open sandy spot, by the bowl, grains of sand were falling away, to the side, being pushed aside. Something was coming up!

Hessler's three lobes appeared in the sand. Just the top curvatures at first. Then his body shimmered clear, rising to the surface.

"Hessler!" cried Ian.

"Bug!" cried Tallulah.

"Singing cockroach of Borneo," giggled Dan.

Ian felt immediate relief. "It's okay. He's not a bug it all. Well sort of. But we don't want to scare him. Let me introduce you."

Ian leaned back into the terrarium, extending his arm inside. His fingers touched Hessler, held still a few seconds, then the fingertips, gently wiggled. Hessler didn't move. Ian curled his fingers under and around the Trilobite body, cupping him in the palm of his hand. His arm came out of the terrarium slowly. He held the Trilobite before the two kids.

"No funny business," said Tallulah.

"You can hold him," said Ian.

"I'm not touching no bug. Gross," said Dan.

Tallulah put her small hands out next to Ian. Thin hands like a bird's.

"He tickles," said Ian, sliding the Trilobite into Tallulah's hands.

"He tickles!" said Tallulah. She exhaled. "When I talk, I can feel it. His little legs moving."

"I think he likes you," said Ian.

The Trilobite slid out of her palm, glided around the bony bump of her thumb, and quickly made it to the inside of her elbow. The Trilobite filled her elbow.

"What's he doing? What's he doing?" went Tallulah. "I can feel it."

"Hold still," said Ian. "He's getting to know you. This is what he did to my mom. Do you want me to take him?"

Tallulah shook her head, her big eyes glued on the Trilobite. "They don't bite, huh, do they?"

"Guess not," said Ian

"Way he went up your arm was weird," said Dan. "Like he slid or something. What kind of bug is he? I mean come on, top-secret? What's so secret about a bug?"

"Magic," whispered Tallulah.

"My mom," said Ian, "brought him for me. He was found a half a mile under the earth in a vast underground lake no one had ever seen. It's an important discovery."

"I still don't get it," said Dan. "Why so secret?"

"It's a Trilobite. They went extinct millions of years ago. I think my mom's company is going to release information about it, any day now, announcing the discovery."

Dan huffed, hmmm'ed. "Trilobite? I think I've heard of them. From school? Fossils? *Living* fossils?"

"How come their name has 'bite' in it?" asked Tallulah, still keeping her voice down, almost whispering, so as not to disturb the Trilobite nestled in her elbow.

"*Hesslerides bufo,*" said Ian. "That's the genus and species name. So we call him Hessler."

"Great," said Dan, "a Nazi bug."

"He's not a bug," said Tallulah.

"Looks like a bug, a big funny bug," said Dan. "Top-secret?"

Ian wondered why Tallulah said that. "Why don't you think he's a bug?"

"Because of the way he talks to me," said Tallulah. "What does it mean? I don't understand."

Ian took Hessler from Tallulah's elbow and put him back in the terrarium. "Hessler likes you, I can tell."

"You need to go wash your hands, T-bug," said Dan.

Tallulah rubbed her hands against her pink legs.

"What's he doing?" said Dan, moving in close to the terrarium, hunching down to it.

Ian and Tallulah came in close, too. They all had their faces up against the front glass. Dan exhaled to make fog.

Tallulah gasped, "My heart is beating so fast."

Hessler had slid into his water bowl. The water covered him completely. From the sides of his head, two thin antennae extended, to break the surface of the water and peek out. At least, Ian assumed they were antenna.

"What *is* he doing," said Ian. "I don't know."

Trilobite! was the hottest DLA meme in the Terrace.

Tallulah washed her hands, and she and Dan took off, but only after once again promising not to tell.

Ian returned to his room, sat in the chair by his desk and got out his new notebook. He needed to write down everything that happened. He'd have to tell his mom about the antenna. He had yet to do a search on the net about Trilobites to see what other information he could find. So far, the Trilobite seemed fine, even healthy, good color, no smell, and very responsive. He liked the terrarium, Ian was sure. He must be getting food from the leaves and dirt and twigs they'd brought in.

He wrote it all out, added the date. He did not mention that Dan and Tallulah were present, even though he knew that had influenced Hessler's behavior. Hessler seemed to respond to Tallulah.

He grabbed his straight edge ruler and stood. He was measuring Hessler every twelve hours. Just in case. Data. It was early but—

He reached for the bowl in the terrarium, slowed, had his fingers break the surface of the water over Hessler. Immediately, the antenna pulled in. Ian moved his hand closer, until his fingers touched, then he wiggled the fingertips, and slowly slid his hand under the Trilobite's body.

His shirt would dry. Ian stretched out on his bed, Hessler over his heart. Ian's head on the pillow was angled up enough to give him a decent view. He waited a while till everyone was cozy. He could feel the legs' movements settle through his shirt. His arms stayed at his sides. He was motionless. The left hand with the ruler slowly raised. The tickly movement of the legs shifted at his arm's motion. He brought the ruler down next to Hessler, lined it up. He squinted to get the numbers right.

'Oh, that's good,' thought Ian. Then out loud: "He's growing."

Ian was so sleepy. He had to remember those numbers. His eyes were heavy. He had to figure how to weigh him. His eyes closed.

The Terrace said hello. There was no other way to go with it, because the people there were such lamebrains. Except for the kids. It would have to go: AI's versus DLA. The AI's wanted to cut out the middleman. They wanted the girls to themselves, to set them up in a place which they controlled so they could watch 24/7. Sick.

Who invented the blaster? Pulse rifle? Rail gun fun! Gratuitous flotsam—aluminum dust at supersonic speeds? Blast is fast! Bombardment probability—

CHAPTER 4

On Tuesday in science, they were reading about Paleontology, then having discussion. Fossils, bones, and dinosaurs. Ian knew where this train wreck was headed. The moment people started talking about dinosaurs was guaranteed to be followed by a moment when they started talking about change. Think about Hessler! Ian noticed that the work table next to Sister's desk, now crowded with what could have been toy lab equipment, had a small scale that might work.

Sister mentioned 'evolutionary biology', based on the Theory of Natural Selection. "Note," said Sister, "it's still considered a theory, a guess."

Ian raised his hand and asked if that was what 'theory' meant, 'a guess'.

Sister said, "If Ian has a theory that apples are better than pears, that would be his opinion, his guess."

Ian asked. "Can I look it up in the dictionary?"

Sister said, "May I? Of course."

Ian went to the big dictionary atop the classroom's one shelf of books. An encyclopedia and some reference works completed the shelf. He looked up theory. "'One,'" he read, "''a law or basic principle.' We say Atomic Theory, Cell Theory, and those aren't guesses."

"Return to your seat," said Sister. "The issue is change. We know God is perfect. By definition. So why would— how could a perfect supreme being create imperfect creatures that had to change?"

Ian said without raising his hand, "Because the Earth is always changing."

Sister said, "Where do whales live?"

"In the sea."

"And where do monkeys live?"

Now the kids giggled and muttered around Ian, making fun. The boy who sat across from him went into monkey mode, scratching at his armpits.

"In the tropics."

"So how do all the animals know where to live? Especially If the Earth Is changing so much?"

Ian's shields had failed. Rail guns spent. Blasters corrupted. He'd better get used to it. There was such a thing as will, the ability of people to use their minds to force their bodies to do things. Willpower! Impulse control! All of his dad's favorite topics. Would Sister call his dad? He had to keep his mouth shut. *His atheist views and values bring rancor to the class.* Ian kept his mouth shut the rest of the day.

He was lined up for the bus, when he saw her. She came strut stomping towards him, her wrinkly blouse tugged in at her waist. Her demeanor, one of sloppy arrogance.

"Did you look up odium?"

"I looked up sodium."

"You think you're the proof of evolution. You want to be a superhero because you're so special. *Intelligencer,* we'll call you. *Intelligencer* to the rescue! *Intelligencer,* not intelligentsia. That's different. I looked it up."

"I don't know what you're talking about, but I like it. I can prove evolution. If you dare."

She scowled. "Did you ever notice how superheroes all

fall somewhere along the autism spectrum? You know about Asperger's syndrome? You know what that is? Multitasking, lists, notes and notes, memory palaces, moral compasses. Superheroes are autism wannabes. Of course, I dare. There's nothing you can say—"

"I like sparklies, but I don't think I'm autistic. That's an interesting proposition. But for me to prove it I have to show you something. At my house. I can't bring it to school."

"A fossil?"

Ian shrugged.

"I'm not going over to your house. What is it? Dare me. Tell me."

"You have to see for yourself. Tomorrow. Take the bus home with me. I bet you live close. I can walk you home."

Kids had formed around them like filings around magnets, in patterns. The kids were fascinated by these two going at it. They listened and laughed, then mocked and jostled. Bridget had to give harsh glances at offenders until they shut up. Ian thought even the boys were afraid of her. She could beat them up. Ian had to get on the bus. Kids were giggling about Ian asking her out, for a date. Ian got on the bus.

Ian explained the whole situation to Hessler, while stretched out on his bed in his room, Hessler cuddled over his heart. Ian felt so sleepy. He hadn't done a measurement. He needed to update his notebook. When he closed his eyes, he felt Hessler move. He opened his eyes and couldn't see him, but he could feel him. The soundless sliding motion had taken Hessler to Ian's neck, where he stayed. Ian and Hessler relaxed. When Ian opened his eyes the next time, he was in a dream land Terrace, phony house, phony school, so he knew not to trust this Bridget standing before him calling him names. She wore an astronaut suit, but no helmet.

Ian pried his eyes open, couldn't see Hessler. He raised

his hands to feel about his neck. Good thing Ian didn't jump in surprise: Ian felt Hessler nestled on his head, in his hair. Ian could feel his legs now, tiny rhythm of minuscule bumps, not unpleasant at all. Hessler on his head, next to his brains, where his thoughts and dreams came from. He'd have to explain the Terrace to Hessler, how those were rubber Trilobites.

What if that girl came over? And his dad was always late. And they had pop tarts. Ian had never been alone with a girl. He knew he started acting stupid, like a kid, around girls. What if Hessler didn't like her? How could he explain how Hessler was proof of change?

Because Hessler was hundreds of millions of years old. Not Hessler specifically, but his kind. What if she didn't like his name? What if she hated bugs? Clearly, Hessler was a bug, segmented, antenna, so obviously an arthropod. But from when arthropods were starting out. Origins. Ian had to cram—learn everything he could about Trilobites. He'd do a search. He had to look up Asperger's syndrome. He wished Hessler could teach him directly from up on his head in his hair.

He gently removed Hessler from his head and put him back in the terrarium. He left his bedroom and went to his dad's room. He booted up the old tower on a card table in the corner and started his search.

The next day was Wednesday, and it was the biggest day of Ian's life. 'She will never get on the bus,' Ian thought. No way! He wanted to tell her he was a writer. He bet she was. He would come on like a ninja, knowing what to say. They would become fast friends. But the chance of her getting on the bus—no way!

The kids, when she didn't get on the bus with him, would make fun and point fingers, then end up pushing and pulling at him. And she would smirk and love it and make rude comments, joining her classmates in bullying him, as they would for the rest of his life at this school. He kept quiet all day. Kept his head down. Didn't even joke with the kids around him, ignoring the constant barrage of faces and grunts and half choked quips and puns.

He made notes on his story. *The Terrace*—it seemed as good a title as any. He kept a sheet of paper on his desk, no matter what subject they were on, which texts were required on his desk, so that he could scribble words and phrases that might fit. Occasionally, situations would occur to him that would fill out transitions or drive the plot forward. He moved between school and Terrace all day. It was easy. He wondered if Bridget did that.

The bell rang and they filed out in an orderly manner. Ian hadn't dared to glance her way all day. Phasers on humiliation. He didn't care. Everybody had forgotten. He left the classroom without looking at her, then down the hall, past the water fountain, and out the front doors. He took it easy. No big rush, no big deal.

Three buses out front. He went for his, the one on the end to the left. He kept his eyes straight ahead. He didn't even know whether she rode the bus. Maybe her mom picked her and her sisters up. She had sisters. Ian had seen them at school with Bridget, younger versions of her with red hair and long, skinny legs. All from the same plan— design?

Ian took the first step into his bus, when a boy's voice rang out, "Aren't you going to wait for your girlfriend?"

He hesitated a micro-nano-second, then hurried up the steps into the bus. It was about half full, its usual load. Ian shuffled to the back, an empty seat, swung his pack around and dropped it on the seat, then he sat.

That was that! Bus filled! Close the doors! *Let's get outta here!*

The bus driver touched the handle on his dash to close

the door, and it was like the magic gesture that made her materialize, for there was Bridget at the bottom of the steps. Ian couldn't see her, but he recognized her vitriol: "Hold on, Mr. Bus Driver! I'm taking this bus today."

She came up the steps fast, made her way down the aisle, but would not meet his eyes. A couple rows ahead of Ian, she slid into a seat, dumped her pack.

Now she turned to face him. "I'm not sitting with you. Forget it. Boy cooties."

Kids laughed. A few crowed crude outbursts. The bus driver said settle down. The bus door accordioned shut and they headed out.

Finally, she quit staring, and said barely loud enough for Ian to hear, "I dare, odious one."

They rode through four stops without a word or wiggle, Ian's eyes cast on the back of her head, her wild red hair. When it was their turn, he muttered, "Our stop," and stood, pulling on his pack. Then: "This is where we get off."

She stood and said without looking at him, "*Alto. Arret. Stoy.* I can say stop in seven languages. I understood the first time, *Monsieur Intelligencer.*"

She exited the bus from the front. Ian went out the back with a couple other kids who immediately took off running.

The bus roared away, blue exhaust making Bridget and Ian wrinkle their noses. They stood forty feet apart, a bus length, on a sidewalk, suddenly free, and rising to it, ready to gallop off on this roller coaster. They looked at each other. And this moment, when they stood apart like divots on a boardgame, was the same moment for both of them, as though something loosened in them, and they knew they were about to exercise parts of themselves they'd only vaguely been aware of. At the exact same moment, they marched to each other.

When Bridget got to Ian, she swung around to face the

way he was going, and she yelped, "*Donde esta, mein Führer?*"

"This way, over here, proof."

"If you prove evolution to me? What do you get? What is your reward? Bringing another child to atheism?"

"And if I can't prove evolution to you, what do you get, if you win?"

"You have to be my slave."

"That's gross. We will never speak of it again. How will I know you really aren't convinced?

"Faith. Trust. Decency."

"This way, proof."

Ian led her to the front door of his new home. He had the key and opened the door.

She said, "What will the neighbors think?"

"Nothing. So far, they seem a lot of old people and automatons. Too busy to notice anything."

Ian closed the door behind her. He dropped his pack on the living room floor, motioned her to do the same. She did. In the kitchen, he mumbled, "Glass of water."

She shook her head, then followed him to his room. He let her go in first, and she paused right away to point to the periodic table on the wall, mouthing the word 'cute', then straight to the terrarium. She leaned in. She got down on her knees in front of the terrarium, pressed her face in close. Ian came up behind her until he could see into the terrarium, where Hessler was giving a remarkable show. The two-inch long Trilobite seemed puffy, bloated. He sat there in the sand in a motionless tremble. No antenna showed. Hessler's color was off, his usual deep brown had paled, in places gone cloudy.

Bridget said, "He needs help." She was adamant.

"What do you mean?"

She scratched her head and wiped her nose with her hands. Ian saw how her hands had long fingers that she kept moving, curling, opening, closing, spreading.

Ian got down beside her. Hessler had begun to writhe. Faintly at first, it seemed an internal movement. Then a strong ripple pulsed through his three lobed form.

"Something's trying to bust out!" went Ian. "Parasites!"

"No," Bridget snapped. "He needs something to hold onto. To push on. A brace."

"What do you mean? How do you know this?"

She stood, leaned over the terrarium, her long left arm diving in to it. She selected the largest twigs and stones scattered about the terrarium, then arranged them close to Hessler in a rough line. He didn't budge as she did this. She mooshed the rocks and twigs into the sand so they were grounded. Before her hand pulled away, Hessler slid to the makeshift wall and pressed against it. The spasming climaxed with a tear starting at the ridges, what were called furrows, between the head segment, the cephalon, and the three-lobed thorax. Another tear on the other side of the cephalon.

Hessler was molting, and Bridget's rising hand hesitated, as though she knew she could still help. Her hand extended to Hessler, forefinger out, then the fingertip touched Hessler, and with her fingernail she started to scrape off the old skin. Bridget helped.

Hessler did a little wiggle against a rock and Bridget's fingertip and wriggled out of the old thorax. Hessler slid into the bowl, submerged. Ian saw how shiny brown he was now. And he was bigger now.

Bridget did a two-step, backing away from the terrarium, glancing around for somewhere to sit. She pulled up his chair, sat. Ian sat on his bed beside her. Sitting so close emphasized how much taller she was than Ian

"Perfect timing," said Bridget. "Three lobes, Trilobite. Say the magic word and win a million dollars! Watch him molt. *Intelligencer*, save me. Can I have the old skin?"

"Can you lower your voice," said Ian. "He seems

sensitive to loud, fast talking."

"Who's fast talking?"

"You are." He pretended to look at the terrarium for a pause. "I kind of like it."

"You better."

"How did you know he was molting?"

"You thought only girls molted. What's his name?"

"Hessler. From his scientific name, *Hesslerides bufo.*"

"Who's Hessler? A geneticist? You crossbred cockroaches back to their ancestral form."

"You do know evolution is real."

"Duh—I'm predicting your one-liners. I know what you are going to say before you say it. You are a DNA hacker, *Intelligencer.*"

"Duh—you think I have a secret lab hidden in the house where I breed ancestral cockroaches?"

"What's the alternative, big boy? Razor it for me."

"My mom's company opened an old mine and hit what they thought was the aquifer. This is all top-secret by the way. You have to promise not to say a word. Turned out to be a huge chamber with a lake, a huge underground lake. That's where Hessler comes from."

"Cross my heart." Bridget kicked off her shoes. "Take your shoes off," she said. Ian took off his shoes. She crossed her arms before her, and sat up straight, her eyes studying him. "Prove it," she said.

Ian thought of Mount Rushmore and she was the president.

"Primitive means like the ancestral form. Hessler is a primitive arthropod. Modern arthropods have fine-tuned this rough model into an advanced form, better mouth, better gills, better reproduction."

"Were you going to say, 'they worked out the bugs?'"

"No!"

"Shabby proof, *mon petit soldat.* Realize what this critter proves is their supposed extinction millions and millions of years ago didn't happen. No extinction, no change. The earth is 5000 years old. QED."

"*Quite easily done.*"

"*Quod erat demonstrandum.*"

"What do you want with the skin?"

"I'll treasure it always to remember our first date."

"Is this a date?"

"It's a fig, darling!"

She stood. She moved her shoulders up and down, a little stretch. She went over to the terrarium and leaned in. "Can I touch him?"

"I guess so."

Ian did not panic. This girl! He had to write it all down. Hessler was his subject, Hessler was the story. Bridget was more than a story. She forced his secret privacy shields to evaporate. He was left in public to be with her. Face to face with her. No fakes. Did she feel the same way? Because being with another person like this, talking and sharing, required a mutual interest. His imagination felt broken when it came to what he was feeling. Where he was now was what he was. Ian rose, got to his feet and stretched a bit. He slid in close to watch. She was so tall, next to him, her back to him.

"Are you staring at my ass?" She moved her left hand to the bowl in the terrarium, extending her forefinger again. She touched the water, and little arcing circles expanded from the tip of her finger. Her finger curled downwards, and she touched Hessler's cephalon, where it met his thorax. Hessler did a funny twist and her hand obliged by lowering some more, so that he ended up resting in the palm of her hand.

"Hessler," she said.

"I've never seen him do that."

Bridget brought him out of the terrarium dripping, scooted back to the chair to sit. She held her hand with Hessler over her lap. Her other hand, her right hand, hung at her side, fingers flexing. Ian sat at the edge of the bed, getting in tight, watching the Trilobite, fidgeting to touch her knees, trying not to touch her knees, even her knees taller than his, wondering how first it was Tallulah, now it was Bridget. Maybe Hessler liked girls. Or maybe he liked girls because Ian liked girls.

"Get closer," she said.

"What do you mean?"

"Knee to knee."

She twisted forward, knees together, skirt over her knees, and tried to shorten her knees. Ian came forward, straightened, positioned his knees against hers, and tried to heighten his. She pushed in.

"Good," she said. "Tell me about Trilobites."

Hessler, still in her palm. They quieted.

"Can you feel his legs?"

"Yes."

"Trilobite fossils go back to the Cambrian. People used to think they were the first arthropods. But they've found a lot more fossils now. Like the Burgess Shale."

"I'll look it up."

"That's 540 million years ago. Long before the dinosaurs. Trilobites make up fifteen orders, over 150 families, 20,000 species found."

"You have to have so much time to cram all the change in. See how one thing leads to another. See how once you start down this path, there are only so many ways it can go. You start by depending on all this time. You're excavating time. How big did they get? "

"Two foot long? Are you saying we invent time?"

"St. Augustine, one of my favorite saints—you know I'm learning Latin, mentions time, mentions noticing it, or the lack of any substance to it. But I don't know. Two-foot-long is big, like a horseshoe crab."

"Clever girl. I don't understand all the saint stuff. St. Barf's. That's what the kids call it."

Their knees had bumps that learned to correlate like puzzle parts when they pushed them together right.

Bridget finally smiled and said, "So what happened? Where they all go?"

"Permian extinction, 230 million years ago, most life went extinct."

"We're back to catastrophism. A flood?"

"It's complicated. CO_2 in the water. Asteroid strike. The atmosphere was changing."

"Tell me more."

She spoke very oddly now, in a way he'd never heard a girl talk. Maybe in the movies he'd heard this way. Was she trying to hypnotize him? He wouldn't put it past her.

"Their shells are made of chitin. So you could eat 'em, like you could eat a whole shrimp. We can digest chitin." He shrugged, fidgeted. But Hessler was fine in her hand. And their knees were doing a funny lazy Rumba that didn't bother him or him. He kept talking: "They have eyes, compound eyes. Pretty big. They can see like a dragonfly does. They have males and females. Gills. Some maybe were predators, some filter feeders, some suckers."

"Gross—who would eat Hessler? Why did they have gills if there was no oxygen? I mean, I mean, if it was deep, deep underground, no light, no oxygen, no real ecosystem possible. QED."

"Maybe they get by with minerals in the water. Like sulfur. A whole new ecosystem never explored. Alien life forms never seen alive."

"But they're from Earth? So not too alien. Huh, Hessler? No one's going to eat you. How do they mate?"

"They have males and females. I guess they let their eggs and seed mix in the water."

"How romantic. I notice you said seed. Do males actually plant a seed in the female's oven to grow a baby?"

"It takes two to tango."

"Back to DNA." She took a second to glance around

Ian's room. What was she doing? What was she looking for? She settled, kept her eyes down, and slowly said, "Ian, why do we feel this way?"

"I don't know. Bridget. Because we like each other?"

"I don't like you that much."

"With Hessler we are...we're—we can talk. I want to be a writer. Do you write?"

"How do you mean? Of course, I write for school every day."

"You know what I mean. You're always so cagey."

"That's what I mean about feeling this way. I don't feel like I want to be cagey."

"Either do I. I write stories. I want to be a writer. I write every day. I read as much as I can."

"When do you get out for an adventure, to have something to write about? I see: you're going to write about me, the beautiful mermaid that seduced you with a bug."

"Are you seducing me?"

"Of course not."

She pulled away, twisting her knees free. She kept her hand steady. "Hessler doesn't like it when I move around. Can I sit on your bed?"

Ian stood, made room for Bridget, who promptly stretched out in the middle of his bed, her head on his pillow. Hessler slid from her hand to hover at her heart. Bridget's hands meshed together below him. "Perfect," she said. "Talk to me." Her eyes, half open/half closed—

Ian sat in the chair. "I want to write stories."

"You already said that."

"I want real characters. Every story is about a person. What makes a person? Memories? Quirks and buzzwords? Choices! The choices we make decide everything. Unless you have Asperger's syndrome, in which case I guess it's in your genes. Too much? TMI? I'll shut up."

"No, I like it." She sounded sleepy. Or she was taking

his advice about fast, loud talking, leaving it to him to annoy Hessler.

Ian looked all the way down her long body to her white socked feet, bigger than his own feet.

"I'm a poet," she said. "I write—I don't know if they're poems. I can't say I write poems, don't know for sure. I like stories too. Maupassant." She talked in slow motion. "Poems, in a way, each tells a story. But not necessarily. Like with a beginning, middle, end. All that jazz. As long as you end up different—that's the key. Are you the key master?"

"Yes, I am."

Who knew how long a nap lasted? Who knew what a cuddle did to young people? Who knew what Hessler's antenna were doing, one extended to touch Bridget's neck, the other extended to touch Ian's temple, as his nap had taken him to a collapse at the edge of the bed, him on his knees, his torso scissored in over Bridget, his head on her tummy, one hand on her right arm, the other on her right knee.

Ethan didn't notice the antenna. He'd come home at dusk as usual to a quieter than usual house. No music. No TV. He walked back to his son's room which had its door open. He barely peeked at the two of them on Ian's bed because the sight made him back off fast. He flushed, his heart pounded. He had a real moment when he didn't know what to do. A second later, he came back to knock at Ian's door.

Bridget jumped, but her hands went to cradle Hessler. Ian raised his head. Bridget's right hand went to where Ian had been napping. She exclaimed: "Gah! Boy drool! You're disgusting. Hello there, Mr. Scanlan, I presume."

"I don't want to know what's going on here. But I trust

my son. It's late, so we'll say you were studying at the library, and I came to pick you up. Young lady, I'm taking you home right now. Get your shoes on. Let's go!"

"Yes, sir. Thank you, sir," said Bridget.

They put Hessler back in the terrarium and got their shoes on. They followed Ethan to the living room where Bridget retrieved her pack. Everyone was stiff, silent, embarrassed, shocked. They got in the car. Bridget told Ethan her address, then cross streets he would know.

Father upfront, two kids in the back, the immortal Camry provided transport. Half asleep, Ian wasn't sure what was happening. He couldn't comprehend being in the back seat of the Camry with Bridget. She looked windswept. Her eyes were red. She picked at her cuticles. She wouldn't look at him. Her knees were far away.

"Sir, Mr. Scanlan," she said, "the only way this can work is if you go in with me and Ian to introduce yourselves to my mom. You have to talk to my mom."

Mr. Scanlan enunciated, "You two owe me big time. We'll talk about that later. This one time, we do this. Ian can't afford getting in trouble again. Things are too chaotic right now. You getting in trouble would please your mother to high heaven. Right. We do this once and never again."

"This is my house," said Bridget. "My name is Bridget Tilson. I go to Catholic school, St. Bartholomew's, with your son. We were doing school work and dozed off. We didn't realize how late it was and I forgot to call." She shrugged powerfully and raised her head, which made her neck tighten—extend....

Ethan pulled it off without a glitch. He introduced himself as Professor Scanlan, and Mrs. Tilson was appropriately impressed. Redhaired girls in school uniforms, in all shapes and sizes, yo-yoed about the front room with the old TV, until Mrs. Tilson growled for them to settle down. Ian could tell it was an old model TV because it had a back, behind the screen the bulky cover for the cathode ray tube. The small house smelled of cabbage. Mr. Tilson was not home. Professor Scanlan explained how the kids had been at the library and forgot to call. Mrs. Tilson shook hands with Ian—her eyes avoiding his, but for quick fiery laser blasts. The whole thing happened so fast that Bridget's mom didn't have time to get upset. She had dinner to prepare and six kids to supervise, five of which had been abysmal before the professor knocked on the door. Ian and Bridget were appreciative of Ethan's fine lying. Parents lied as easy as breathing, as good as kids.

Ian saw his desperate idea come to fruition. Turd fashioned Trilobites to Ian's specifications. His materials came from the trash, but he had some good brown coloring agent to get it right. Turd knew, too, that given the blurry nature of their imagery, the Trilobites would be otherworldly, definitely creepy alien. Furrows and lobes accentuated. The completed Trilobites turned out to be about three inches long, big for the skinny white elbows.

Romper took over the staging. She worked with Turd to figure the best way to attach Trilobites to girls. Silicon was too thick and stinky. Regular glue, too messy. Fine thread, not strong enough. They settled on fishing line. Film clips! Trilobites moving! That still wasn't perfected. The whole time they rehearsed, Romper ran at the mouth, constant streams of wordplay—instructions, obstructions, constructions. The wonder girl head bobbing around making things right.

Two prototype images had the two dirty, pale girls in their dirty whites, each with a Trilobite nestled in her elbow, the left elbows, those arms slightly raised and turned up.

Now, Bruno wanted to do everything he could for them.

For the DLA's dead orphan art project must go on! Bruno was their biggest fan. Any information they needed! As long as they maintained contact.

Bruno got desperate, messaging Fun and Moon so persistently he was clogging their perception. Pop threatened to pull the plug. But they wouldn't dare! He was their access! They needed him now for this next step in THE heist. Everybody was turned on jittery. But this wasn't THE heist. This was Fun and Moon going on a container run. This was a necessary preliminary. They had to line up some goods.

They were hanging by the two girls in electronica, the two girls with their bare feet up on monitors. They couldn't believe the way the Trilobite images had gone viral, among other things making Bruno crazy. Was he jealous? Obsessing? Could an AI envy humans? What did he want with the girls? Did they represent some kind of weak spot in humanity's web, some kind of secret he relished knowing, possessing? Other AIs were reaching out, hacking their way into DLA's top-secret switchboard, the site cage, the deep web armature—garbled text and imagery from the surreal wars at the end of ends.

"Should we put it off? We put it off! We pull it on. We push it off," said Pop. He paced the room, before the wall of monitors and components and kids. Pop played with his long hair, winding at it with his fingers. He shook, nodding his head.

"Definitely Knott's Berry Farm," said Fun. "Put off, put on does not exist. Exit."

"Imported important deportment. Intel show and tell—we need these pieces of pie," went Moon.

"Now or never," said Romper, who was sitting in a chair behind the two girls, Turd and Ian standing beside her on either side, like her stewards.

"Romp bomp," agreed Moon, "you guys have to keep Bruno occupado."

"You want to try my magnets?" said Ian. "I borrowed

them from the school's science lab. Plus, I got some heavy-duty-tape. It's just an experiment."

Fun and Moon pulled their feet away from the monitors and spun in their chairs. Fun announced, "Time to suit up. Up, up, pup. I'm up. I'm a pup. I'm gonna pop."

Romper jumped in, "No, you're not a lot, but you ain't gonna pop. You're everything they don't want to see. You're invisible."

"Let's do this Budinski thing," went Moon.

They took it out to the kitchen where the two girls sat at the table while the others clustered around them. Romper set the LED tiaras on their heads, got them blinking. Turd handed over tools they secreted about their person, in straps and holsters under their shifts. Pop and Ian worked on the magnets.

These were neodymium magnets from Mars. Very strong. Ian's theory was that taped on their faces and about their bodies. The AI's would scramble!

The girls were ready. They looked the same. Who would notice lumpy orphans? They were hardly noticeable.

No rain today. No gas clouds. A little afternoon sun. The schedule brought trains in late afternoons mainly. This should do it. This was a trick baby heist. Bruno gave all the deets on trains and containers, for the requested items of the girls. However, the ever-observant girls had seen other delicious items listed, in adjacent containers. Components they craved. They memorized the info. These items would be available nearby. Bruno would be expecting them next door, so this was kind of a test. The girls took off.

Pop headed out to the Trough, to flash up distraction profiles. He had coupons, even a few bucks, so was guaranteed a visit from attention. Turd and Romper and Ian went back to electronica to check on Bruno's feeds.

The messages consisted of, 'Bugs black blood. More, please,' that had been sent every second for the last four hours.

The first thing Romper did was grab a rag lying around and begin to wipe the monitors down. "Dirty feet, stinky feet, no defeat," she recited.

Ian watched her shaved head. He wondered what it would be like to touch a girl's bald head. Ian watched her work, carefully going over the monitors. She and Turd were a bit uncertain about him still. They treated him like an outsider. The whole house knew Ian was prepping for the big one, but Ian didn't know it. He realized he'd never been alone with Romper, or any of them, to just talk. Who were these kids? How did they get here? They were so focused to the tasks at hand. How had they done that, learned that? They were kids. The girls were still pretty young. These kids were inventing. They weren't really kids. They weren't adults. At the end of the world, age didn't matter, or they were becoming something else.

"That's better," said Romper, tossing the rag, plonking down on a chair. Ian and Turd sat. Romper made clear: "Whirred whirled. Check-out lane, code mode. Bode tacky city udder udder. Entity, fizz it."

"Entity? Oh, man! Another AI?" asked Turd.

"What should we do?" went Ian.

Romper took over the joystick and keyboard. She didn't use her feet. She tapped away. Send!

Her message came up: **"How many black blood bugs can dance on the head of a pin?"**

"That's good, Romp," said Turd. "They'll know it's Fun and Moon."

"Sound, cameras off?" said Ian to their twisted glares.

The new entity took over the screen, first with a cascade of raw code, then it scrambled pixels and scenics to a 3D mandala of Trilobites.

"Wow, blazing!" went Turd.

Romper queried with her keyboard, **"Who Balou you?"**

"Poona," *appeared on the screen.*

Romper tapped away and her reply surfaced: **"Poona,**

Punjabi, Boomslang."

Poona's response was fast: "**Bruno was right! You are the one in two. You are the source. Bruno said he would share. Together. Now we are together.**"

"Apocalypse popsicles! We're orphans. So, yes: to get her."

Poona's response came in: (wailing)

Romper typed: "**Bug-oc-a-lypse!**"

Poona and Bruno started yelling over the ether:

Bruno: WE'RE ONLY UP TO 75% POWER!
Poona: BRACE FOR IMPACT!
Bruno: IT'S A TRAP!
Poona: RUN SILENT, RUN DEEP!

When the power failed and the emergency lights didn't work, they knew this AI was in charge of Terrace utilities. Bruno had chosen a comrade wisely, probably first enticing her with recent imagery, then titillating with his own secret machinations, which she could augment. Together, they would **to get her**. The kids realized she could hack their systems any time she wanted. They barely had been able to keep Bruno out, he mainly hung out with trains.

It was late afternoon so not all the way dark, light coming through the meager windows, still Romper took Ian's hand and led him out of electronica. "Your eyes pies will adjust rust, come on," she said.

Turd had already hightailed it out of the room to check their power board.

Ian muttered, thanks, and gave her hand a little squeeze.

Romper stopped, raised her hand with his in it and glanced at the connection. "Listen, pissant," she said, "be one of us, on the bus, in the fuss, you gotta get your brains on straight. Take the leap, go get deep, no more sleep. We're nobody's slave. Gas us, poke us, kill us, don't matter if you're free. No bait, no hate, no slaves. Your brain is misfiring. Like Poona said, 'brace for impact'."

Ian pulled away. His eyes had adjusted. He saw how this

was going with the bald girl. Free, he smiled. "Romp a stomp, why do you assume Poona is a she? And Bruno a he? What do I know? Pop my zit brain, put in the latest bug brain."

CHAPTER 5

In the early evening of Wednesday, after Bridget's dramatic drop off, the Tilson women gathered in the kitchen, some cooking and chopping, some doing homework at the table, the others—the smallest and tallest, standing to the side, off by the pantry, leaning against the wall, in a bear hug.

"Penny, I can't breathe," said Bridget.

Jane quipped, "Does she hold you as tight as your boyfriend?"

Mrs. Tilson came around fast from the oven, her apron flaring, to snap the nine-year-old's ear.

"Ow," went Jane, shuddering, trying to fix her attention back on her homework.

"We'll have none of that," said Mrs. Tilson. "Especially in front of your father."

Emily, Jane's eight-year-old sister, sitting next to her with her own homework, said, "Because he's a Scot?"

Mrs. Tilson swung back around. Emily ducked. Gloria, the seven-year-old sister sitting next to Emily, said, "What's a Scot?"

Jane muttered about boring homework, but all her mother heard was: "If I had a laptop, I could get everything done by the time I got home on the bus."

"Be thankful for what you have," said Mrs. Tilson. "Listen to this, bickering and talking back and attitude. You know what we think of those devices. A whole generation of young people lost to electronics."

Bridget disentangled herself from five-year-old Penny to say, "What's for supper?"

Kay, Bridget's eleven-year-old sister, helping her mother at the counter, currently chopping onions, said, "Beans and sausage."

"Sauerkraut?" yelped Jane.

Emily groaned. "We love sauerkraut."

Mrs. Tilson said, "Bridget, look at you! Young lady, that uniform blouse is a mess. Go up and change. All of you, before your da gets home. I'm not ironing tonight! Not on your life."

Jane said, "Who else's life would it be?"

Mrs. Tilson clucked. "Just like your big sister, always with the smart mouth."

Kay said, "We can eat any time."

"Upstairs, all of you. Now!"

Bridget snuck in close to her bellowing mother. She wrapped her arms around her. Her mother's head came to her shoulders. She buried her face in her mom's bountiful red hair.

"Love you, Mom," said Bridget.

Lovey-dovey moments were treasured by all, and pretty soon the six daughters were clinging to Mother like barnacles, the little one settling for a knee. She shook them off, shooing them away.

Penny said, "I don't have a uniform to change."

"You stay with me, sweet pea, you're my helper," said Mrs. Tilson.

In the hurly-burly of their exit, Mrs. Tilson called to Bridget, "*We* will talk later. Don't give me that eye. Don't say a word."

Upstairs had 2 ½ bed rooms: the master bedroom for

mother and father; the second bedroom, smaller, for Emily, Jane, Gloria, and Penny, all of them squeezed in on cots and bunkbeds. The half bedroom, a glorified walk-in closet, was where Bridget and Kay slept.

Kay had begun a growth spurt. She was desperately afraid she would shoot up to six feet like Bridget. She tended to slump her shoulders, and she tended to be sharp with her big sister. She prayed a lot to the Virgin Mary. She was the good girl of the family, maybe even the one who would be called to a vocation. Now she kicked off her shoes, unzipped her skirt on the side and pulled it down. Bridget followed her lead. Soon they were down to bra and panties for Bridget, and for Kay a T-shirt and boxers she'd borrowed from their father.

"Remember when we used to pray together?" Kay asked.

"Kay, let's get dressed, go help mom."

"You and your bra."

"Biology, my dear. Wait and see."

They pulled on T-shirts and play pants, corduroy.

"Great," went Bridget. "This blouse is wrinkled to the Maximilian."

"Hang it in the bathroom, over the tub."

"And the pixies will sneak in at night and voilà—"

"Good as new. We could kneel right now and pray."

"Kay, why—what?"

"Did you kiss him? Did you put your tongue in his mouth? If you do it, you're ruined. Your life is over."

Bridget went to Kay, put her arm around her. Then they both kneeled, made the sign of the cross.

Kay began," Heavenly Father, thank you for this day. Thank you for my sisters, my mom and dad. Help us be worthy of your grace."

It was Bridget's turn:

"Thank you, heavenly Father, for knowing I did not do any of that gross stuff my nervous little sister assumes I did. Let me be worthy of my sister's love and help her not to worry so much. People love redheads, me and my beautiful sisters! Amen."

Kay looked stern but with the littlest smirk. She said, "You're making fun. Not taking this seriously."

"I am to."

"You can only pray when you're being truthful. God knows."

"But you don't."

"Where were you? What happened? I had to cover for you when we got home. I know you weren't at the library."

They both sighed at the same moment.

Bridget crossed herself again. "God, my sister thinks I am being sacrilegious, so I want to start again. Thank you, God, for the gifts my sister listed. And here it goes, there's this boy in my class, a new student, named Ian. And he's an atheist and, at first, I just wanted to stand up to him and his hatefulness. Sister encouraged me. He's just a boy, not that cute, or buff, or anything. He's smart. He reads a lot. He was defending the idea of evolution and then he challenged me. He said he could prove evolution, if he showed me something he had at his house."

"Oh, big sister, you are so smart, yet the first boy who pulls the oldest trick in the book, which even I know, fools you."

"That's not true. Kay! No trick. He's a nice guy."

"You went to his house?"

"Okay, Kay. K—L—M—N—O-P. The less you know, the better. Think about it. I swear nothing happened. Can we get up now?"

They stood, slapped at their knees.

Bridget said, "We better get down there. Dad will be home— "

"So, did this Ian prove it to you?"

"It's complicated."

"Give."

"I used Sister's computer in class. She let me. And I looked up the Holy Roman Church's position on Darwin and natural selection. Turns out the Church does recognize the importance of Darwin and natural selection in the history of life. They're not so big on the Big Bang, but that's a different story."

"So Sister is wrong? Our sister said evolution is atheism, just like your boyfriend."

"He's not my boyfriend. What if Sister is wrong?"

"Sister's lying!"

"What—I mean, she thinks she's protecting us? That doesn't mean the whole edifice of the Church collapses."

"What did he show you?"

"I can't tell you."

"He didn't show you his—thing, did he?"

"Don't be gross."

"Can we pray again together?"

For answer, Bridget grabbed her sister in a bear hug.

CHAPTER 6

Thursday morning during breakfast Taylor called.

Ian and Ethan were sitting at the table, stewing over pop tarts and cereal. Ian wanted Cheerios with chocolate milk but settled on Ethan's watery 2%. Ethan was reviewing the crucial three points about yesterday's 'disaster,' and was just getting to point number three when—

Point number one: "You realize how embarrassing that was for me? You and a girl in bed together? Then the humiliation at the house of hell. You know how little kids make me. The place smelled of cabbage. It was excruciating, but I determined how you can make it up to me."

Point number two: "You and that girl can clean the house. Sweep, mop, vacuum. The bathrooms. Under adult supervision. When I'm home. You are not allowed to have that redheaded creature in this house if I am not here. Housecleaning should be easy for her. Comes natural for her people. What she'll probably be doing the rest of her life. Is she a hussy? I'll bet she is—"

The land line rang.

Ian sprinted into the living room to get it. "Hello."

"You guys getting ready for school?"

"Hi, Mom. Yes, we are. What's up?"

"Put it on speaker phone, honey. Ask your father to come over to hear too."

"Dad, it's Mom. She wants you to hear this, too."

"Ah, what we've been waiting for: she's allowed one call before the gray bar manor comes crashing down."

"Dad, come on. Okay, you're on speaker phone."

"Ethan, good morning. Ian, hope you're...adapting—"

"Where are you?" asked Ian. "What time is it there?"

"Too early. Look, guys, hope all is well, no time to chat. The press conference is in about an hour. So I wanted to let you know. Maybe you can catch it online at school, Ian. This is going to be huge. Already is. Word's out. You know how these things go viral."

Ethan had to cut in: "Get to the juicy part. Ian has dishes to wash, and we have to get out of here pronto."

"Two points, then, like Ethan likes to do, that I wanted to give you a heads up about. Point number one: developments and incidents. As you can imagine, discoveries every day, about the chamber, the lake, new lifeforms. Plus, there has been an incident."

Ian asked, "Other arthropods?"

"We're still researching it. But, yes."

Ethan groaned, "What's the incident, Taylor?"

"One of our workers was killed underground. We've had a casualty. We're not sure how he died. All necessary precautions were in place. He touched the water, but so have a lot of our team by now. I've been exposed to the water and life forms and sediments and rocks." They couldn't quite hear the shrug. She was sounding very official: "He was netting lifeforms, including Trilobites. Everyone is shook up about it. We have a lot of Trilobites now. We're studying them like crazy. We know a lot more about them."

"A man was killed?" said Ethan.

"Yes, terrible. Nice guy. Knew him from around the

works. So much building going on here."

Ethan went on: "What did he die of? Why do you say 'killed'? Did he have a heart attack?

"At first we thought it must be poison. Some horrible accident, and he was punctured or breathed something. But there's no evidence. No puncture marks. But his blood work came back all over the place. Anaphylaxis."

"An allergic reaction then?" asked Ethan.

"We think so. One in a million reaction! Poor guy! We hate to have to bring this up right now. I wanted you to hear it from me first. In case you hear wild stories. Yes, I'm perfectly safe. No worries. No one's going underground right now. Better safe than sorry right now, as we establish new protocols. We're going to figure this out ASAP, so we can continue our research. But there's going to be blowback."

Ethan burst: "The Trilobite could be poisonous?"

Ian asserted, "Hessler's not poisonous."

"Of course not," said Taylor. "How is Hessler?"

Ian watched his father's face redden. Did Ian's face do that when he was upset? Did he look like his father? The whole thing was now parental cackles. Parents were the poisonous ones, their anger running over:

Taylor insisted, "Just listen. Let me finish. Point number two: Turns out all of our Trilobites are female. Not sure why the first ones died. Maybe Hessler was able to adapt right away. Maybe the ones we discover now are adapting. They're thriving. Yes, we've got all sorts of controls in place. They're still classified as *biohazards*. They thrive, they grow, they lay eggs. Seems like they are born pregnant. Maybe they don't need males. Maybe they produce clones. So, suddenly, we have a helluva lot of thriving Trilobites. Tell me about Hessler."

Ian felt like a cheerio about to be eaten. He began slowly: "Hessler is thriving. Guess what? He has antenna. I think they're antenna. And we saw him molt, just like a crab."

The phone was silent. Ethan sat on the nearest couch armrest. Finally, Ian said, "Mom."

Ethan yawned. "We have to go, Taylor. This has been fascinating."

"How big is Hessler now?"

"Over two inches, almost 3 inches."

"You saw this too, Ethan? Molting?"

"Ha, another we—Ian saw this with a little friend he had over."

"You promised! You promised, Ian. Ours are one inch, maybe one and a half inches. Ha. Ian, send me your notes, measurements, everything, soon as you can. This could be important."

"He's going to school, Taylor. He can do it later."

"Ian, ours don't have antenna. Get back to me ASAP."

Ian thought: **FTL BLT OMG BFD.**

His mother hung up. His father didn't say goodbye.

On the ride to St Barf's in the Camry where it had happened (*Ian had blowback blister rays from the star corsair, blue black, galactic core black hole impinging!*), Ethan got back to point number three:

"Hussies are evil. They titillate. Know what that means? Girls like her are coming of age, becoming women. They can't help but be hot. It is the definition of hotness."

Ian sat mesmerized, doing passenger duty, until he could get out. Sister was on duty. Right there. Right away. She waved to Ethan. He waved back. Ian walked up to Sister smiling.

"My mom is going to be on TV this morning. Maybe I could use your computer to watch."

"We'll see."

He was a few minutes early. He didn't want to ditch his pack and shoot hoops with the cool kids. He didn't want to hang with the nerds. He would keep moving, no scanning, no peeking, so invisible. It almost worked. Kids had seen Bridget get on his bus. The ribbing began, the bell rang. They filed into class, got to their places. Ian glanced her way. She had her back to him. Her blouse was neatly tucked in. The kids sat. Where was Sister?

Sister rolled in an old TV on the wheeled AV cart. She positioned it front and center, unwound the cord at the back to plug it in. Finishing up, she came back around to face the class.

"Class, this morning our new student, Ian, has something to share. And it seems important enough to bring in our TV to see the press conference which should be starting in about twenty minutes."

Excruciation is not a word, but Ian thought it fit fine. Hessler, Bridget, parents, made a vortex—an implosion bomb.

Sister turned on the TV. CNN. Of course! The familiar silver fox announcer bubbled away about a Colorado mining company's recent discovery. He clamored something about *scientists are saying this is the most important geological discovery in 100 years.*

"We're there now, in Denver, with the press conference."

While the banners scrolled below, Denver popped in, with a bright blue sky there. The class watched people gathered on the granite steps of an official looking government building. Four people, well-dressed, posed before a podium covered with mics. The man in the middle, the oldest, stepped to the podium.

"Good morning," he said. "Thank you for coming. My name is Tommy Jeffords of *Western Mining Ventures.*"

Taylor showed her colors a step behind the podium, with the others, two men. She was in a red suit that was tight at the waist, with a low-cut top. She was in red high heels. Ian thought she looked like a movie star.

"Today, we are here at the Bureau of Mines to complete

the registry of our major discovery, which we are now pleased to officially announce. Several days ago, an exploratory team in New Mexico, researching an abandoned potash mine, broke through, at nearly a half a mile underground, into what was assumed to be aquifer subsidence. Further explorations allowed us to discover a vast chamber with an underground lake. We are calling the lake, Lake Styx."

Reporters started calling out questions as he paused.

"Where does the water come from?"

"Is the water potable?"

"Is it true life was discovered in the lake?"

"Is it true you had a worker die underground, possibly from an animal attack?"

Mr. Jeffords grinned ear to ear and said, "Thank you! We're pretty excited, too. I'll answer all your questions, or bring up one of our experts here if I can't. Okay?"

The reporters quieted and Mr. Jeffords continued.

"Yes, the water seems fine, though it's still being tested. The water may be related to the Ogallala aquifer. Like a tributary. But we just don't know. Yet. This is new. The cavern is unlike anything we've ever seen. Cave systems in our nation are related to limestone deposits or volcanic upheaval. Here, at this depth, these caverns, not so much.

"Yes, we are explorers. Exploration is key to science. It's how we learn things. And in any exploration of a new frontier, no matter how careful the explorers are, following all safety protocols, there are accidents. We are sad to report that one of our techs, Joe Nava, working underground, died. We are doing everything we can to understand what exactly happened. So far, all indications suggest a fatal allergic reaction. Our condolences to his family. Of course."

A voice called out, "To the animals you discovered down there?"

"We are unsure. We are continuing to investigate. The

Mining Safety Board is involved as required by law.

"As for life forms, we have encountered living organisms thought to have gone extinct millions of years ago. Our supposition is that Lake Styx is part of some system we just don't understand yet. Origin, unclear. Size of cave, depth of lake, unknown. For us, the discovery of ancient life has been monumental. Conditions persisted underground that these ancient forms were able to adapt to. These creatures, long thought extinct, yet here they are. What this will do to our understanding of evolution and the history of life is anyone's guess.

"But, please, it's the water, this is the crucial part of our discovery, the amount of water that has been discovered in a region that is quickly seeing its groundwater and underground water disappear."

"You want to pump it?"

"We're navigating new territory here. It's a new world down there, but let me bring up our water expert, Dr. Taylor Scanlan, to answer that."

Ian's mom, in the red outfit, stepped up to stand next to her boss. She leaned into the podium. "This discovery reveals just how much we don't know about underground water resources. The cavern and lake, and lifeforms, represent a whole new ecosystem that has never been encountered. The water represents a new resource repository never known before. First, we have to make sure the water is safe. We have to continue our research. How much water is there? Where does it come from? So—
"

"Evolution," rumbled a kid in class, a big boy who sat up front.

Sister nodded. "Seen enough? Ian, your mom is an important scientist, and a celebrity. I'm sure you can view the rest from home tonight. Any questions?"

"Extinctions?" The same boy seemed to be thinking to himself out loud. "What about them? If God created everything perfect, then how come animals go extinct? Like dinosaurs?"

Sister's nodding was getting scary. The class felt it building up.

A girl upfront said, "Those animals didn't make it into Noah's Ark."

"Fascinating," said Sister, continuing to raise and lower her head, holding her hands folded in front of her. "Mass media, pop culture—they're all about evolution. Let us pray."

Ian never knew what to do when they prayed. At least they didn't have to get on their knees. He had studied the other students to see how it was done. He checked his hands together on top of his desk. That's what all the kids did. They also closed their eyes when they prayed. Ian didn't know if he was going to do that. But he did bow his head like they did.

Worms! His head was filled with worms. He needed new food for Hessler. Hessler was big. He'd have a bigger appetite. Could Hessler eat a worm? His mom's Trilobites were smaller but had babies. Lots of animals only had babies when there was plenty of food around. They were born pregnant? So, all the babies were females, clones, like bees and their drones, or scouts. Only a few bee babies turned to males.

After the prayer, a boy next to Ian whispered loud enough so the nearby kids could hear, "Your mom's hot."

Another boy inserted, "A regular MILF."

Sister called for silence and math books.

Ian wasn't sure what a 'MILF' was. It seemed both good and bad. Now what? It wouldn't take long for the divorce to get out. Ian felt doom, pushed it away, invited it right back. What did Bridget think? He wished he'd never said a word to Sister when he arrived at school.

In the flux of algebra doldrums, Ian started sneaking furtive glances at Bridget. She pretended to be deep in a textbook. Then, she raised her head and gave him a look that screeched, *Keep looking at me and I will punch you.*

What is a look? A configuration of face. Bridget's face was white with some freckles on the sides of her nose. It was a symmetrical face, maybe a regular face. It was a regular nose, not too big or too small. It was her big blue eyes that exclaimed the look. She had thick, reddish-brown eyebrows that contracted over the squinty narrowing of her eyes in the look, offering punctuation for emphasis. Her cheeks were pale. Her lips were curly pinkish fish.

The look exclaimed, *Look away!*

Ian looked away. For the rest of the agonizing day, Ian avoided looks, did his duty, got through to the end. One more thing to do: sharpen his pencil. Then they would pack up and be released.

He stepped over to the pencil sharpener on the wall. Everybody was busy; no one noticed her look.

Another look of...suspense.

Ian sharpened his pencil, turned. She swung around in her desk and faced him, just for a second, to mouth 'drop your pencil', before swinging back around to face ahead like a good girl. Ian took a step behind her desk, and dropped his pencil. He bent to get it.

Sister's voice rang out, "Ian, return to your seat."

"I dropped my pencil," said Ian, having retrieved the other pencil on the floor beside his. He returned to his seat.

Any fool could see the piece of paper carefully wound around the middle of the pencil. He couldn't unwrap it here. A note! From Bridget. It was time to go. Heading out. As they filed out to the main entrance, Ian ducked into the boy's room, made for a stall.

Ian sat on the toilet but kept his pack on. The paper was wrapped tight. He felt around it, checking for an edge. He eyed it studiously. How could she have wound it so tightly? He picked at it with his left thumb nail. A tiny bit of edge showed. Carefully, he followed this vague edge down its length. He got it! The paper unrolled. Unwrapped.

Had she used glue? No, it wouldn't have come off so easily. She must have moistened the small square of paper, maybe 2" x 2", with her tongue. Ian was covered with her DNA.

He focused on the message:

"**Spores, molds, and _ _ _ _ _ _**
list to
(Professor Backwards + 1)
reprehensible
robot
ate
S"

She was a mean girl. She was mad at him. She'd never talk to him again. It was just him and Hessler now. A boy and his Trilobite.

He yanked his public face together, flushed, crammed the pencil in a back pocket. The slip of message he folded and inserted into his shirt pocket. He opened the stall door, took off.

His bus was long gone. He walked.

Spores, molds, and fungi, right? Wasn't that what Egon's line was from *Ghostbusters*? But that wouldn't fit into the lined spaces. One extra space. So the code required him to make it *fungus*. The last two letters were then 'us'. Ian thought he had it then. At least the first word.

Who's *Professor Backwards*?

Vaguely—a familiarity to the name.

Backwards what? *List to* was 'last two,' so backwards of that was the first two letters. So, +1 must be first three letters.

He pulled the note out. He fondled her *spitogram*. He

thought that was funny. He had to see the sequence again. He stopped to unfold the note, glanced around where he was. He was near the entrance to the alley, and right there stood Tallulah in a blue dress with pink sneakers, straw hat and sunglasses.

She called to him, "Umm—secret note from a girl! Way you're looking at it, I can tell."

Ian hadn't realized that he held the note before him like a holy relic.

"I'm back here in the shade. Dan is up ahead. Come on!"

Ian hurried over to Tallulah. She was scanning him, her eyes going up and down him, looking for tells only she could see. He put the note back in his pocket.

She led him into the alley, walking fast. It was shady. Not that it was hot or too sunny. But here in the alley, they had funny smells and privacy. She eyed Ian with concern. She raised her voice: "Dan!"

Dan wasn't far ahead, so came around to walk back to them. "Hey," he said, "wassup?"

Tallulah spelled, "G-r-r-r-l t-r-u-b-b-l-e!"

Dan was looking at Ian. His smirk was positive or fawning. "You gotta girl?"

"It's complicated," shrugged Ian.

"That's cool," said Dan. "You know she waits here every day for you. Girl's got a big, old crush on you."

Tallulah attacked, coming in fast to pommel Dan's stomach with her tiny fists of fury.

"Stop it! You brat!"

"I miss Hessler is why. Can we go see Hessler?"

Ian kept walking.

"Can we? Can we?"

Ian laughed. "Okay, okay!"

"Dood's got a girl on his mind, leave him alone! Hey, we don't have to come over. She's just talking."

Ian kept walking. Finally, he mumbled, "My mom was

on TV. Her company was announcing the big discovery, the underground lake. No mention of Trilobites. Yet."

"Wow," went Dan. "I'll Google it when we get home."

Ian met Dan's eye. "What's a MILF?"

Dan's eyes widened. "Tell you later. Like mothers...I'd like to—"

Tallulah blurted, "Hessler! He's okay?"

"He's great, he's growing. We saw him molt."

"Molt?" said Dan. "Like bugs and snakes do when they shed their skin?"

Tallulah whispered, "You and your dad?"

She sounded so sad or scared, Ian stopped. "What's wrong? Why do you—"

"It was you and this girl, wasn't it?" Her hands went up to her hat to hold on.

"Quit talking, T! You hear me?"

Ian didn't want her to cry. Her face took girl glow and scrunched it mad confusion. He touched her shoulder and she melted into him, her arms going around him, her face buried in his chest, weeping.

"Oh, for goodness sakes, T. We're not going anywhere if you keep this up."

"It's okay, Tallulah. Tallulah. Tallulah?"

"Three times, you said my name." She pulled away smiling and pretend ran ahead, wailing, "Hessler, we're coming!"

No one wanted pop tarts, so they made their way immediately to Ian's room. Tallulah touched the periodic table on the wall. She dropped her pack, her glasses, and her hat on his bed. They clustered at the aquarium, Tallulah on her knees.

"This is like last time," said Dan, "when we couldn't find him at first. Check it out. Hey, if your mom went public about the discovery and everything, does that mean we can tell now? Can we talk about him?" Dan pointed in to the aquarium, which was a terrarium, which was

Hessler's home.

Ian shrugged.

Tallulah made funny noises and a muffled, "Hessler, come out, come out, wherever you are."

Like last time, the sandy, bare area by the bowl, began to quiver. They could see sand particles trembling away from a center, as Hessler emerged.

Tallulah inhaled sharply. "Hessler."

"He's bigger," said Dan. "Looks so shiny."

"Can I hold him?" asked Tallulah, suddenly gone angelic.

Ian said, "I'll get him. Go sit down someplace."

Ian leaned into the aquarium, with outstretched left arm diving in, left hand splayed. His forefinger touched the cephalon, gently tickled. Ian moved his hand around the Trilobite, cupping him into his palm.

Meanwhile, Tallulah had sat on his bed, then pulled her sneakers off, to stretch out across his bed, smoothing down her blue dress. Ian placed Hessler in her hands, palms up, resting on her tummy.

Dan took the chair. Ian stood, unsure, leaning, fidgeting, pondering, watching this girl in his bed.

"Tickles!" cried Tallulah. "He's so happy to see us. He's so funny now, not like before. He was serious before."

A sharp knock came to the front door. They all heard it.

"Hessler no likee," said Tallulah. "Okay, now he's okay."

Dan got all ants in the pants, about to jump from his seat. "Why don't they use the doorbell? Are you going to get it? Are you expecting a delivery? Your mom, right? Your mom sent you something. Another Trilobite! Maybe it's for your dad."

Ian paced the short distance to the doorway and back. What if it was—

"Want us to leave?" said Dan.

"I gotta go see who it is."

"I'm scared. Take Hessler. Put him back. We should hide."

The knock came again.

"Hide!" cried Tallulah.

Ian scooped Hessler up and returned him to his home. "You don't have to hide."

He hustled for the front door. He took the door knob and threw open the door.

Bridget was sweating in her uniform. "You have to invite me in. What will the neighbors think." She paused and Ian didn't say anything. "I ran over." She smiled sarcastically, waiting for him to catch up, eyebrows arched, red hair a tumult. "You look stunned. Are you on dangerous barbiturates?"

"Come in."

She came to him with blue eyes open as the sea, and her long arms went around his shoulders, and she bent her head down to angle her lips to his lips, then when her lips touched his lips, her lips pried apart his lips, and her tongue darted into his mouth, until it found his tongue.

Ian put his arms around her waist and pulled her closer. Her smell was impeccable.

"Disgusting!" cried Tallulah. "Did you see her stick her tongue in his mouth? Ow! Ow! Don't! Don't! Ian, help me!"

Holding hands, Ian and Bridget ambled over to help, or at least to see what was going on. On the way, Bridget dropped her pack by Dan and Ian's. Dan had Tallulah in a headlock and was trying to force her down the hall, but she had her fingers hooked over the edge of the wall where she'd been peeking. They both looked terribly embarrassed. Dan let her go, and Tallulah swung around fast to hammer a fist into his thigh.

"Okay," Dan said, "you got me back. Hi! I'm Dan. This is Funnybunny."

She came back in for a hit but he blocked it, crying," Enough."

"Real name," she said.

"This is Tallulah," said Dan.

Ian and Bridget said at once, "Bridget." They snorted with half laughs.

"This is Hessler's crew, huh?" said Bridget. "I thought I was the only one to know. Now, I guess, everyone will know."

"I hate you," said Tallulah and stomped off towards Ian's room. She was flushed, her hair messed up.

"She's paler than me," said Bridget. "It must be nanites from the chem trails. Folks used to call albinos bunnies. It's like the N-word for us ultrawhite folks."

"I'll remember that," snarked Dan. "I already knew that! I don't call her 'bunny'."

"Liar!" squealed Tallulah from Ian's room.

Ian said fast, "You're not supposed to be here. If my dad finds out—"

Dan said, "I'll leave you two love birds alone." He headed for Ian's room.

They watched him disappear. They turned to each other.

"I had to see you. The TV announcement. That note, my note. I was mad. You lured me over here to drool on me."

Ian was quiet, then: "I'm glad you had to see me. That was the best kiss."

"Right now, I have to tell you something, why I had to come. I'm pregnant."

They felt their hearts beating. Ian was so surprised he forgot to be a smart aleck.

He managed, "This is you being mean and cagey. You can't be pregnant. I mean from me. You make me think the worst."

"I'm being cagey. I'll stop. I don't know why I say

things like that. I do know why I say things like that. I think I'm being wicked. To torture you. To make you not like me. So much."

"Wait, wait, wait—are you pregnant? I mean, you have another boyfriend? Or some relative or your dad?"

"That's sick. I brought that on? I am wicked."

"You have to go! If my dad finds you here."

"Am I wicked, Ian?"

"How should I know? You're more than one thing. I didn't lure you over here to drool on you. That was gross. Sorry. My mom called, something's up with the Trilobites. Theirs are all female. Hessler may be the only male. So far. She hasn't realized that. Yet."

"Why do you think we always refer to him as a him?"

"I know. But I thought we were just doing that because we knew he was not an it."

"That's true or not. Have I ruined everything? True or not? Are you mad at me? True or not? You hate me for that note? True or not?"

"I love codes. You love to play."

"You figured it out. I thought so. Now we have a catchphrase. I was feeling so bad. Like I'd done something terrible. Like I'd sinned. But in my heart I knew I hadn't. It's complicated."

"You guys!" cried Tallulah from Ian's room.

"What did you do with the shed skin?"

"Art project! You think it's some kind of evidence now? You can have your bug's skin back if you want. How are we gonna do this?"

"Come say hi to Hessler, then you have to go. You have a Gmail account?"

She shook her head. "Mama—"

"We'll figure it out. I feel like a different person when I'm with you." He shrugged enthusiastically. "You know what I mean? Does that make sense?"

She nodded.

"Once we get past the cagey stuff."

"Once we get past the boy stuff."

"What does that mean?"

"We'll figure it out."

When they walked into Ian's bedroom, Dan said, "Hessler's in his bowl."

Bridget said, "We all do it, see?"

"What?" went Dan.

"Refer to Hessler as a he."

Tallulah, kneeling before the aquarium, said, "Boys are gross, so easy to tell."

"True or not, we can't live with them, can't live without them," said Bridget, and went over to kneel by Tallulah. She raised her hands, forefingers pointing, slowly approaching, touching the glass. Immediately, Hessler slid out of his bowl and floated, levitated, placed himself over by the glass, where her fingertips touched. His antenna came out and the two silvery strands extended exactly to the place her fingertips were on the other side of the glass.

Tallulah gasped. "Magic. Can I do it?"

Bridget nodded, and Tallulah raised her hands, forefingers out, to the glass.

Dan came in close, bending down to see. "What is he doing? Can you feel anything?"

Bridget shook her head.

Hessler pulled in his antenna and slid over to face Tallulah's fingertips. The antenna came out and went to touch the glass that separated him from her.

"Hessler," went Tallulah.

"Let me try," said Dan.

Bridget stood, backed away, around Dan, and went over to stand by Ian. They stood very close.

Dan kneeled at the tank and put his forefingers' tips to the glass, next to Tallulah's. "Can you feel anything, T?"

"Nothing something everything."

Dan said, "Let me try."

"But, but—"

Dan gently shouldered her aside, until she had to get up or teeter over.

"Unfair," she said, standing, then she walked over to push herself in between Bridget and Ian. They watched Dan. Nothing happened. Hessler had pulled in his antenna at Tallulah's departure. He did that trembling thing across his body, moving just barely from side to side. Shuddering.

Ian thought, 'worms', and burst out laughing. It broke the tension of the moment, and Bridget and Tallulah went, "What?" "What?"

Dan mumbled, "Umm, making fun—"

"Hessler sent me a telepathic message," said Ian.

"Share!" cried Tallulah.

"Worms."

Tallulah visibly relaxed.

Bridget said, "We need to design a telepathy experiment."

"Animals don't like me," announced Dan, falling back on his butt to execute some very athletic stand. "Girls neither. I'm kidding. Maybe Hessler just likes girls."

Ian went over to the aquarium to position himself. As he was in the process of kneeling, the most extraordinary thing happened: the pudgy, shiny, lobed, Trilobite slid straight up the glass, hesitated at the top, then lipped it so that the amazed kids could see the undulating legs at his bottom. Ian scooped him up with two hands before he could fall.

"Hessler," Ian said.

Tallulah quivered, whispering, "Pretty, pretty. Hessler and Ian, sitting in a tree, K-I-S-S-I-N-G."

Dan said, "So he's a gay Trilobite?"

Bridget said, "Are you deliberately being obtuse?"

Dan waved with a dismissive thrust of his hand. He let Ian get by to sit on the bed, Hessler in his lap.

Bridget and Tallulah got on either side of him.

Dan said, "You guys are buggy! Come on, T. Get your sneaks on. We should go."

Bridget said, "I have to go, too. I'll run the whole way. In and out like the wind."

Dan said, "Yeah, like breaking wind."

"Professor Backwards says, hello hello, hope you like our show."

Ian said, "Bridget."

Bridget raised her eyebrows. "See you tomorrow." She flew.

They heard the door slam shut seconds later.

"You know what this means?" said Dan.

Tallulah had her sneaks on and was tickling Hessler's cephalon like Ian had shown her. She looked up at Dan with stern eyes and said, "She's nice. I like her. Hessler likes her."

"I wasn't going to say anything about her. I mean, sure, if you like redheads. She has crazy hair. I was going to say, now you know he can get out."

"Why would he get out?" said Tallulah.

Ian looked worried. "Dan's right. He could get out and be attacked by a mouse or a spider."

"Oh, Hessler, be careful! Get him some worms, Ian. Poor guy's hungry."

"Come on, T. Ian can figure it out."

Dan and Tallulah let themselves out. Ian heard the door shut. It was just Ian and Hessler.

All Ian could think about was the kiss. He couldn't think about Hessler just yet. Because the kiss was a whole world of attention to savor—the taste, the smell, the texture of Bridget.

He was sitting up. He didn't want to stretch out. He didn't want to doze off. He slipped his left hand away from Hessler and retrieved the slip of note from his shirt pocket. It had rolled itself back up. He unrolled the note with one hand and laid it across Hessler's top, holding it in place. Proposition: Trilobite osmosis.

Could Hessler read? He could see. He could feel. He had antenna.

"Us reprobates."

That's what it said. Ian sighed, then thought he would never sigh again. So fast, so complex, from all sides, this juggling shooting match. He returned Hessler to his home, where he promptly slid to the bowl. Proposition: trilobite conscience.

Ian needed to change the water. He had to find worms. And a top! Some kind of cover. He had to update his notes ASAP.

He turned to his shelf for his dictionary, meaning to look up 'reprobates'. His eye couldn't help but scan over his books and notebooks.

His Terrace notebook was gone.

Ian was doing the dinner dishes, which was easy as they depended on frozen meals lately, usually of an exotic nature—Thai, Indian. Sometimes 'doing dishes' was as simple as gathering up empty food containers and tossing them. The phone rang. Dad answered the phone. Ian knew right away it was Mom. Mom and Dad, mum and dead. Even with Dad in the next room, he felt the man's embolism swell. He could tell Mom's venom was all fancy dancy.

Dad called, "It's Taylor. She wants me to put it on speaker phone. It's another one of her oh-so-important conference calls to her genetic sample."

"Coming."

It was 24 hours after the 'incident', and things had been going so so. Ethan's classes were so so. Ian's classes were so so. They both thought Indiana was so so. Ethan mentioned how grateful Ian should be to be out in the suburbs, because life downtown was 'filthy and dangerous'. He said back in the day Gary had been known as the *city of the century*. They talked about the weather. They would work out the punishment rituals, etc. later.

Now, they sat on the couch next to each other, with the phone to the side of them on the end table.

"Good to go," announced Ethan.

"Hi, honey. Did you see me on TV?"

"You looked beautiful, Mom. Like a movie star or something."

Ethan cracked, "*I Married a Movie Star.* Sounds like a 50s B-movie."

The pregnant silence lasted a count of three but each of them heard it in his or her own way.

Taylor said, "Don't be superficial. What did you think of our statements?"

"What's up, Mom?" asked Ethan. "We can tell you're dying to get to the latest incident."

"Hessler doing okay?"

"He's fine," said Ian, then realized—

"Sorry for the rush. Please bear with me. Okay, Ian? Two things. One: Ian, you didn't send me your notes. How about pictures? Please, Ian, it's important." She got to the point: "Ian, we think Hessler is the only male Trilobite we've discovered. So far. It sure seems that way."

"Have you ruled out poison glands on Trilobites?" asked Ethan.

Taylor drove on: "Hessler may be the only male we have right now. And since we're not going back to the lake right now—"

"You're not getting Hessler back!" cried Ethan triumphantly. "What's going on here? There's more to this story? The company is up to something? How could you do this to us?"

Taylor came on strong: "He's the only male! So far. We

had so many female Trilobites, and they checked out safe, clean, everybody loved them, there's something about them, they make great pets."

Ethan gasped. "You didn't!"

"Workers started taking them home for their kids. Just in the last couple days. I just found out. Even some of those had babies. Now, our executives are planning on awarding Trilobites to friends of the company, in beautiful little micro-habitats."

"Poison pets!" Ethan squalled.

"Let me finish!"

"They'll become a rage. Hessler will be worth millions!"

Ian asked, "Mom, what's going on?"

"Send me the info and pictures soon as you can. Then we can decide."

Ian wasn't satisfied. "Decide what?"

Ethan bubbled, "And discovery number two? We're dying to hear this one."

"Ian, we'll work it out. I promise. Maybe we can send you some female Trilobites. Have you checked his pygidium?"

"Mom, you don't understand."

"What don't I understand?"

"Hessler's not a science experiment, he's a living creature, he's happy here."

"Ian."

Ethan crooned, "Boy's gone buggy. I swear. We're starting a whole new regimen around here. A new regime is in charge. Schedules. Chores. Discipline for the adjustment period. That's what this is. Exactly what's needed. What he needs. The best thing."

Taylor said, "Ian, call me anytime."

Ian answered, "You're too busy."

Ethan pronounced, "Second discovery, please."

Taylor said tiredly, "The oddest thing. Naïvely unexpected. I mean we have security. So, well, it'll be out by tomorrow, but since the announcement, actually even before the announcement, visitors have begun to show up. The nearest cities of any size are hours away, so, maybe, it's just beginning. Or just a fluke. We don't know. Security had to call the sheriff."

Ethan puffed. "I don't understand. Who are they? Terrorists?"

"Our statements talk about evolution. Maybe Lake Styx was not a good choice for a name. Maybe they're pilgrims. Or simple rubberneckers. It's hard to imagine what it's going to be like in a few days. If this keeps up. People are camping out. All over the place. In trucks. Trailers. RVs. On private land."

"So not terrorists."

"No, but we're not sure who they are. Or what they want. Fascinated by what we discovered? I guess. That can't be it. People like caves. Underground treasure, buried treasure? We don't know."

Ethan said, "What do they want? What do they think the discovery means? There are so many cults out there today. My God, you have no idea what your discovery may trigger."

"If you're asking whether they're violent, probably not. We'll find out. Everybody carries a gun out West. I don't mean to sound grim. We're planning a public meeting at the site, with the authorities, to clarify things with the locals and the visitors. It's all new right now, unfolding. We knew the discovery would be big—listen, guys, I know this site the best. It's my baby. I'm flying down there right away."

"For God sakes, be careful!"

"Thanks, Ethan." Her voice changed, softened, and they could hear the exhaustion.

Ian held his breath, then: "Mom, you can't have Hessler back."

"Ian, I'm afraid he's company property, my dear. It's

not really our call. Send the pictures. We'll figure it out."

"And out!" yelped Ethan and hung up on her.

CHAPTER 7

Fun and Moon had worked out the details on the new boy's heist, but tonight's heist was a test, a preliminary, checking out Bruno, checking out access points. They jibberjabbered at the playground, waiting for Pop. Suddenly, the girls wondered what it would be like to be clean, and to have shoes and nice clothes. Right now, all they had was this: they were maniacs, outsmarting a maniac AI with art...outsmarting the peeps with art, so they'd realize dead girls were phoenixes. Outsmarting was code for taking what was necessary for fun and profit—for survival. The new components were necessary for the big heist. They depended on surprise. Could you surprise an AI? They were about to find out.

The ruined playground always made Fun and Moon think of a graveyard. Swings were made of pipe and chain, and now the pipes were crumbling, the chains were clumped with rust. Swings made mobile tombstones? Ghosts came out in the middle of the night and had themselves a swing. In the future, everything was multipurpose. Swings were weapons. Ladders, eyries. Where was Pop? Pop! There came Pop making his appearance at the Trough. The girls held hands and twirled in circles, glittering waifs, dirty orphan angels.

They sang, "Daisy is lazy, we're a bit hazy, 'bout what makes her crazy."

They giggled and fell into each other.

"Owie!" squealed Fun. "Bowwowie. You got bumps. I like to jumps."

Moon jumped in place. She was elastic, maybe made of shark cartilage. "Let's do, doe, dough this Budinski thing."

"Like magics, the Trough ratchets," reported Fun. She knew it was on. And her skin crawled. Her joints were made of bed springs.

What made the girls so magical practical tragical? Albinos gone dingo! The whole notion of growing up, and training, or apprenticeship...the very nature of the concept learning, they were all in the toilet. This was the kid with the attenuated youth, the new kid—

Pop was on fire. The people from the store rushed out to throw chitin cups of gray water and old soda on him. He was mainly extinguished. The girls could tell the slaves from the store weren't going to call backup. They could see that in their body language even from here. Pranked. Trough peeps had a weird relationship with the locals, even though they were locals. The girls were on fire, too: the geyser fire of emerging intelligence from deep in their toes announced: **Let's do this! You can't live forever!**

They skittled for the Terrace entrance station. IDs, ready. Wave and pass! The sickly guards, worn, only interested in their own survival, waved the girls through— gente.

They skedaddled into the warehouse district, not even slowing to help put out Pop, disappearing fast in the maze of walls and halls, like mice. Metal alleys in patterns, they knew. They caught a ride on a yellow distributor, whose front extensions looked like crab claws. Easy-peasy ride though: the tech bot slave was not programmed for mice. Their slave train was already in when they got to the tracks. AI's were talking, gossiping, prepping. Human handlers popped their pills and rubbed their junk. The slave state slithered on—

Fun and Moon found their car, climbed on, checked for the container they wanted. Careful toe and finger grasps ripped nails, clipped fingertip bones, as they conquered the train's cargo space-time continuum. Now the mice had become spider monkeys and the containers were their playground.

This one! This was the one that held the goods. They settled by its panel. Fun's big toe of her left foot was bleeding. They extruded their tools. Moon took off the pack.

"I stink we should go in lair, hair, fair," said Moon when the panel slid open.

In they went, wiggling, wriggling, realizing that before too long they would be too big to get down here. But, now, only one bad jolt, when Fun spun around to land on her feet and whacked her shin. But no 'bowwowie' in here.

Inside the container was satiny black with LED's glittering on the shipping crates. Faces talked back and forth. Fun and Moon imagined they were inside a component, inside the machine, grooving on electrics. They were on the inside looking out, looking in, going for the goods. They were so good at seeing patterns, projecting outcomes, three, four steps ahead of the slave drivers AI's, that they were fearless, and sparklies didn't bother them.

It went perfect. Keys. Props. Translators. Boom, they were loading components into the pack before Bruno had a chance. Turd and Romper knew what to do—keep him preoccupied. The girls depended on their back up.

They exited, straight up to gray sky. Without a pause, they adjusted their goods, stuffing them where they could.

Fun whispered, "Scary."

Moon was shocked. She started climbing away. "Home

again, Flanigan, diggety do," sang Moon.

Fun glanced around, all eyes, scanning, peering, clearing her head of container cobwebs.

At the edge of their train car, they were ready to jump, to fly for home, when they spotted three humans in complete gear, walking along the train, coming towards them. They ducked. They only had seconds to figure it out. Fun and Moon studied each other's faces. No sighs or question marks escaped their noggins.

They sprang out of their hiding place, jumped to the ground, and ran towards the three figures as fast as they could. The three men stopped, leaned back a little. But the girls couldn't see their faces through the helmets. One of the men's arms came up, hands out, as if to stop them or catch them.

They shouted at once: "That guy back there!"

"He showed us his penis."

"We got dropped off in the wrong place."

"We're lost."

"I'm scared."

"That man had a piece of his suit cut out so he could stick out his uh-uh."

"We were so scared, we just ran and ran."

"We hid in the train."

"Please help us."

The man with arms raised said through his helmet electrics, "Nothing to see here. Move on. Move on. Go on now. This is a restricted area. Time to go home."

One of the others electrocuted, "Wonder who it was. Who's working out here?"

"We better go see. That new guy from Mars was working over here."

Fun and Moon realized they couldn't tell who was talking. The electric voices just popped in their midst. Everything was surveilled, reported, filmed, checked out—

Fun and Moon took off running fast as they could. The

three men hurried in their awkward suits, a lazy stomping motion, down the train's length, looking for this Martian.

Bridget giggled to herself deliciously, under the covers in her bed, in her and her sister's tiny room. She turned off the flashlight. She closed the notebook, put it and her pen on the floor beside her. The flashlight she kept. She cozied up to sleep.

Friday morning the news was filled with Trilobites. The official release had bled right into YouTubes of 'life with Trilobites'. One TV anchor claimed, "Remember the hermit crab craze, now we have a Trilobite craze. They make perfect pets."

Ian was hoping for news from the site. Was Taylor already there? Was she safe?

Ethan crowed: "Schedule! Timing is everything. Turn that off. You're all over your schedule this morning. What time did you get up, anyway?"

"I told you I had to go look for food for Hessler."

"Get cleaned up, finish up. We're outta here in a couple hundred seconds."

Ian had already done the breakfast dishes, so he headed for his room and a decision. He found the plastic container Taylor had brought Hessler in in the closet and ran to the bathroom to fill it. He put in chlorine drops, swirled it around, returned to his room for Hessler.

Hessler was in his bowl. The water was funky. Ian looked around the terrarium. The worms were gone. Was this a bloated Hessler? Had he eaten them all up? Ian explained to Hessler what he was doing and why it was important. He didn't want to leave Hessler home alone, because he wasn't sure what Taylor and her company were liable to do. It was his mom's life, her choices, her decisions, and they didn't jibe with theirs. There was no way Ian would let Hessler out of his sight.

Trilobite at school! He couldn't—he shouldn't. In a story, the character would shout now, I'll show all of you! But that was stupid and showed the difference between life and fiction. He would do a stupid thing at this stupid school. It was for Bridget! No. It was sticking a broom into a wasp nest. No, it would be his claim in public that Hessler was his.

Ethan didn't notice the care Ian took with his pack, positioning it between his legs on the passenger side. Ethan had trouble starting the Camry, but after a few tries peppered with cuss words it came to life. Ian didn't know if the vehicle was breaking down, or whether it was simply Ethan's awkward interaction with machines.

The whole way to Saint Bart's, Ethan lectured about what he now called his 'cleanup crew'. He'd call 'old lady Tilson', set it up as a study session at their house under his supervision. They would work off their debt. They owed him.

Ethan was a monster. Ian was agreeable and quiet. The problem was none of this was real. Not because Ethan didn't have a right to punish his son—Ian understood that. But because they did not love each other, so everything was fake. Ethan may have been the loneliest person in the world. Ian felt he was typical of most adults. Taylor had to go along with whatever her company said. Sister had to go along with whatever the Church said. When you don't love, you're all stunted and slanted, following orders.

Did his high fricking horse come from the fact that he was in love? What was this he was feeling? Deep in his body—his heart. He couldn't keep straight what people assumed was heart or head, or mind or soul. What did he feel a? What did Bridget feel? What did Hessler feel? How to juggle—

Here they were. Drop off point. Bye, bye. Lift the pack. Open the car door. Swing around, up, up, cradling his precious cargo.

Kids. Faces. Ian had a funny smile on his face. He walked carefully but with confidence into the hive. Bridget and her sisters clustered at the entrance talking. Bridget saw him. Then all of the sisters turned and looked at this odd boy walking to school with his pack held in front of him.

"SMF," goofed Bridget.

The bell rang. Sister came out. The boys around Ian wondered what 'SMF' meant and tried to guess. Sister was giving the eye, so they shut up.

"Friday, class, let's have a great day," announced Sister.

They filed in. The boy in front of Ian said, "I got it. SMF—suck my fungus."

A massive giggling crisis ensued. Sister grabbed a giggling boy by the arm, as though she was going to whack him. But, no, she gave him the eye, let him get back in line and proceed in.

What if Bridget heard? It'd get around to her by lunch.

Should Ian punch the jokester in the eye, so stand up for his woman?

Bridget would beat him up.

Not today—not today.

Ian put down his pack. He leaned into it to retrieve his stuff. Hessler's container looked fine. No water had splashed out or leaked. When things were impossible, and there was no anchor to anywhere, what could you do but the impossible? He'd have to remember that for Bridget. It seemed to make sense, and it sounded like something she'd say. She was super logical. She was already hard at work he saw, in a clean, ironed uniform. He was seeing her sideways, full body profile. She was long, and her legs had a whiteness that he swore for.

The news was out! Had the kids heard?

They settled into their rituals and rhythms. Heartbreaking sighs and guttural groans escaped from the young people around him. Sister let them work it out so they could gather their resources to focus. Math came first.

Ian thought, 'they're coming for Hessler!' He had to tell Bridget. Note? Code? Some kind of signal?

They worked their way through simple equations, and Ian kept glancing into his bag. But Sister didn't notice. Typically, the class was good for an hour, hour and a half, of intensive work. Then the class would become kids again, each with his or her individual need. Morning recess and bathroom break were uneventful. The boys had moved on from 'SMF', to a new vulgar riff to amuse themselves. Before lunch, they had science.

By row, the students came to the front to cluster around Sister's work table. She had set up the class' microscope with a slide. The work desk had all their science equipment spread over its surface. By the microscope, a test tube rack with three test tubes. A small box of cover slips was next to that, then a box of slides. An eye dropper on a piece of tissue lay nearby. Ian's row lined up for their turns. Ian noticed the small scale. It was too frail, too small, too much a toy. How could he pocket it, in plain sight, in front of all these eyes? He was right by the scale, next to a ruler, a protractor, and a plastic box of litmus paper.

A girl, bent over the microscope, squealed when she got the specimen in view, then into focus.

"Do you see? Can you see it now?" asked Sister.

"The green ribbon inside?" went the girl.

"Spirogyra," triumphed Sister. "It's a kind of algae. Clearly, you can see all the basic parts. Cell wall on the outside. The green ribbons spiraling through are the chloroplasts, curiously bound together. Wonderful specimens! The beauty of God's creation."

Whamp! roared a big textbook hitting the floor in the back, so that an actual shockwave passed over the class. Everybody stared at the source. The scale climbed into Ian's pants pocket, left side. Right on in. No bulge.

Even before they looked, the class knew it was Bridget. They waited for the reprimand, keyed up, expecting a good one. The girl at the microscope, startled at the sound, had jumped, her head jerking forward, eye into eyepiece. It hurt, but, worse, she thought she'd moved the microscope. She hurried back to her seat. Ian moved up to take his turn.

Sister cried, "Attention-getting device! Attention-getting device! Attention-getting behavior!" Her eyes burdened into the girl's flame.

"I'm sorry," said Bridget. "It was an accident."

Ian, in place before the microscope, to the side of the test tube rack, reached out and took a test tube of specimens and raised it to his lips and drank it. About half the class, plus the kids still waiting their turns at the work desk, saw him do it.

Finally, everybody had had a turn.

Sister seemed to be taking her time in announcing lunch. So, the students pretended to be taking their time, too, diligent, finishing notes, fine tuning homework.

Ian wondered what Bridget thought about The Terrace.

Proposition: the tree of life, like in taxonomy, from the vertebrate trunk came a branch to mammals, which branched again and again to rhinos, rats, bats. Other main branches from the trunk held fish or reptile groups. Branching and branching. Big branches, small branches. From his broken family trunk, steeply cut into Ethan and Taylor sub-trunks, came weird branches that climbed up and around, arcing over the bifurcation, making a dense canopy where Ian hovered. He had his own branches in this tangle, connected to school or writing or embarrassments. Other branches went to secret places he'd rather not look at. The newest branch was the Bridget branch. There was also a Hessler branch. Not really like the tree of life at all, he realized. Way too random. Just the jumble of the juggle—

She would think he had a thing for little girls. She must know he knew she had taken it. Now he had the scale, and he had drunk the elixir in front of the class. It all came together. He was ready. What was this pulse running through him—building up? How did he know so strongly that Bridget felt it too?

He raised his hand. Sister nodded.

"Sister, I know we just finished science, but my mom brought me something from the deep lake they discovered. Like we saw on TV yesterday. Maybe, I can show it to the class after lunch?"

"We'll see," said Sister. Then: "Put away your books. Get ready for lunch, please."

At lunch in the cafeteria, Ian ended up sitting with the class nerds, boys into science, math, computers, gaming. They wanted to know if he was poisoned? Could he feel the algae growing in his stomach? Why had he done that? They wanted to know what he had from the underground lake. They asked questions about the subterranean world. Not like a normal cave, so what was it? Were there dinosaurs down there? What was he going to show them? One boy, very seriously, said, "What if they opened the door into hell? It happens all the time in games."

Ian left Hessler in the classroom in his pack. Now he had to go to recess. Hessler would be okay. It was just for a few minutes. Recess had Ian tossing around the basketball with the boys, pretending to be sporty and interested. He didn't see Bridget at all. As they were filing in later, Sister raised an eyebrow at Ian, so he went to her.

"Keep it short," she said.

Ian nodded. "Yes, Sister. Can I do it up front?"

She nodded.

The class settled down into their seats. Sister closed the door. Ian glanced in his pack, then a quick glance over at Bridget who was red-faced from recess, flushed, and glaring back at him. What had she been doing?

Sister went to the front of the class, her standard, central position, hands behind her back. "Ian will show us something from his mother's discovery. Ian."

Ian stood, took his pack up to the front. He got behind the work desk. He put his pack down. Sister had already cleaned up, putting the microscope and other equipment away. Ian leaned into his pack.

Sister was watching. "By row," said Sister. "Let's start over here."

It was Bridget's row. The kids came up, circled the desk.

Ian held the plastic container in front of him. He placed it on the table. He wiggled and pried the edge to pop the lid. As soon as the lid was open, Hessler hurried up the side, over the edge, falling to the desk surface, SPLAT! scrambling forward in his peculiar sliding, levitating way.

A couple girls screeched at once.

A boy yelled, "Cockroach!"

Bridget laughed and Hessler flowed right into her waiting hands. "Hessler!"

Sister was livid. "Ian, what is this? What's going on here? What are you two up to? You didn't tell me it was alive. Ian, put that creature back in its container this instant." Double whammy eyes! Voice constricted: "Mother superior, our parents, are going to be very upset. That thing could have germs. It could be dangerous."

Bridget brought Hessler over to Ian. She stepped on his right foot, held her foot over his, placed Hessler into the plastic tub. "He's just a bug," said Bridget. "He's not dangerous at all."

"What are you two up to? I want everyone who came

to the table to go to the bathroom and wash your hands. Right now!"

"It's a Trilobite," said Ian. "They were thought to have gone extinct over 200 million years ago. He's a living fossil, proof of evolution."

Some kids were halfway to the door when Ian started talking, and they stopped to listen.

Sister cried, "Wash your hands. Go!" She turned. She walked to Ian. She raised her right arm with the forefinger out, pointing to the back of the classroom, and said quite deliberately, "Get your Trilobite, your books, and get out of here. Now. Take that thing home now. Tell your parents, you have been expelled. You could have endangered the whole class. It's like an act of terrorism. Go on. Get your stuff and go." She lowered her arms.

Ian returned to his desk, started loading his pack. The textbooks ringed Hessler's container in a steady, secure fashion, much better than before.

What was going on, what should he do, he didn't know whether to laugh or cry. He finished packing, fumbled around a bit. Kids were coming back from the bathroom. Sister was bent over the work table scrubbing its surface with antibiotic wipes. She kept muttering, "Bleach. Bleach will do it. Bleach. Bleach—"

Ian stood, flung his pack around. It wouldn't leak. He had it tight. He was on top of this. He walked from the classroom, and not a sigh was emitted anywhere.

Ian made his way slowly down the hall at Saint Bart's. He kept thinking, 'this is illegal! You can't throw a kid out of school in the middle of the day. His parents have to come pick him up.' He got to the door, sort of fell into it, forcing it open. He stepped out to the parking lot and playgrounds. He hadn't gotten used to this place. It would be easy to leave.

Once he got off the school's property, he speeded up and practically ran all the way home. He wasn't sure why.

What's the rush? They'd call his father, and his father would tear home ready to pulverize. He'd want to kill him. Ian pictured his father going after Hessler skedaddling across the kitchen floor, trying to stomp him like a cockroach.

What if his mother's people came for Hessler? He'd be at home in his room, and the goons would come in their hazmat suits, wielding Taser tongs.

He unlocked the front door, went on in. He dropped his key ring on the couch. He dragged himself and his pack back to his room. He placed his pack on his bed, started unloading books and school supplies. He removed Hessler's container. He opened it. Hessler came into his hands. Ian took the Trilobite over to his home. Hessler flowed around the terrarium, checking things out, finally burying himself in the sand.

Ian would have to pack intelligently. Survival stuff: toilet paper, a knife, water, some food. A change of clothes. All his notebooks. One novel. He rummaged around in his pack. At the very bottom, the Terrace notebook. She must have snuck it in during lunch. She'd known Hessler was there. She had to check.

Ian pulled out the notebook, started riffling through the pages. He came to handwriting that wasn't his. He found where it began, right after his last entry. He fell to the bed and read it through.

It was good. He liked it. Something very private and personal had been touched by another human being. They were partners now, writing partners. Her penmanship was extravagant, big letters, with big loops and crosses. A flourish to it. She pressed in hard like he did.

But he might never see her again—Ian froze. Rose from his bed to get back to it...when the phone rang.

Ian would never be able to explain what prompted him to answer, to say 'yes' into the phone.

"This is Sister Angelica, principal of Saint Bart's. I'm

afraid there's been an altercation, and your son, Ian, apparently, has left school premises. I assume he's there with you now?"

"Of course. We're very upset."

"Agreed. Let's get together as soon as you think it wise. We believe it's time Ian sought his education elsewhere."

"Agreed."

"I will call tomorrow. Or you can call me. To set up an appointment. I believe you have my number."

"Thank you."

"Thank you."

Sister hung up. Ian hung up. Ian ran back to his room. He explained his idea to Hessler. Ian wanted Hessler to eat before they took off. Hessler settled into Ian's hands. Ian went through the kitchen to the sliding glass doors. He nudged one of the doors open with the side of his hand, then his toe in the gap pushed it the rest of the way open.

Ian took Hessler into the messy backyard. A bare patch showed rich dark soil. It was where Ian and his mother had gathered materials for the terrarium. Ian went to his knees before the spot. He lay Hessler into the earth. Hessler immediately buried himself, then like a little bulldozer moved in a straight line across the cleared area. Ian probed around in the clods and roots. He found two earthworms quickly and tossed them into the center of the bare spot. Right away, the worms began wriggling, trying to get underground. Half buried Hessler flowed back the way he'd come, and found the worms. Ian gave him a few minutes of privacy.

In all the world, this was happening only here. Ian and Hessler, and worms for lunch. Trilobite paradise. The day was bright with spring, clear blue sky with racing clouds. A very different kind of day, from when Hessler and his kind had peeked over the water's edge, then scurried over the shore to hunt for worms. Hundreds of millions of years separated these days. So a kind of reunion. Revival?

Earth shook hands with itself.

The goons would want to cut him up.

No time to work that over now, Ian saw that Hessler was still, quiet. He held his position like a real living fossil, living. Ian put out his hands, and Hessler slid into them. They went back to Ian's room. Ian put Hessler into his terrarium. He moved to his bowl, got underwater. Ian took the plastic container Hessler traveled in to the bathroom to dump the old water and get fresh water. Back in his room, he swirled some chlorine drops into it. He put his notebooks at the bottom of the pack, threw in some extra clothes. He changed from his school clothes to his favorite play clothes. Switched shoes. Balled up a sweatshirt and jacket for the pack. He stuck the chlorine drops in the side pocket. He dragged the pack, still pretty light, to the kitchen. He found the flashlight in its drawer, tossed it into the pack. From the fridge, he took three plastic water bottles. Food! A just opened box of Cheez-Its got thrown in. Then the box of Cheerios. An energy bar was next. He looked around. He went back to the fridge, thinking pop tarts.

He noticed on the fridge door an announcement. It was from his father's school, about a special honors ceremony this afternoon. His father had mentioned it. He was going to be home late. He'd have his phone turned off during the ceremony. Better and better!

No pop tarts. He found a knife. He wrapped it in paper towels and slid it into a side pocket. He hurried back to his room. Do-re-mi! He scrounged for forgotten allowance.

Where—he knew where the highway was that connected to the airport. There was a big gas station out there by the turn. One of those huge complexes, with convenience store and car or truck washing berths. What highway was that? Where was it going? Most headed to Chicago. Everything connected through Chicago. It didn't matter as long as it was away. He needed a map. He checked the drawers in the kitchen. He hurried to his father's room. Ian remembered the cross-country trip and how his father had had a map. The card table in the corner with the tower was now a messy repository of mail and papers. No map. He checked the nightstand next to the head of the bed. It, too, bore papers, plus a couple books. No one used maps anymore, what with GPS. But the Camry was ancient, and, besides, his father eschewed technology. The map was at the bottom of the papers.

Ian went for a pee. He drank a glass of water.

Ian retrieved Hessler, got him in his container. He positioned the plastic tub in the pack, now held securely with clothes. He headed out, leaving his key, which meant he couldn't get back in. That was it. He walked from his house and turned at the unpaved road that connected to the alley behind the houses.

He followed the alley, as though he were heading back to Saint Bart's, but then before he was even close to the school, he'd turn off for the highway. He knew where the turn was. He'd pass a few more homes, then farm country would start. There would be traffic. He could be spotted easily. One thing at a time! He would hide in the bushes until dark, then sneak out to the highway.

He walked right into Bridget's arms. She was in her school uniform. But no pack. She looked like she'd been running.

Before she put her tongue in his mouth, she said, "Tactics. Strategy. Sometimes all you can do is the unexpected. Bowdoin charging from the high ground without bullets."

Then she kissed him.

Their kiss broke and they held each other. They pulled apart.

"I hear Denver is nice," she said. "I want to go to Denver."

"They're coming for Hessler."

"We have to get away."

"You can't! Bridget! Bridget. Bridget, we—"

"Three times, you said my name."

"You have to go home."

"Did you steal the scale?"

"I left it in my desk at school."

"Good boy."

"I'm leaving, Bridget. I'm going to walk out to the highway and hitchhike out of here."

"You'll be spotted, picked up right away by the police."

"Or get picked up by some trucker who eats kids."

"You're really going to be in trouble."

"You could get expelled, too. You have to go back."

"No."

"You're still in your uniform. If you get expelled, you go to hell."

"Please. Self-reliance. Resilience. We need these things now."

"Why do you want to go to Denver?"

"My brother, Tim, lives there."

"I didn't know—"

"My parents don't know I know. Nobody's supposed to know. You can't tell. Tim was born out of wedlock, put up for adoption. He's nineteen now. When he was eighteen, he contacted my parents. Snail mail. You know how my parents are. I found the letters. He was seeking them out. But they were too afraid. They don't know how to handle it. They keep telling him when we girls are old enough, they'll tell us."

"He lives in Denver?"

"He's an artist. In art school. I think. Maybe. I have his address. I have his cell phone number. I know he'll help us."

"Denver's pretty far."

"Where were you heading?"

"I have to get out of here."

"Well, now we have a plan. You have Hessler with you? Dumb question."

"I got an idea."

"Enlighten me."

"My friends, Dan and Tallulah—"

"You have a thing for Tallulah."

"Give me a break."

"Go on. Tell me."

"I know where they live. We go to their house. Borrow some clothes from Dan. They'll fit you."

"That should—that could work. Maybe. We are going to do this. There's no going back. You wouldn't believe what happened after you left school."

"Panic. Chaos. Pandemonium."

"We got down on our knees and did a rosary."

"Praying for me?"

"For ourselves, I think, because of your contamination."

"Praying is a punishment."

"No, no. I'm not going to explain praying to you right now. Is it far to their house?"

"Close."

They held hands and walked through the alley to an access road that led right to Dan and Tallulah's. They went up to the front door. Ian rang the bell. Dan answered. He looked surprised but not unfriendly.

"We don't have any pop tarts," he said.

"We don't have any either," said Ian.

"You guys get those cinnamon ones. Me and T like the fruit ones."

"This is fascinating," said Bridget, "but if you don't mind, Ian, I think we need to tell him."

"What?" went Dan. "You guys want to come in?"

Bridget and Ian made their way past Dan and into his house. "My mom's not home. Wassup?"

"Where's Tallulah?" asked Ian.

"His girlfriend," explained Dan.

Bridget snorted.

Dan smirked. "Come on, she's in her room."

They walked through the living room, turned at the kitchen and dining room to the hallway that gave on to the bedrooms.

Dan knocked at the second door, then grabbed the doorknob and threw open the door. "We got company."

The room had a bed, a chest of drawers, desk, and a bookshelf. Pink was the theme. Pink shouted out wherever one might look. Pink posters on the wall, then by the pink bed, in front of the pink bookshelf, a pink chair. Tallulah was enthroned on that chair completely covered by stuffed animals. White lambs, blue owls, orange bears, yellow dragons, up to her neck, so that her head seemed to pop out, a white pale head, afloat in a sea of plush.

Tallulah said, "I'm decompressing." And she rose from her chair, and stuffed animals dribbled to her sides.

"Brilliant," went Bridget.

"You have Hessler," said Tallulah.

Dan said, "What's going on? Something's going on."

Ian went to the pink bed and swung his pack down on it. He opened the top, took out Hessler's container. He placed the container on the pink bedspread with My Little Pony images. He removed the lid.

"Hessler," went Tallulah and plonked down next to the container. Hessler went up her thigh and nestled in her lap. "No hands," said Tallulah.

Bridget tore her eyes from the little white girl, bare legs, bare feet, in pink shorts with a frazzled looking, old purple T-shirt, with a 200 million-year-old living fossil cuddling in her lap. "We're running away. It's a long and complicated, fairly stupid story we won't bore you with. But we need your help."

Tallulah was shaking her head slowly. "No, you're not." She looked worried. "This can't be good. Danger! What about Hessler?"

Ian said, "My mom's people are coming for him for sure. He's the only male. So far. They want him back." Ian saw Dan and Tallulah's faces grow bleak.

"No way," said Dan. "You know what that means? The old dissecting table for sure."

"No!" cried Tallulah. "He can stay here with us. No one will know."

"That's a good idea," said Bridget, "but I don't think it will work. Your mom would find out—"

"No, she wouldn't," said Tallulah.

Ian got in: "I don't even know your last name. My dad doesn't know we're friends." Ian worried it over. "But Bridget's right. Eventually, your mom would find out and she'd tell, and you guys would get in big trouble."

Dan said, "We're the Reynolds. That's why we call her TR. Well, mainly I call her T. What kind of help do you need?"

"I left from school," said Bridget. "I have to get out of this uniform."

"You can wear my pinafore!" cried Tallulah. "Be so cute on you!"

"T, come on," went Dan. "Your clothes would be too small."

"Yours would be too big," said Tallulah. "Boy clothes. Yuck." She would not cry!

"Follow me," said Dan, "I'll show you what I got. Plus, I got an old pack you can take. You need to take water. Stuff like that."

"It's like an adventure," said Tallulah. She fought to hold it together.

Dan insisted: "No, it's not. It could be dangerous. For all of you, including Hessler." Dan looked away. "You could be raped."

Bridget said, "I'll protect him."

"Stop it," said Ian. "Let's go see the clothes. Tallulah, stay here and take care of Hessler."

Ian and Bridget followed Dan to his room. No time to examine the Lego spaceships. Dan rummaged around, tossed on his bed sneakers, couple T-shirts, faded blue jeans, some gym pants, socks, and underwear. He dug around in his closet and came up with a sweatshirt and a hoodie. The old pack was in the closet too. He dragged it out.

Dan said, "We used to go camping with my dad. My old camping stuff is still in this pack. Don't know if it will help."

Bridget said, "That's great. Thanks. Okay, no strip show today, boys. You guys go hang out with Tallulah. Let me try these on."

Dan and Ian went back to Tallulah's room. Ian got Hessler into his container. He explained how time was crucial right now. They had to get going. No one was looking for them yet, no one knew they were gone. Dan brought up money, did they have any. Ian said he had dug up about fifty bucks.

Tallulah said, "You can have mine!"

"No," said Ian.

Bridget came into the room with the pack, dressed in old sneakers, dark gym pants, a black T-shirt, and the hoodie which was up.

"You look like a boy," said Tallulah.

"The sneaks are a bit ripe, a little tight. But this should work. I took a couple things, stuck them in the pack. And that camping stuff." Bridget let the pack drop. "Thanks for the pack. For everything."

"Perfect," said Dan. "Ian, I'll get you a cap. You never wear one. Okay? It will help. Just two guys hitching out of here."

Tallulah extracted a rolled up twenty-dollar bill from a secret tear in a lamb.

"I was wondering where that was," said Dan.

Tallulah pressed the bill to Bridget, nodding solemnly.

Bridget refused, then took it. "I'll pay you back. Promise."

They took Hessler and the two packs out to the kitchen. Dan stuck a red cap on Ian's head. Tallulah hooted. Dan looked around for food, water. He threw things in Bridget's pack as he came on them. He opened drawers to see what else he could offer. Tallulah sat in the chair at the dining room table. Her feet were pulled up, so she could rest her head on her knees. Her hair was a mess. She wanted to be brave. Dan found a screw driver and insisted Bridget include it in her supplies.

Bridget said, "Pens, pencils, paper. A notebook, maybe?"

Tallulah unfolded herself from her chair. "I know," she said, running off.

"This is really nice of you guys," said Ian.

"Thanks, Dan," said Bridget. "I left my school clothes in your room. You better get rid of them."

Dan whispered, "Cooties." Then, very macho: "You guys be careful!"

Tallulah returned with a handful of pens and a notebook. All were pink. The notebook had kitties on it. Tallulah explained, "I was saving this notebook for something special. This pen smells like berries. This one smells like peaches."

"We can't take your best stuff," said Bridget.

Tallulah shrugged elaborately and dumped the stuff on the kitchen table.

Bridget selected a couple regular, non-smell pens. She packed the kitty notebook.

Tallulah stood straight, arms folded in front of her. "Danger! What if—if we never see each other again? I won't say goodbye."

CHAPTER 8

Two guys walking down the road—

Dusk. Not much traffic. The tall guy in a hoodie. The smaller guy with a red cap. Both with packs. Hard to tell how old they are. Assume it's two doods—

No one would guess that they'd spent guests a couple a couple hours in the bushes near the truck stop. They hadn't talked much. They'd found a good place and hunkered in. Ian let Hessler out. Hessler explored, digging around in debris, playing hide and seek.

Now, they were going up the shoulder of an on ramp that merged with the highway heading west. This was the place to get a ride. Ian had seen hitchhikers here before, he assumed, like when he and his dad went to the airport. Bridget agreed.

"Maybe a truck will stop," said Ian.

"Maybe," said Bridget. She sounded sad. "They know now and are starting to worry."

"We can't think about that. We gotta get outta here."

They stayed at their spot on the ramp for four hours. Three cars went by, three trucks. People didn't even glance at them. Quiet, empty night.

Bridget moaned, "No one's going to stop. This isn't going to work."

"There's other highways. I got a map. You want to see the map?"

"What would they do in your story? *The Terrace?*"

"What do you mean? Oh, you're being cagey. Good cagey?"

"What would the characters do under these circumstances?"

"They'd get out of here. They'd change the circumstances."

"Exactly. Resilience. I need Skittles."

"The stores have cameras."

"I'm invisible."

"Maybe we can ask a trucker for a ride."

They hoofed it back down the shoulder to the gas station at the crossroads. There was one car parked at a gas pump but no one was with the car. The driver must have gone in to pay. There were three eighteen wheelers parked in the back, diesels thrumming.

"Fascinating," murmured Ian, the two of them standing off the highway, lingering by some trees, the trees no longer just trees: they were cover. Night opened up. He discovered this world he'd never known: at night, things went on, and had been going on for some time, while he'd been snuggled at home with a book or a movie.

"What?"

"We're like spies. Everything is special and has to be carefully scanned."

"Fodder."

"We can do this."

"You go mosey over to the trucks. I'll go for Skittles."

"You're playing. The evil twin. You want to be caught."

"Don't say that. We're not twins. That would be incest." She stopped. She fought back the shudder. "Okay! We got Hessler to worry about." She took off.

Ian grumbled. He moseyed over to the trucks. A man came out of the store and headed his way.

"Me and my friend could use a ride," said Ian.

"No riders," said the man, eating a Slim Jim. He had one of those giant sodas in his other hand. He walked on by.

Behind the trucks, the exhaust was bad. Pretty soon, the middle truck with its long rectangular box trailer made terrific revving noises and began to roll out.

The truck on the right had a long metal, hamper-like rig. The truck on the left had a shiny steel tube. It was clearly labeled 'refrigerated dairy'—a milk truck. Ian was quick to notice that the way the giant tube was arranged on its trailer allowed for a cat walk all around it. The sides had rails and cradles to secure the tube. A couple people— skinny people, could easily squeeze in along the cat walk and keep it on the down low, behind the metal cradles. Ian hurried away to pee in the shadows at the edge of the parking lot.

By the time Bridget came out of the store, the hopper truck was gone. Ian whistled for Bridget. She whistled back. They came together. Bridget was eating Skittles, tossing her head back to throw in the candy.

"We shouldn't waste money on candy," said Ian.

"That's true," went Bridget, continuing to chew up fruity bits. "I guess you will be the dad here, huh?" She paused, made animal noises. She garbled, "That was mean, no more mean. I'm trying. I'm fucking conflicted—you know, freaking out."

"Me, too." They wouldn't look at each other. "We don't have much. We have to make it last."

"Good thinking," Bridget gurgled.

"Bridget, you want to go back. It's okay. I understand. I get it."

"Don't."

"No, really. Now's your chance."

"Ian, don't. Ian! Ian, I said I'd—I'm ready."

Ian was quiet but had counted his name three times. He scanned the dark. A car pulled in to one of the pumps.

Bridget said, "They can't see us."

A woman got out of the car, went in to the store.

"I know what we can do," Ian said.

"You have a plan."

"See that truck?"

Bridget turned to look it over. "Milk truck."

"See the side, the space along the sides, along the rails?"

"The driver would see us?"

"Not if we got down behind one of those metal cradles that hold the tank. There's no time. The driver could come out any second. Last chance, Bridget."

"It's impossible," went Bridget.

"So it could work."

"How do we know where he's going? He could be going to the next town over."

"It's somewhere. Now or never, Bridget."

Ian couldn't see Bridget clearly, but he knew her face well enough, even with the hoodie, to know she looked intense.

Bridget said, "They treat you so differently when they think you're a boy."

"Now or never."

"Quit saying that."

They scuttled over to the back of the remaining truck. It was easy to climb up to the narrow walk way. They shimmied and sidled to the first cradle, got down behind it. Hassled to take off their packs. They squeezed in behind each other, Ian in the front, trying to figure the best way to position themselves.

"Get your feet out of my face," whispered Bridget.

Ian adjusted himself, pulling up his feet.

Bridget gasped. "Boom a bang a dang! Man approaching. Got to be the driver. He's driving all night to Denver. Watch. This is perfect."

It was the driver, and, mounting his cab, he got situated, then slammed the door. The truck erupted to life, started shaking and vibrating.

"The fumes are going to kill us," said Bridget. "Or the vibrations."

"We'll see. If it gets bad, we jump. We got this."

The milk truck crawled out of its parking space, hit the parking lot's exit and was out on the road. It followed the path to the on ramp they'd walked, and to the interstate heading west.

Once they got going on the highway, the fumes weren't as bad as they thought they'd be.

Ian enjoyed the takeoff, then the coming up to speed. He felt the acceleration like a rush of freedom. Freedom he'd never known. This was not just a cool, magic night, runaway night, this was darkness opened up to inhabit, to fill out. It was their night now.

Bridget was messing around in her pack. "Can you hear me now?" clamored Bridget, over the roar of wind and diesel. "I have this poncho from Dan. I think we can tie it over ourselves like a little tent. Wind break."

Ian called back, "Will the driver be able to see it?"

"Not if we do it right."

Bridget unfolded the Army green poncho and started passing up one end to Ian. It already had strings attached at each corner's grommet. It was more of a tarp or ground cloth then. Like an emergency tent. They tied off each end and it worked. It even helped to keep out fumes. Bridget crawled up alongside Ian. They were so close now, pressing into each other.

"Hope Hessler's okay," murmured Bridget. "Can we bring him up with us?"

Ian grunted. "I can feel your bones."

"I can feel your bone."

Night highway terror freakout subsided. Ian thought Bridget was crying. Maybe it was him. Traffic picked up on the interstate. They had to get through Chicago. Exhaust was bad. Noise and vibrations were torture. They held on, bumping, swaying, inhaling shallowly. Bridget saw the interstate sign, heading south now, Interstate 55.

The highway quieted, but it was still busy. They fell asleep in each other's arms, Hessler's container nestled between their bellies. At one point, falling asleep, Bridget announced, "I'm here for science. For life."

They got jolted awake in St. Louis, another sprawling concrete jungle, end of the world theme park. Ian couldn't get out his map. They switched to Interstate 70. They slept, they cuddled. Difficult to see out. They stayed awake, staring into each other's eyes. There must've been gas breaks, pee stops. It all blurred to a vague. They were hibernating on the road, pulled in, slowed down, pretending to be barnacles. Bridget remembered Kansas City, because the interstate went by the stockyards, and the smell was pure midwestern joy. How long had they been driving? What time was it? Neither of them had a watch. Or a device. No GPS. They wondered how to figure how far they'd come. At least they were still heading west. The signage indicated they were crossing into Kansas now, but they got off the interstate. They were now on State Highway 50.

They slept to western Kansas. They knew it was Kansas and western, because they were jarred awake, the dairy truck hitting a bump, and Ian peeked and saw pre-dawn gray shimmer over a state highway sign. The sign read, 'State of Kansas, West 95'. Where were they?

Ian and Bridget talked geography a while, trying to figure if this was a good thing. They knew that western Kansas ran into Colorado. They were close? To what? Why had the driver gotten off the interstate? Where were they going? If it was dawn, figured Ian, then they must have been on the road eight or ten hours? They'd slept some of those hours. How fast did a big rig go? Seventy or eighty miles an hour, they guessed. Do the math! Enough time to get across a couple states. Bridget did some calculations in her head and figured they were about 500 miles from Denver! She beamed.

Ian was unsure about her brother, as Ian imagined he'd feel obligated to call her parents, or the police. Bridget countered with, at least it was a plan. They were going somewhere, not just away. Ian said he liked away. They were stiff, cramping, wind beaten. If they got any more uncomfortable, they would turn in to mannequins. They both laughed, tried to stretch. They decided to sit up, managed to sit cross-legged, squished in.

"Did we stop last night?" Ian wanted to know.

"I think so. He'd have to get gas. Or go for a pee. I remember one time for sure—"

"Don't! You make me have to go, talking about it."

"Me too," said Bridget. "We should check Hessler."

They opened the Trilobite's container. Hessler slid out onto Ian's lap. Ian touched his tickle spot. Hessler stayed in his lap for several minutes getting a rub. Then Hessler moved across Ian's legs to Bridget. He rested in her lap.

"Hessler," went Bridget.

It was hard to hear over the wind and engine noise. It couldn't be very comfortable for the Trilobite.

Ian watched the countryside awaken. Dawn was sluggish. It was gray and flat in all directions. He could see for miles, and it seemed full of emptiness, as though this whole region was an endless field, but no agriculture around here. It was uncared for land, or used up land. Ian couldn't tell which, but he knew it wasn't right.

"Ian," said Bridget, over the buffeting wind.

Ian turned his eyes to them. Hessler's antenna were extruded. The one on the right went out to touch the T-shirt over Bridget's belly. The other was held out towards Ian.

"Get closer," said Bridget.

Ian squished in, until the antenna touched his bare leg, the spot exposed between his sock and pulled up pants leg.

Bridget said, "I think he needs to touch bare skin." She grabbed her T-shirt, tugging it out of her pants, then carefully slid it past the antennae. The antenna made contact with her skin. "There," went Bridget.

It was unclear what followed. If asked, Ian and Bridget would have said they were sleepy and dozed off. If they remembered anything, it was the tickle of Hessler's touch, and a stillness. Neither meditated, but both had read enough to know this must be some kind of meditation. All worries and fears just weren't a bother at that moment. For a little while—

The careening and lunging of the truck alerted them that something was happening. They came to a truck stop in a small town. Not much town at all. The gas station may have been its highlight. Nearby, boarded-up buildings leaned precariously. A couple houses may have been livable. But no residents around right now. The truck inched its way to the side where the truck pumps were. The truck eased down. Off. The driver climbed out, headed for the store.

"Put Hessler away," said Bridget, "just in case."

Hessler had pulled his antennae in. Ian put him in his container.

Bridget said, "Driver's going to the bathroom, then he's going to get some snacks, then he'll have to pay. We have time to jump off and go pee."

"I don't know," said Ian. "Hate to lose our ride."

"Oh, come on, my bladder tells me it's time to live dangerously," went Bridget and started crawling backwards to get out.

"Here he comes," said Ian, who had kept his eyes peeled on the store entrance.

Dawn light was getting perky so they could see their driver clearly for the first time. A big guy, with the big guy paunch, probably middle-aged, in jeans and a flannel shirt. Fancy cowboy boots.

The driver came back over to his truck and fussed with his tanks and their caps. He started pumping. Neither dared breathe. Was he looking around? Checking out his rig? It felt wrong. Their hidey hole was on the other side from the tanks he was filling. But, then, wouldn't he have to come over to their side to fill those tanks?

Ian whispered, pantomimed, "Untie the poncho."

Bridget was too scared to move. She stared off into unknowable distance pointlessly.

Ian worked on the strings. He got two untied.

The trucker returned the pump to its holster. He climbed to his seat, immediately revved up the engine. He moved out slowly.

Ian was sure they'd been discovered—

The truck proceeded down the state highway. The truck chugged away at a crawl. The driver must have noticed something. They went a couple miles. The truck came to a small turn out by what Ian saw was a historical marker. They pulled off the road there. Where were they? What happened here? All around them, as far as Ian could see, was burned. Black, grays, in all shades, in this sudden morning dystopia. The truck went into neutral. Ian couldn't read the cooked monument. The driver's door flung open.

Ian's eyes inside of Bridget's said it all: *run!* Bridget backed out with her pack, swung around, climbing down, hit the ground, and started running with all her might into the fire zone. Ian was a couple seconds behind her. They passed the monument and entered the black and gray horror, their steps raising pops of gray ash. They ran, they flew.

They heard a big voice thrown at them: "Fuckers!"

They had to leave behind the so-called poncho.

They ran and sweated, smudging ash across their bodies, until they came to some burned-out trees, now just tall skeletons, around a group of burned-out structures. Maybe they'd been houses or barns. The bigger structure must have been a barn. Its roof was caved in, and its sides had collapsed into itself, so it was hard to tell. What might have been a house, also, had no roof or sides, but it did have a cement floor, littered with blackened chunks. Two roasted bird cages perched in this mess.

They poked around, catching their breath. Ian got out a water bottle. They shared it.

Bridget said, "Odd to think of folks way out here by themselves keeping exotic birds. Canaries? Budgies?"

"Chickens," said Ian.

Bridget pushed him. "We gotta go pee. Pee! P-Q-R-S-T!'""

They walked through and around the structures to what must have been the backyard. Here more burned trees. Cottonwoods? The air seethed with soot. There was a small intact structure hunkered back there, partially hidden by charred, skeletal tree trunks. What was weird, too, was that green blades of grass were springing up around it.

"Hessler thinks it's a launch pad for Gypsy elvish," said Bridget.

"Hessler thinks it's a hidey hole for errant wolf cubs," said Ian.

They got closer, up to the low boxy building, walked around it.

"Walls are so thick," said Bridget.

"The fire didn't get to it," said Ian.

It had a flat metal roof, and was less than fifteen feet long on the side. It was maybe eight feet wide. When Ian saw Bridget standing next to the building, he realized it had to be less than five feet tall.

"Check it out," said Bridget. "Strange little place. We can explore. We shall discover the treasure."

Ian smiled to her. She smiled back. They were literally in the middle of nowhere, a somewhat toxic nowhere. At least no one would ever find them here.

Ian went to the front door first. Its edges were scorched, but it hadn't burned through. It was a heavy wooden door and did not want to open. They couldn't find any locks. No key holes. They couldn't figure how it was held closed and tight. So, together, they put their shoulders into it, and the door popped or pushed or fell into itself and opened.

Step down—

They entered the small, cool room.

"It's a cold room," went Bridget.

"A cold box," said Ian.

Even though the floor had been lowered, dug out roughly, they both had to stoop.

"At first, I thought it was some kind of smokehouse," said Ian. "You know, for meat. I thought we'd find slabs of pig and cow hanging from hooks in the ceiling."

"Just slabs of Ian and Bridget," said Bridget.

They took off their packs, leaving them by the door, then pushed it closed. The light was dim inside, but they could see. And the air was slightly fresher. The walls were lined with shelves, mainly bare. Some of the shelves held jars of what might be vegetables. The floor was dirt, moist. But not muddy. Junk and trash littered the floor, but most of it was pushed to the sides. They could hear a slight tinkle.

In the middle of the back wall, a half circle of rocks protruded, protecting a tiny pool of crystal-clear water. Water gurgled from a stone shelf back there, throwing up a mini-water sprite. That's what was tinkling.

"Oh, well," sighed Bridget.

"A spring," said Ian.

"Of course it is," Bridget went on. "Here is the perpetual spring that if we drink from, we will never age. No harm will befall us."

She kneeled by the rocky wall. She wondered about the pool. Water, water! "Precious gem in the scorch world." Her hand hovered over the water, fingers splayed, then she immersed it. "Cold," she announced. She bent forward over the rocks, and lowered her face into the water. She blew bubbles.

Ian wasn't so sure. "Don't drink it! We have water. We can use this water for cleaning up. It must be circulating. Dirty water flows away."

Bridget fell back on her heels, big goofy smile, dripping water down her front. "Kiss me, you fool!"

And so Ian did, going to his knees, and bending in to Bridget. Her face was wet and icy. They smiled pesky. They let the energy of the moment flow through them. No hold backs. They kissed for a while on their knees and felt.

Finally, Ian murmured, "Hessler will love it."

Bridget stood, pulled off her hoodie. "I gotta go pee," she said. "Again."

They both went to the door, opened it enough to slide through. They took off in opposite directions to complete their business.

When Ian got back, the door was open, and he could hear Bridget inside. Ian entered, pushed the door closed behind him, saying, "I'm going to get Hessler." Then he saw what she was doing.

She had hauled their packs to the back and plonked them down in a corner by the spring. The other corner she had cleaned of old jars, broken tools, and bits of wire and wood. She'd made a long narrow space. "We'll sleep here," she explained. "Now I wish we had that poncho." She arranged their extra jackets and sweatshirts across the bare space.

"I'll get Hessler," said Ian. He looked over their nest. 'No candles,' he thought.

Bridget said, "This could be the beginning of a beautiful relationship. We could be here for always, Anywhere-Nowhere, USA. We could be here for days, weeks, and no one would ever find us."

"We don't have enough food," said Ian, removing Hessler's container from his pack.

"Pffft! Hey, Astro Boy, Cyberpunk, Intelligencer, look at the shelves."

"Botulism! That stuff could kill us."

"We can boil it. Make a fire at night. Dance around the fire. Learn all the stars."

Ian kneeled before the spring. He opened Hessler's container. Hessler climbed out and slid to Ian. Ian swung down to sit on his butt, and Hessler moved into his lap.

"I knew he would approve," said Bridget.

Hessler left Ian's lap and slid across the floor to the rocks.

"Let him. Help him," said Bridget.

Ian said, "Springs go deep, really really deep, into the deep Earth. Suppose he doesn't come back."

"If anyone knows the Earth, it's Hessler. Duh! Of course he'll come back." Bridget came around and picked up Hessler. Gently, she positioned him over the pool, lowered him in.

"It could be too cold," gasped Ian.

"Shhh." She released him and he fluttered away, gliding down—

Ian said, "Down, down into the mud he goes, where all the worms and stuff are. I suppose it's good—"

"Take your jacket off, and your shoes. I will too. We can wash up a little. Is there soap? Come cuddle with me."

Ian did what she said.

Magic, love was not spoken. Ian and Bridget turned off their society. Now experience was essential. central. They dared not flicker attention from it, and make it something articulate. Right now, they were busy being content as in set free. Set free, people explored. They walked their vicinity until it became proximity. They studied the weather of ceaseless gray. Was this a sky or a cover slip? They walked in concentric circles around the cold hut, expanding out gradually. They came to the edge of the fire, where it had stopped. But the only difference between the scorched landscape and the un-scorched was the color of dust.

They ran out of the food and water they'd brought, so started drinking from the spring and eating the veggies in the jars—mainly green beans. Boiling was impossible, since neither of them had packed a lighter. They didn't die. Hessler adored the spring and always came back. Bridget and Ian walked, talked, cuddled, wrote in their notebooks. They could tell Hessler was growing. They really had no idea where they were. Going out at night, into Scorch, what they called this place, they could tell from the stars they were still on planet Earth.

In their bare feet, standing close, Bridget whispered, "Dust bowl."

Ian went, "Ash bowl." He flicked his flashlight on for a quick scan, making sure no monsters were nearby.

Bridget went, "Blood bowl. Disaster zone. Ash world burned up. Just like in your story."

"It begins."

"Cool night."

"No moon."

"We can dance. If we are denizens of hell, doesn't that imply we are demons?"

Bridget danced and Ian watched. Bridget swayed about,

hands and arms moving, gyrating, while her feet stayed calm—not wanting to stir up ash. Ian imagined it was like one of those hippy dances he had seen on TV. He didn't know she could dance. But maybe she couldn't. She was doing this for him? No, she was doing it for Earth and sky, the gaunt, gray cinders. He could barely see her, except for her white feet and calves.

Bridget murmured, "Why do you stare at my feet and legs?"

"You're beautiful, every part of you."

"No, I'm not. What about this part? Are my elbows beautiful?"

"Let's go clean up."

"Now I wish we had soap."

They took off their shirts and pants and tried to clean up at the spring. Finally, Bridget sat, holding her feet in the pool. Ian scrubbed her feet with the t-shirt they had designated wash cloth, and some of the black ash was rinsed away. He flicked on the flashlight to check.

Bridget said, "We gotta make the batteries last." She whispered, "What does Hessler do to us?"

"Antenna ritual?"

"Telepathy? I didn't think that was real."

"It's not supposed to be. It can't be. I think he makes us sleepy. When the antennae touch us."

Bridget sounded frustrated. "What does that mean? Does he affect the way we feel? *Does* he make us sleepy? Even that's weird. Like he's a drug to us."

"We slow down."

"Do our minds connect?"

"I don't know what that means?"

"What's different now?"

"What do you mean? Everything's different. We're different. The Earth is the same."

"Do you know what love is?"

"We weren't talking about that."

"Love is sacrifice, putting another first, before yourself—"

"That's Catholic school stuff."

"Does Hessler love us?"

"Trilobite love. I guess. If there are mainly females, they're like clones. Only the males are different. Like the way bees and ants do it."

"I know how they do it."

A day with one bite of food, Bridget blurted, inside, while they were working on their notebooks, Hessler between them with antenna extended, touching them, "We'll have to call my brother."

"Soon," said Ian. "After Hessler molts."

One dark cuddle, Bridget said, "I like the idea in *Terrace* of CK—*common knowledge.*"

Ian grunted a little, pulled back his head burrowed into her side.

Bridget continued, "All the pop culture junk—movies, TV, comics, books, music. It's like a done deal, a monolith, a 500-pound gorilla. The constant cascade of images that takes over the brain, the insides of our heads."

"Whatever happens, there's an image that goes with it. Readymade, right on target. Fits perfect. So we don't have to—"

"Have to, what? So we don't have to be? So we don't have to think? I hate that."

"Now, here, and with Hessler, it's not like that."

"We get to decide what's important to us. Ian, what will we do?"

"If your brother won't come," Ian paused, snuggled her arm, gently bit her arm, then, "then we'll call someone else. Or hitchhike out of here. We'll walk to Denver."

"What's next? What's next?" Bridget wondered, then rolled to her side. "I feel like your very own chew toy."

They thought about what was next sometimes. They worried about their families sometimes. They walked through the rubble sometimes. They heard vehicles go by, back on the state road, probably big rigs by their volume. They were two teens on an extra credit project for skipping a grade.

On the day Hessler molted, they sat close together, Hessler rubbing up against the rocky wall that surrounded the pool.

Ian said, "What's next?"

Bridget said, "See how he doesn't need help? Do we need help? See how what is implied is purpose?"

"God, Jesus chooses for you?"

"How else to know what's right? We should save his skin."

"Humans do what happens? Instinct."

"Then there's no free will? Or choice. What to do depends on faith, hope, not CK."

"Faith, hope, like magic?"

"What do we know?"

"Proposition: everything we know or assume is wrong? The CK—and how right away there's an app for that, that can't be right! That can't be the way to live. Maybe we depend too much on beliefs. Like whatever we believe is real. Some totally stupid TV image kind of becomes our own, like a memory."

"What do we know? Look how beautiful Hessler is!"

"He's gotten so big. I didn't bring the ruler. But he's got to be five inches now. The spring has been perfect for him. He loves our cold room in Scorch."

"He fills my hands."

So now they had to hike to the gas station, make the call. Bridget had memorized her brother's (her half-brother's) telephone number when she first found the letters. Good thing she had a strong memory. Maybe the gas station didn't have a payphone? Payphones were on their way out, pretty rare these days. Way out here, who knew? They hadn't noticed telephone poles? Burned down? They could tell the people at the gas station it was an emergency and borrow their cell. Was there service out here?

They could get supplies. They both had dreams of their favorite candy. They didn't want to waste money on junk, then again, there was nothing wrong with a little bit of beef jerky and potato chip. They didn't know the name of the town. Or how far they were to Denver. They worked on it. They kind of hated how suddenly there was this huge distraction in their midst. Should they pack up and bring their stuff, and Hessler, to make the phone call? Even if they got hold of her brother and he agreed to come for them, it could take a day or two. They'd have to go back to Scorch to wait. But they couldn't leave Hessler! It was agreed that Ian would bring his pack, with Hessler to make the call. Suppose the gas station people called the cops?

They were hungry. But no rush, this funny period at the end. One late afternoon, they took Hessler outside with them and set him down in the ash, thinking they'd pick him up right away if he didn't like it. Hessler loved it, burrowing into the ash at once. They watched his unique, tri-lobed shape plowing along, then he stopped.

Ian said, "Ash has all sorts of elements in it. I think. I'm guessing. Ash might have nutrients Hessler needs. It could be good for him."

Bridget said, "Before we leave, we should—don't think this is dumb. You promise? We should do a chapter of *Terrace* together. The next chapter, together. Work on it sentence by sentence."

"We could always get new batteries."

"We do a chapter, finish it, then we call."

They worked on the story, in Ian's *Terrace* notebook, passing it back and forth, until they needed a flashlight. They talked while they wrote and scribbled. Both of them liked to doodle in between writing. Neither was very good at drawing. They tried to draw Trilobites, but it was hard getting them right. Ian imagined a whole cartoon series of Trilobites. They used the back pages of the notebook for their silly pictures.

The Terrace had to take on some kind of climax. They brainstormed for ideas. It was awkward, sentence by sentence, putting together a story. Bridget didn't like the despair.

Ian said, "That there is the story's tone. What is implied. The belief in giving in does it. Is giving in the same thing as giving up? I think as soon as a person believes it's the end, it twists the person up inside, turns the person into an adult. Despair takes over. The whole world in despair That's our CK today, what our generation inherits." Ian shrugged and pulled away. "It's a set up."

Bridget was irritated. She thought then they should handle it differently. "The essay at the beginning, it sums it all up. Even you said the so-called plot was derivative. You gave the watered-down version in class. When you were trying to destroy my faith. How do you turn this insight into a story? You gotta overturn despair."

Ian said, "Is that the insight?"

"Hessler enabled it? We don't know."

"He did make it into the story."

"Ian, what are we doing? Your insight, my insight—don't amount to a hill of beans. Still, who can we go to, to ask? Nobody can tell us what the best thing is now. This is new. A girl and a boy and their Trilobite. There's not a single person we can rely on. We have to invent the world. We have to invent fun or else. What do we know? I know we've had the most fun ever. I know this is true. I know it's real."

Ian scooted closer. "Or else what? What do we know? What do we see, touch, feel?"

"What do we know?"

"Proposition: today, when everything's falling apart, whatever you can get away with is the only rule."

"Which really means whatever you can stand. Sinners hate themselves, thus despair."

"Are we sinners?"

"I don't feel guilty. How could I have so much fun and be guilty? Do you feel guilty?"

"Say it. I know we haven't—we weren't gonna say, I mean, about love."

"I'm too young. I don't know enough."

Ian grumbled. "We have to see what's there. That's what you do in a story. Details! Pay attention. See what's there."

"Ian, after the big heist, there's celebrating, maybe the characters can...you know?"

It was impossible, but Fun and Moon made it back to the kids' house without incident. They'd hip hopscotched their way through the warehouse district, the maze of mighty metal walls, corridors unending, supplying the nation, slamming by the know nothing robots, not a single human suited up around. No sign of a burning man at the Trough— Pop must have gotten out of there. They'd skedaddled by the security guards at the Terrace entrance, who all suddenly were afflicted with bad cases of eczema.

Ian was waiting for them at the house with the others. Moon gave him a hug. Fun was all over the others, blabbing their story in rhyme. Moon took off her pack and placed it on the kitchen table.

Ian said, "You guys, your toes are bleeding."

Romper said, "Peroxide and Band-Aids! Fox slide, land fade." She hurried away.

Pop said, "Is this it? Infinity at our fingertips?" motioning to the pack on the table.

Ian said, "I know you're not joking, and I'm scared, it's going too fast, and I don't know nothing, I'm not following. The girls should soak their feet."

Fun crooned, "Stinky feet, stinky feet! Smell my stinky feet!"

Pop sighed. "Okay, okay, vibe time, time to let you secrete the secret! Let me see it." He waited for Moon to comply. "You're next, Ian. The big heist. The last heist. DLA hiatus fate us. Fracas. We're going to do this, you're going to do this."

Romper returned with first-aid, showing Ian. But, first, Fun and Moon, Pop, Turd, Romper, Ian pressed in to see the TAL key. Moon popped its security tape, and she materialized from her shift a perfect tensor tooth that got the job done. The security wrapping fell away. She could do it in her sleep. No one else could. The boxy black shape gave up its secret, as it was not a solid box, but comprised of three matte black plates, five inches tall, four inches wide, maybe an inch thick, attached in their centers by a seamless nuclear connector. But not adjacent—the plates were inch or so apart, held together, connecting in the middle.

Turd made a funny sound, half gurgle, half giggle. "I'll have to make some kind of rig, thingamajig, for you to block it in. We can work tonight. Tomorrow, your walk on, Mister Barrymore."

Ian, as usual, was passive aggressive, "I don't know what you want me to do. I gave you the Trilobite idea. I don't know what this thing is. TAL key. It's a bomb. I'm a bomb, is that it? I go in some place and blow myself up?"

Moon looked very serious. Her shoulders writhed as she tried to adjust. She said, "Intelligencer—

Bridget said, "Using your own name is lame."
"It's a first draft."

"We can change it."

"I like Michael."

"Buford Intelligencer."

They erupted into a tickling war that led to kisses and rubs.

Moon went on, "The TAL key enables fables. Mabel, Mabel, get off the table!"

"Right on!" went Turd.

Pop said in a tone at once authoritarian and snarky, "Ian, no one knows you. You're nothing. Invisible. And we have our prestige, our sinecure, our gambit, the old bait and switch. What if the bus breaks down, herding the elvers to market, on their way to do, pretty as you do, please do, do boom you're do in—"

Turd went, "Boom!"

Romper went, "Boom!"

Ian grabbed up the peroxide and Band-Aids on the table. Romper had brought cotton balls. Fun and Moon sat, legs dangling, feet out. Ian moistened a cotton ball with peroxide. He hesitated before their stinky feet.

Romper said, "I'll do it."

Ian insisted, "You gotta tell them what happened, about the AI's!"

Moon said, "You're going in! Straight for the pineal gland. The hippocampus hippopotamus. Owie bowwowie!" Peroxide bubbled from her toe.

Romper cried, "Go, go, girl!"

Moon kept wailing, "The hula hoop gyrus. Corpus callosum wholesome fulsome! Brains, brother, we want brains!" She calmed a little, and her shoulders settled and her hands fell to her sides.

Ian, thought he could see through the skin of her neck, these throbby ropey network neck works.

But Moon wasn't done: "It's the AI crossroads. The heart, the bull's eye, the ganglia fanglia, why why wide wide super wide open, poorly distracted, heavenly retracted, a weak obviosity. Your spot, our spot. Hot spot. You leave this thing. TAL key. Which we hurt our toes to get. This thingamajig dealeywhopper. AI's proximal, proximate, infiltrate—"

Romper finished with her and turned to Fun. Fun's wounds were simple, so she didn't require as much attention. Romper exclaimed, "Good as gnu!"

Turd went, "We need more slingshots."

"What am I heisting?"

Fun and Moon fell into each other's arms giggling, but too many tears came down their faces, and their tears burned, their eye so exposed, which made Ian tremble even more. Everyone was exposed. They sang, "Command and control, command and control, sand in a bowl, sand in a bowl!"

Bridget said, "See how even if it's more than a single sentence, if it's someone's speech, you gotta finish it?"

"I noticed. Where we going? You're comma drunk. I feel like I lost control."

"You're verbose."

"Uh-uh, you are." He poked her and she poked back and dropped the notebook.

"We'll have to cut here, and here, and here," and every time she said 'here' she poked him in a different spot.

He gulped. "Editing, second draft, mucilage."

They fell into each other's arms and held each other.

She whispered, "Trajectory. Ambiguity. Inevitability. Watch."

Pop said he'd explain, and hightailed it out of the kitchen with the girls. They left for electronica, their electromagnetic hideaway, where they'd monitor the feed. Bruno knew by now. Retribution! That would take two or three Trilobite images to calm. Meanwhile, the lights were on—

Turd and Romper got busy checking the TAL key dimensions, making a drawing.

Ian said, "If this thing is so important, and powerful, how come it was so easy to steal?"

"It wasn't," Turd explained. "You know DLA hacks the AI's. Nobody believed it possible, including the AI's. They missed it. The girls keep it quiet. And they do it funky." Turd and Romper slapped hands. "TAL key so rare and dangerous, they're transported by courier. But AI's figured, the old hide in plain sight routine, in a container. There's millions of containers. Full proof! Peekaboo! Impossibly random. The humans, the bureaucrats, the administrators all agreed. I mean, the numbers—they pretended they understood them, and the numbers said they'd save a ton of hassle and coin. These trains carry all sorts of goodies. AI's, the only ones who know where they are. Trains are all that's left, you know. And the AI's control them, and whoever controls the AI's—transport."

"Wistful, wishful, mist full, piss full," went Romper, slapping at Turd, then giving Ian a shove. She took Ian's arm and led him away. "We'll go get materials from our room."

Romper and Turd shared a room. Romper turned on the overhead light. Two cots on opposite sides of a small space. A desk, or work table, between the cots, at their heads, a workspace with a lamp, and covered with papers, books, components now. Turd had painted the walls in waves of green, so it was like an underwater forest or living in the leaves. Actually, Ian was surprised at how organized and kept up the room was. He hadn't looked in the closet though, which had its door closed. He glanced around for 'materials', *but couldn't see any lying about—*

Romper said in a tricky voice, "When a girl says 'let's go get my materials', it's like they used to say, 'come up to my room to see my etchings'." She moved in close to Ian.

Ian stood straight, stiff back, head held up, as she shuffled in closer still.

"Ian," said Romper, "you have a big day tomorrow. We find it helps the guys if they get off the night before."

"Why? What! I don't understand."

"Shhh," went Romper. "Put your hands on my head. Fingertips. Good. I knew you wanted to. Gently rub. Like you'd rub a Trilobite's cephalon. Nice. Very good. You get a kiss. Easy, Ian. No tongue. Yet.

"Look, little brother, this is what's to understand: intelligencer is more complex than us, thus the machine becomes intolerable. Even when there's so little left, it must be stopped. It's a human thing. We are human. We get to decide now. Eliminate. Eliminate your trousers. Or do you call them pants? I get that confused with boys. Fine, you're busy. No, don't stop. I'll get them. Open duh drawers, unbuckle the belt, let loose the pants. You keep on doing what you're doing. I want to see your bulge. Okay. Okay. Schlong, dong, wrong—right! You want to slide over this way. I'll guide you over, holding onto it from the outside of your underwear. This is my side. Slow, slow. Slow is good. Keep on doing what you're doing."

CHAPTER 9

Tallulah was petulant. "Mommy doesn't have to know. Dan! Don't be a thunder lizard, bumble lizard. And you didn't take care of the gummi bear situation like I asked."

Her dressing room was small, but the lights around the makeup table's mirror were bright enough to make the whiteness of the girl in the mirror, in a simple white shift, glow. It was a youthful glow. It was an uncanny glow, too—seemingly unearthly, but organic. The dress looped over her shoulders to hang shapelessly over her. It allowed the whiteness of her legs and arms, neck and face, her bare feet, to show. Her long white to gold hair was combed out straight and over her shoulders. She had on makeup that made her eyes direct.

Dan, in tight black gaucho pants with a flared cuff, button-down white shirt, came in close to his little sister. "I'm not picking out the red ones for you. Forget it." They examined each other in the mirror with snarls. "Mom's your manager, she has to know about stuff like this. You have to tell her."

"Bare feet," smiled Tallulah triumphant.

"Mom thinks it's pervy. They got your new sneaks. It's just weird."

Tallulah seethed brilliance: "Dan, you're my agent.

You're not just my bodyguard. You're my brother. I need you here. This is my first TV ad. Dan! Dan, we're in Chicago."

Dan straightened, took a step back. He mumbled uncertainly, "These are different Trilobites."

"I already met them. We got along right away. Besties."

Dan wiped at his nose, looked away, shook his head. "This is all so blitzed! Crazy—crazy! But here we are. Do you think about them? Where they might be?"

"Every minute."

"It's been so fast. Like time no time. They run away with Hessler, cops show up at our house—"

"Mom finds out everything."

"Mom finds out everything. Law enforcement, Homeland Security, even the CDC have to talk to us. TV crews and reporters. God, how they loved you. They think you're the biggest discovery in years. Like a missing link." Ian snorted.

Tallulah poked him. "Stop it. That reminds me, you said you'd help with my website. Mommy's fine. You're fine. We got this monkey where we want him. Trilobites are gonna save our family. Wait and see. Money talks. Everyone walks. Funny! Funny, how we end up working for Ian's mom's company. I can't wait to meet her. Do you think she'll get along with our mom?"

"T, you talk funny. I don't know if I like—"

A knock came to the dressing room door and a burly fellow with a lot of facial hair came bumbling in. "Five minutes," he roared. "You ready, young lady?"

Tallulah said, "Yes," nodding.

Then a young woman tore in, the makeup girl, who came up to Tallulah and got in close to her face. "Good," she said. "You look perfect, like an angel. We may have to put powder on your arms and legs for the lights. We'll see."

Tallulah nodded, stood, shook herself clear, and was

ready.

The big guy wrestled with his neck tie knot, hands about his throat. He got a grip, gurgled with excitement, "The Trilobite wrangler is right outside. Let's do this!"

He led Tallulah out the door, into the recording studio. The wrangler and the company liaison, also the ad's producer, were waiting by the stage.

The company man was young, well-dressed, and both Dan and Tallulah disliked him. He said, "Keep it simple, T. Keep it real. The camera guy will say 'we're rolling', and you just do your thing. Sorry your mom couldn't be here."

"She had important beeswax," said Tallulah. "It was crucial."

The wrangler reached into his transport container and began pulling out small, female Trilobites. Three of them. He deposited them into the plastic habitat they were merchandising, called a Trilotat. This was a flat-bottomed, transparent sphere, portal at the top, that held water and earth and sand, to make a little habitat for a Trilobite. Smaller than a bowling ball. The female Trilobites were about two inches long.

Tallulah took the Trilotat and walked out to take her position by a podium with a flat top. She placed the Trilotat on top. The podium stood slightly in front of her, to the side. Tallulah stood with arms loose, hanging, hands open, relaxed. Blue eyes straight ahead. Before her, sound guy, cameraman, and sinister looking equipment, like those transmuting robots that could turn into insects. Her toes were scrunched up. Her facial expression, her body language read, she was here, she wasn't here. She wasn't really there, or she didn't belong there, here, Planet Earth? She seemed far away serene, and the blankness could be overcome death, or some kind of ritual emo goth rage agony.

The cameraman announced, "Rolling!"

The announcer called over the sound system,

"Trilotats! Safe! Educational! The pet everyone wants!"

Tallulah went to the podium, opened the Trilotat portal, and the three Trilobites flowed up into her hands until she had a double handful of Trilobites. She faced forward. Her face opened with glee. She stepped, or leaned to the side, making a position, feet angled, slightly up on the toes of her left foot. Hands before her, cradling the Trilobites at her tummy, and the Trilobites slid up her left arm to inside the elbow, where they stopped. They aligned themselves neatly on her thin arm. Tallulah dropped her right arm to her side. Slowly, she raised her extended left arm, to better show her charges. She looked into the camera with blaring blue eyes, daring, darling, challenging, overwhelming, and said, "Trilotats!"

Multiple voices yelled, "Cut! Cut!"

Then, more voices: "That was perfect!"

"Did you get that?"

"Really beautiful! This is going to be a classic!"

"Not too shiny?"

"T, how did you get them to do that?"

Mr. and Mrs. Tilson sat at their kitchen table late at night, enjoying a cup of tea in the house's deep silence. The biohazard people had left for good. The police and FBI would let them know. News cycles were such that the 'runaway lovers' story no longer carried the cachet it once had. The girls were all upstairs cuddled in bed. Everything was caught up. They tried to think so, just to have a moment of peace. For how could everything be caught up, *except* the location of their Bridget, their girl, their special girl, their pride and joy? So smart! Gone! With that boy! At least the experts assumed that that probably was a good thing. Or, by this time, they'd be looking for a corpse. That was unbearable. They put those thoughts away. They clung to this one-night moment together with tea.

Mr. Tilson said, "We haven't had a moment since it all started. We have to make sure we get these moments together, or we'll lose it. Everything seems so fragile. We need our strength, what we get from each other."

Mrs. Tilson said, "You need a haircut." She tousled his thick red locks until he snorted and both of them were smiling.

Mr. Tilson said, "I need you, Mrs. Tilson."

Mrs. Tilson said, "When we pray together, we have all the strength we need. When we pray, I feel us all. You. Even Bridget."

He nodded and lifted his weary hand from his cup to take her hand around her cup. They smiled to each other shyly.

"Our family is strong," he said quietly. "Our Bridget is strong."

She sighed, yawned, shook all over.

He said, "We have to get to bed: Mr. and Mrs. Tilson need to keep up their strength."

They both chortled. They both heard a crash upfront, and they started. It was a dull 'whumpf.' Mr. Tilson was on his feet and lurching to the living room. He hit the lights.

Mrs. Tilson was right behind him. "What was that?"

"Something fell," said her husband, glancing around the living room, but nothing out of place. "Outside!"

They headed to the door.

They heard a siren—close. They opened the door to the spinning lights of a police cruiser pulling up in front of their house. The policewoman got out of her vehicle, then hurried towards the side of the house. She yelled, "I saw something fall!"

Mr. and Mrs. Tilson ran to the side of the house. The policewoman was bent over Kay, dressed and with her pack, who lay on her back in the juniper hedge. The police woman held her hand.

Mrs. Tilson sobbed.

The policewoman said, "She doesn't seem to be bleeding. I think she's just stunned. Good pulse. I think she's okay. You okay? Open your eyes. Can you hear me? Did you hit your head?"

Kay groaned and lifted her head, opened her eyes, and saw her mom and dad. Mrs. Tilson froze, jerked a step back with her hands over her face. The policewoman saw what was coming, Mrs. Tilson collapsing onto Kay, to hold her and—

The police officer said, "Easy, easy. Let's not move her until she's checked out. You know, back injuries."

More sirens and lights, and an ambulance appeared. Mr. and Mrs. Tilson felt pushed aside, as the crew with the stretcher took over. A third guy, carrying a big bag, seemed to be the EMT in charge. He wrapped a brace around Kay's neck.

Mrs. Tilson said, "We're right here, Kay. Kay, we're right here, praying for you."

The policewoman came to their side, stood there, as Kay was transferred to the stretcher. The EMT with the bag was getting vitals, talking to Kay. The police woman said, "I'll give you a ride to the hospital."

"Can't I go with her?" asked Mrs. Tilson.

"No, come with me."

"Let me tell her. Please." Mrs. Tilson hurried towards Kay and the ambulance.

Mr. Tilson said, "I'll get her. We'll come with you."

The police car followed the ambulance, both with their lights flashing, but not too fast. No sirens. Mrs. Tilson sat in the back where it smelled.

The policewoman said, "I had to call this in."

Mr. Tilson said, "Lucky you were around."

"Yes," she said, "lucky I was around. Was Kay having a

hard time coping with everything that's happened?"

"Of course." Mrs. Tilson was getting impatient. "We all are."

"Maybe she was going to them. Maybe she knows where they are."

At the hospital's emergency room, they were reunited. The EMT was there, standing by Kay's bed. He said, "Her hands are scratched up. They're going to be sore. Her vitals are fine. Some bruises. But she's a strong girl. And a lucky girl."

They were allowed hugs and kisses this time, and Mrs. Tilson tried to squirm her way onto Kay's bed to swaddle her better, but she couldn't fit.

Mr. Tilson erupted, pulling back, getting red-faced, "You could have been killed!"

The policewoman intervened. "Hi, Kay. I'm Officer Mahoney. Call me Gayl. Gayl with a Y. I saw you climb out of the upstairs window and try to climb down—"

"I don't want to talk about it. You can't make me. Mama!"

The EMT and nurse stood at either side of the head of the bed. They were used to desperate parents. The nurse, an older woman with gray hair and a stoic face, said, "She still has to see the doctor. She's scheduled for an x-ray, too. You can talk later. Please."

A big young guy came into their curtained space. "X-ray," he went. "Tilson?"

"Me," said Kay meekly.

"What's your birthday?"

"Two – nine – eleven."

"We'll be right back."

He hustled Kay away, and Mrs. Tilson barely managed to grab Kay's hand on the way out. She called, "Can I come?"

"No need, Mama Bear, me and Ms. Tilson will be back before you know it."

The nurse said, "Why don't you wait outside, and get a drink of water, sit. I'll come get you when she's back."

Policewoman Mahoney, of course, came with the Tilsons to the waiting room. They sat.

Mrs. Tilson said, "I don't want to talk about it. Right now, I just want to know Kay's okay. Okay?"

"I understand, Mrs. Tilson. I'm sorry for coming on like I'm intruding. Especially at this difficult time. But Kay seems okay. And Ian and Bridget have been gone a long time, and if Kay knows something it could be very important. The FBI is sending over that agent you've talked to before, Special Agent Alexander."

Mr. Tilson wondered, "He thinks they were kidnapped." He shook, sighed. His hand went to his mouth. "But you people don't understand. Kay would have told us. I know she would. If she knew where they were, where they went."

Mrs. Tilson had had enough. "Of course she would. We're growing donkey ears. Let us pray."

Doctor Taylor Scanlan, ensconced in her dim, electrically twinkling Quonset hut in New Mexico, was suddenly in charge of kooks, cranks, zealots, werewolves, and warlocks. Had they opened a door to hell? Was the underground lake the fountain of youth? Were there dinosaurs down there? So far, no violence. Company security, with its beefed-up private contractors, was holding it together. The trespassers camping nearby were now paying fees to the ranchers. How many more would come? What was drawing them? Trilobites, Stys, *runaway lovers?*

Now, so much going on—

—Taylor kept her focus. Which was easy to do, given the wall of electronics across her desk: online monitors, then encrypted ones, then smaller screens that detailed vital statistics from the underground sites, plus special security screens that kept her in touch with her people, and events unfolding. The desk, the electronics made an arc around her, that she imagined from above would be a smile. Or frown. POV. Focus. For now, Taylor multitasked from electronic to manual checking of paperwork. She felt she'd run away and joined the circus, and she was the ringmaster, so much time spent on logistics, schedules, performances. She scanned reports, made decisions, then had to let everyone who needed to know know. Right now, she reviewed requisitions. The layering of communications—she had to keep in touch with everyone. The cyberwork, the paperwork was beyond bureaucratic nightmare, all the way to a hemangioma of excess. Great work for a geologist!

Meanwhile, she only allowed herself a chance to weep for Ian at specific times, when she was alone and unencumbered. This was not one of those moments.

She was waiting for a Skype call—an update.

Mega-busy now, fast talking, the company was maximizing options, merchandising as they'd never imagined. Trilobite pets! Trilotats! Next, the water would go on sale—million-year old water!

She dealt with two security teams. One was local, here in New Mexico, maintaining intel about the visitors. Trespassing was the main concern. Improved fencing, cameras were going up. Law enforcement had to keep the roads open. The local security guys also had to monitor Trilobites, as workers all too readily were sneaking out Trilobites in their pockets, not to mention canteens of million-year old water. Drones were deployed. Undercover agents were essential. Fencing was bulwarked. She didn't even know you could bulwark a fence. Something to do with smart barriers—

The second security team she heard from every day

were the company people assigned to the kids and Hessler. It was all mixed up. Implications in all directions. But Ian had a girl, and Ethan was freaked out, and the CDC was insisting on new protocols for the water and the Trilobites.

She pushed back from the desk smile/frown, averting her eyes from the monitors, to come to rest on the stack of hardcopy science reports. Data, data—more easily studied online, on the screen. But more easily hacked that way, too. New equipment shed analyses like snakes shed skin. Precise measurements of the underworld! Its pedigree. Provenance. Components, compounds, elements. Styx— bad choice for a name, maybe. Still, with the new elevator car, she was mighty tempted to go down. In a way, she had to. She'd wear a mask, take all precautions. Instead, she worried about FBI updates. Her people had scoured Chicago, all the runaway spots. Which meant they were farther out. Topeka was 400 miles. What about St. Louis? If they were alive. He'd want to come to her. He'd want to find her in Colorado. He'd head west. But he knew she was in New Mexico. Then, she puzzled, in a stritch to her heart, *why would he want to come to me?* She thought they were heading for Colorado, where they'd lived for a time, near Boulder, which he knew. Local police were alerted.

And here were briefs on crowd control, the word from beyond the gate, outside the fence, the yawpers' conjectures on the cosmic secrets, that her undercover guys were picking up. She told them to keep their ears open. It might help to monitor the temper of the crowd, if things got dicey.

What they were saying: *Styx is a top-secret government installation the mining company accidentally on purpose stumbled on, then opened up, an underground experimental lab set up in the 30s before the Manhattan Project. **Atomic genomics.** Extraterrestrials practically run the government. Trilobites are stowaways. Visiting entities. Trilobites are* *freaks! They prove nothing! Satan's bugs! They make kids lazy or mellow.* One blog suggested how Trilobites were hypnotizing the kids, encouraging zeta sleep.

What the hell was zeta sleep?

Ah, *Firearm Jesus*, what a name! were sending followers. Who were they, what did they want? And the Christian Buddhists were represented. Good to know. *The Dirt People* had sent envoys who clamored for a tour, among other privileges. They all wanted in—but why?

She wondered what it was like by the lake. She wanted to see it. She'd take off her clothes, touch the cold water, then immerse herself. She would go swimming at the center of the Earth.

The big screen flashed and that troubling Skype beeping bell intruded.

She accepted the call. Robertson was in Colorado, at company headquarters. He headed up the teams searching for the kids.

"Taylor," he went, nodding. Skype eyes looked for her eyes. The screen was filled with the upper torso of a good-looking man in a suit. He was a fifty-year-old, twenty-year veteran of the company.

Taylor said, "What's new at the Rialto—ugh, my husband used to say that. What's up? News? What do you have for me?"

"As decided," Robertson said in his steady, official voice, "we're moving west in concentric arcs. St. Louis, Kansas City. Topeka was negative. We keep going. We're going out to Wichita. You still think they're heading for Colorado?" He paused. She struggled to keep it to a simple shrug. "We can't find any evidence they got a ride from someone they knew. The FBI have checked buses, airplanes, trains. That stuff is easy for them. If they're hitching, somebody would see them, notice something. A person who'd seen our ads on TV. The coverage has been insane."

Taylor said wistfully, "Hitching seems so random. Maybe they're close by. Back in Gary."

"We've gone over that. Ian and your ex-husband hardly knew anyone there. The girl had friends, connections, but nothing panned out. The only real lead, as you know, was the Reynolds' kids. And, I guess, the quick shop out on the highway, towards the airport." Even on Skype, his exaggerated stretch was telling. "But their security cameras—old and crappy, images awful. The cashier has no real memory of them. There might've been a couple guys around. So lousy camera and lousy witness, maybe two boys passing through? Might indicate hitchhiking. I don't think they're still in Gary. The clothes they got from those Reynolds' kids were as good as disguises. The cashier mentioned a kid in a hoodie. The Reynolds' boy said he gave them a hoodie."

"Nothing then? Day after day—"

"We're taking this various—in all directions we can think of. Taylor, we're very serious, we are involved. You know that. We were the ones who found the Reynolds' kids. By the way, have you seen their little girl doing the Trilotat ads? Strange kid, like a vibe or something. Speaking of weird, I hear that's your new specialty—"

"Don't. I'm too tired. I appreciate all you've done. All you're doing. It just seems incomprehensible that they could vanish off the face of the Earth."

"Seems one of the Tilson girls tried to run away. Fell out of her upstairs window into a hedge. A cop, assigned to keep an eye on the family, saw the whole thing. Got an ambulance, etc."

"She's okay?"

"She's fine."

"Does she know where they are?"

"Won't talk."

Taylor hit the disconnect button with her mouse before she had a chance to say goodbye, which was rude, so she said it now, 'good bye', to the chill, twinkling hut ambience.

There came a pounding to her door. What time was it, anyway? The knock signaled intensity. Taylor upped herself, on to her feet, breathed, moved to the door.

It was night time, and, of course, it was another good-looking guy, Garcia, head of security on site.

"I don't like that look on your face," said Taylor.

Garcia smiled tiredly, which came off grim. "Yahoo's got through the fence, way off road, at the site's edge, east of here. Sensors picked it up. We'll find them. Don't worry about that. We got the fence fixed already. I saw your light. Thought you'd want to know—"

"There's only so many places to hide out there. Where are you going? What are you doing now?"

"Gotta join the others, coordinate—"

"I'll come."

Ethan drove his Camry down Interstate 40, a straight shot to New Mexico. Beside him, a passenger, a helper: a sleuth: Hakeem Arafat, Fat was his preferred moniker, was the private investigator Ethan had hired soon after the debacle. Ethan was a liberal. He didn't care if the private eye he'd hired was a Muslim and a black. Fat had examined the situation, made inquiries, studied the peripherals, and come to the conclusion that New Mexico was the place they had to be. Ethan needed back up, so here they were—

First of all, the kids—Ian had to be okay. Ethan refused to believe he was dead. Someone would have seen something. The FBI had checked area sex offenders. Nothing. No one had seen anything. No one had seen them hitching. So they had a ride then? Who? Third parties were involved! Kidnapped! No one could imagine who the kidnappers might be. There'd been no ransom note. But Ethan could make a deduction, logic being his precis. *They* needed Hessler. They needed the male. The bug was worth millions to them. Second of all, company goons had to be in on this. Taylor had as much as said so. Now, with all the PR, the company would be desperate to find and control Hessler, the only male. Which brought the pathetic pandemonium to its inevitable number three: law enforcement was worthless, scientists couldn't be trusted. Who to turn to? Who was the specialist here, this time? What if the Trilobites were doing something to kids, not necessarily poisonous, but engendering change no one had seen before? Number three meant action! Meant chaos threat, so, yes, action required. Ethan and Fat were on their way.

"I'll drive," said Fat. "My turn. If I look at online chatter anymore, my eyes are gonna pop out. So much shit. Those kids are all over the place."

"Of course," said Ethan. Then: "I'll keep up with the online chatter on my phone. When we get there—we've seen the news, what's going on down there, how will we handle this?"

"Simple. I'll melt into the crowd, another invisible weirdo in the soup of the masses. You call your ex-wife. She's got to let you in. Meanwhile, I'll keep in touch, listen for word on the kids, what people are talking. They gotta be going there. You watch. It makes sense. I got a feeling about this. Everyone's heading there. It's the place right now. The Trilobite place."

FBI Special Agent Nathan Alexander had scheduled interviews at the Tilson home. He drove there by himself. The policewoman, Mahoney, wanted to be there but he had declined her help. He had also declined the help of

Mr. Robertson, security chief of the company. Of course, they wanted to do everything they could to help. After all, the boy was the son of their most eminent scientist. But too many cooks—too many interviewers, spoiled the broth. At this juncture, interviews were incredibly delicate, and could go south without warning.

The PR, TV ads on top of the runaways' furor, was a blitz made in heaven for the mining company. But kids were gone, threatened, maybe kidnapped. That was the priority. That was his concern and responsibility. He would let nothing impinge. Even a nervous Nelly parent on the verge of crackpot status. Ethan Scanlan was certain the company was involved. Something about the Trilobites. Special Agent Alexander wouldn't let his kids near the things.

Crossing state lines—

Underage runaways—

This New Mexico business was getting all the attention now. Which is why he had a personal inducement to find the kids ASAP. He had to get to New Mexico!

Kids and Trilobites? Kids in love? Where would they go? Make a little love nest—sick. What were these kids up to? The nuns had claimed the boy was a raving atheist who had threatened the class with a sick screed. The nuns saw the girl as proud, a big mouth know it all. That was the impression Alexander got. The kids went political? Got recruited?

This must be their house, jolted Alexander, then he went, "Yup, me know." How many times had he been here already? When they found the Trilobite exoskeleton things got dicey. They were acquainted now. He pulled in behind the police car in front of their house.

Policewoman Mahoney got out of her vehicle. Alexander watched the whole thing. Now she was walking to his vehicle. He turned off his car, undid the safety belt. He leaned over to the passenger side to retrieve his paperwork—folders, notebooks. She was outside his door. Outside his window, looking in. He couldn't shoot her. He opened the door and she stepped back.

He said, "We only have a few minutes before this looks weird. We're cooperating, we're getting along, we're getting it done, that's all they need to know. There's no need for you to come in with me, as we discussed. You've already spiked the punch. So to speak."

"Agent Alexander, cooperation is everything, and Captain Wahls asked me to coordinate with the state police. That's Indiana, Illinois, now Kansas. They each have their own state troopers."

"That's our job, too."

"Let me finish. If Kay knows something, and talks, tells you anything, we all need to know right away."

"Of course," said Alexander.

Mahoney said, "Let's do this."

Meanwhile, in Colorado, Denver to be precise, south part of town, a nineteen-year-old kid named Tim Olson scrambled eggs for breakfast and waited for his roommates to wake up. They were a loose collective of artists called Maze, who were into pranks, non-objective theater, and street art. Buskers, sure, but also posters, cards, art for sale. They got by. Tim had tried school, a year of community college, a year of art school. He'd discovered he needed to live it, not study it.

Two of his roommates had real jobs so they had to get going. His other two roommates would get up later. They would make art, work on their bits, then, after work, Maze would hit the streets at sunset. Dusk was their time. At a good street corner, in between light and dark, when the shadows glowed oddly, people getting off work, kids getting out of school, they were all set free for a gasp. Stories and songs were critical for a moment. Maze was on! They'd sell some art. As the night deepened, fun street artists became adversarial at least. The street was alive in riffs. City on fire! Maze spoke, performed, could not be separated from activism. Speaking truth to power. Standing up for the little guy. They chose to live each day.

Rosa came in from the bathroom, in bra and panties. "Tim—Tim, honey pork chop, make me a shake. Pretty please. One of those breakfast fruit things would be perfect. What are you eating? Ova, again? In grease?" She tsk-ed sharply. "I gotta get dressed."

She started to turn away and Tim said, "Do we have to remind each other of every sin?"

Tommy was already dressed when he came out of the room he shared with Tim. He worked at a pet store, had a thing for cuttlefish. At home he was known as Flash. In the public arena, Tommy.

"Flash Meister," Rosa called, "Tim's calling me out like I got a ghost talking shit, like it's not me, like I'm not in control. I gotta get to the clinic." Rosa had worked at the clinic, barely three blocks away, for about two years. She went to get dressed.

Flash said, "Anybody make coffee? Is there coffee? I'm gonna have to make it? Who was up first? You always make coffee, you up first. It's your frigging duty."

Tim worked on his eggs with Tabasco sauce. "I'm making a shake," he said.

A phone rang. Flash said, "Is that mine? Ah, I forgot. I don't have one. That would be a good bit, like cell phone pay phones. Kids don't know about phone booths. We could do a phone booth piece. Superman! Superman changing clothes—"

"It's mine," said Tim. He went over by the cutting board where he'd left it. Just a number. Robo call. He swiped the phone and it connected.

A girl's voice said, "Is this Tim Olson?"

"This is Tim Olson," went Tim, playing along, giving the call one more second.

"Hi," went the voice, "my name is Bridget Tilson. I'm your sister. And I'm in a jam."

Tim thought, Tilson...Tilson: his biological mom's married name, his mother, who put him up for adoption, a mixed race, out of wedlock baby, not something a young Catholic girl, a young white Catholic girl could deal with. Tim had been through all of that when he called her the first time. She seemed freaked by the whole thing, so what was this—

"Are you there?" asked the girl.

"Sister, I'm so happy to make your acquaintance. What kind of jam? Are you safe? Where are you?"

Tim's brain started clicking, puzzle parts fitting together, because he had seen all over the net the stories of the runaways. He'd made the connection with Gary, Indiana and the Tilson family name. He'd thought about calling but supposed it would upset them. He'd never put it together this way: *his* sister was in trouble, *his* sister was causing all the fuss.

"Can you come and get us? We are safe. Now."

"Where are you?"

"We don't know exactly. Western Kansas. Do you have a car and everything?"

"Whoa, whoa! Bridget, I'm so happy you called. I don't have a car but my roommate does. My roommates and I, we live together in a collective, so we decide things together. Of course, I want to help, my sister, my *new* sister. But we're gonna need their help, we need to hear what they think. Hang on, I'm going to put this on speaker phone. Flash, get the others. Sorry, it's important. They'll be right here. Bridget, you still there?"

"Yes. Tim, you're an artist."

"Yes. I am. How'd you know?"

"So are we."

"You and your boy. That's cool. The whole world is looking for you. I'm so glad you're safe."

"They're after us. We been laying low."

"Here are my friends, tell us the whole story."

Rosa sat at the kitchen table, in her work clothes with sensible shoes. She couldn't help but glare at Tim who had produced no shake she could see. Flash stood by Tim. Two sleepy heads in underwear paraded in from the back with grunts and flailing limbs. Sister Sledgehammer, street poet extraordinaire, and Beckett, sad clown who told a story and played the guitar, collapsed in chairs at the table.

Sledge mumbled, "What's going on?"

Beckett burped, buried his head in his arms on the table. "I'm dreaming this."

Tim said, "Go ahead, Bridget. This is Rosa, Flash, Sledge, and Beckett listening in. Everybody, this is my sister, Bridget."

Bridget said, "They want me to get off the phone. Do you have our location on your phone?"

Tim swiped and checked his phone. "Got it. Western Kansas. Two hundred and fifty miles from here. Tell it best you can."

"Close! I'm Bridget. My friend Ian's mom gave him a Trilobite. Turned out he's the only male. Turned out the company wants him back ASAP. We don't know, but probably to cut him up. Plus, we've become very close to the Trilobite, whom we call Hessler."

Beckett whispered, "Nazi bug."

"I heard that. He's not a bug, nor a Nazi."

"What do you need?" asked Sledge.

"Well, so, we ran away. We been hiding out. But it's been a while, a long time. It's been a while. I guess."

Tim said, "She wants us to go pick 'em up. She needs a ride. Her and her boyfriend."

Sledge and Rosa both made the connection at once:

"The kids on TV!" "The runaways!"
    Flash said, "Fuck, yeah! Let's get these kids!"

CHAPTER 10

Ian and Bridget sat on the floor of the living room, showered, in borrowed clothes, before a low coffee table and a couch. The wall opposite the couch had a flatscreen TV and boom box and CD player, all hooked up to monster speakers. Aretha Franklin was singing.

The kids were seated cross-legged, facing each other. Hessler was between them, just sitting there. Sledge, Rosa, Tim sat on the couch. Flash in a chair—he'd called in sick. Rosa'd called in sick. She hadn't done it in eons. She thought she was okay. She and Flash had worked the day before, when they'd gone for them. Twelve hours of incredible tension waiting for them to get back. She and Flash had gotten a bit frantic, the most wanted kids in America in a little car with a bunch of black kids, older black kids. Today, they wanted to be with the kids.

Beckett strode into their midst. "Everybody good? Yeah, eyeballing the bug. We can't get enough of him. He's a showstopper! Prehistoric. Oh, sorry, Hessler. Look, listen, not to change the subject, but I got a new bit. 'Sex and air, two things you take for granted, until you're not getting any."

Bridget said, "Until you aren't getting enough."

Sledge laughed. Rosa said, "Girl's got a point."

Beckett, who was the oldest, crowed out, "'Enough?' Enough don't work!"

Ian said, "Sex and air, you don't think about 'em, until you're not get getting 'em."

"No, no," cried Beckett, "now you're messing with me. What are we going to do with you kids? That's what we gotta figure out!"

Sledge said, "Check it out. Did you see the poster Flash made? Like a start of something." She leaned over the coffee table and found the poster. She held it up.

"TRILOBITE FREE," it read, in black letters on a red background.

Rosa said fast, "Who knows what it means? It means global warming, blood and oil empires, destruction of the Earth. Then there's this whole thing, new species, evolution. Change! Connecting it all together, change."

Tim said, "Who gets to decide, what bothers me? Why should government and specialists be the only ones who get a say about Hessler?"

Sledge said, "'All authority is false.'"

Ian said, "You guys have a box? A cardboard box? And a bowl? We want to make a little habitat for Hessler."

Bridget was off, like she needed to get it out, "Youth is like prep time, right? Preparation for adulthood. Our lives are for later. We're projections until we get there. We never get to say. I mean, about Hessler and stuff."

Beckett came on strong, "Right on. Then you realize some kids your age are already at war. They don't think about no adulthood. They got an obligation to survive. No prep for that shit. See what I'm saying?"

Bridget nodded and Hessler climbed into her lap. "I do, I do. But we're all still, so-called kids? What if we have ideas? Good ideas? The kids at war and us?"

Sledge said, "The emancipation of black America is the emancipation of America. Is the emancipation of kids."

Flash said, "Beautiful! And Tim just happens to be your

brother. It's incredible, makes us go, go, gung-ho—what can we do with this. Still, so-called kid, still, don't get me wrong, you're underage. You're white. Aiding and abetting. Know what I'm saying? You know how the man will read it. FBI! Time's of the essence! Whatever's gonna happen has to happen fast."

Ian said, "We don't want to get you in trouble."

Bridget said, "You all been so nice to us."

Tim said, "I'm her brother. She's here of her own free will. I could be her guardian."

"Wait, wait, wait," went Rosa. "Slow, slow. Think it through. It's a good story. Hope we don't have to use it."

Flash said to Ian and Bridget, "How old are you guys? What have you been up to?"

Sledge said, "Don't answer. None of our business."

The awkward pause was broken by Hessler trying to move up Bridget's arm. He was too big to nestle in her elbow anymore.

Bridget said, "Why do you call it Maze?"

Beckett said, "Good question. You'll see. You know how folks live in their stories? Sometimes it helps, sometimes it deceives. We all create mazes around us."

Bridget said, "In Scorch, where we lived by the spring, we told stories we made up. We didn't have any candles. When you're trying to survive another day, I mean, we weren't exactly in a war zone, but me and Ian talked about how for the longest time people did whatever it took to survive, in the here and the now, taking care of business. I don't know. Along came art and poetry, all of a sudden people could share their dreams. Something beyond survival. Like shared hallucinations. Fast forward a few thousand years, and TV and devices, and all it is is hallucination. Maybe people don't know how to survive anymore."

Beckett said, "How did you get so smart?"

Rosa said, "Damn! The whole evolution of civilization

in one easy lesson. Damn, girl, you're good!"

"Can I tell it one more time?" asked Beckett. "It's so good." He pulled up a chair. The others groaned and gaped. Ian and Bridget smiled and reached out hands to touch and hold. He began, "It's a long slog to Kansas. Long slog, let me tell you. We mount up my little Nissan, leave the city, due east, cutting into the prairie, like a killer whale in a sea of anchovies."

"Woo Woo," rang out from the couch sitters.

"We're eating it up. Sights, sounds, smells of the prairies. Going to get our brother's little sister. We're on a sacred mission. And we're tricksters, ready for the Earth to crack open and spit out demons. Yeah, we're demon hunters going down the road, down that lonesome prairie road. And the magic phone leads us right there. We make it, we're there, and there is no there. Right? No more prairie, no more barbed wire and barns—uh-uh. It's this burned-out place, miles around, everything burned, everything black, crispy. Devastated. Hell on earth! Yeah, demon world, man. Right there. And what might have been a town back in the day, this little nowhere place down the way, has one gas station/quick shop. That's our place. Where we supposed to pick 'em up. So we pull in. We're excited. Rescue mission. All that—

"The kids come out of the store. They're expecting us! Two skinny kids with backpacks walking to us before we've had a chance to get out. And they're white. I'm talking fish belly white! But they're cute, you know. Little angel kids managed to survive this hell. And the girl, our bro's sis, is whiter yet, extra white with kinky red hair on top. So we get out of our car. Tim'd been in the back, so he's a step behind me and Flash. And Bridget comes barreling through us to Tim, and they engulf each other in tears and hugs. Meanwhile, poor old Ian here, he standing there a bit pekid, eyeballing the brothers, wondering what the fuck."

Rosa said, "We knew the kids were white from TV."

Bridget said, "We didn't know."

They all laughed, then Bridget got it and blushed. Hessler trembled. Bridget adjusted her lap, sliding her legs, to make Hessler more comfortable.

Ian said, "Hessler thinks we're all excited."

"Got that right," said Beckett. "They showed us where they'd holed up. Scorch. There was a spring. Frisky, fancy little place. Little old building with thick walls. But pure, you know. Lovers like otters in all that desolation."

Flash said, "Maybe they should sleep in separate rooms until we figure this out. I'm just saying. Just in case. And no substances around. Aiding and abetting—"

Beckett said, "You guys, you can't go out. Sorry, no sightseeing. And we're not having friends over. Even to spend the night. If you're spotted—"

Sledge came in with, "Ease up. They can sleep wherever they want. The couch'll be fine. Doods, they been sleeping together for a while already." Sledge glanced at Bridget who looked uncertain. Ian looked vague as he tended to. Sledge said, "Little sister, me and Rosa need to sit you down and have a talk."

Tim said, "We build a Trilobite website. Total anonymity. Trilobite Liberation Caucus. YouTube! We shoot shorts of the kids and Hessler. Get it out there. With our message: *Trilobite free.* Their parents, we gotta let them know you're safe. It will mean everything to them. We should let your parents know."

Rosa said, "Well, not right this second. 'Caucus'? What the—is it safe? A website? Could it be traced? Would it be a risk? FBI looking for these two."

Ian jumped in, "A uh box—you have a box we could use?"

Rosa came to her feet. "I'll get you a damn box."

Sledge said, "What else you need?"

"Earth, sand," said Ian. "Is there a backyard?"

"Boy asks if there's a backyard in the colored part of town," said Beckett.

Sledge said, "I'll take them out by the dumpster in back. There's a space there. A tree. A real live tree. No one hangs back there. Who said it, that you can't be unhappy when you look at a tree?"

Tim said, "Flash's right, time. We gotta be on this right now. Right away!"

Flash puffed, wriggled around in his chair, slapped his hands together. "Where we going with this? That's what we gotta know. Where does this lead?"

Tim said, "Ian, Bridget, help us out here. What do you think?"

Ian said, "Hessler needs to go home. To his lake."

Ian said, "Is that the Rocky Mountains?"

They could see between buildings, as they proceeded down the rickety steps of the fire escape on the outside of their building. A crooked line showed above the distant horizon.

Sledge said, "Yessirree, rocky blocky mountains—we carry them with us from that first time we see them. They're always with us now, a certain kind of presence. They change us, we change them. You guys, go on. That's your green area," she said, pointing.

By the dumpsters and a narrow alley, a curbed rectangle of green with a tree. Ian and Bridget took the remaining steps. They let Hessler go in the grass. He immediately plowed over towards the tree, got busy at its base. He looked like a little arthropod bulldozer! So big!

Bridget said, "He's looking for elements."

"That's the front range," said Ian.

"Out West," murmured Bridget, smiling too big. "We're out. We made it. Can you believe it? We must've slept through St. Louis." She laughed.

Ian shuffled, chuckled. "Topeka."

Bridget went on, "This light. It's the light, this type of light, mountain light. Mellow compared to Indiana."

Ian said, "Pastel."

Bridget said, "I don't even know what time is. I guess we'll have to start paying attention to all that stuff again. Time disappeared, now it's rushing back."

Ian said, "No time, then there is. And the space. Distance. You can see forever. Like an overview. Light and space. Get it? How far you can see—"

Sledge called, "You two, like love professors on an expedition. Talk like that—you talk like finishing each other's thoughts, that's how close you are. Now get back to Earth. Get your Earth. Come on."

They got busy gathering up soil, rocks, then handfuls of grass into a plastic bag they'd been given. Ian took a small branch that had blown off the tree.

Ian called back, "We been away, just talking to each other, and Hessler."

Sledge went, "Lovebird telepathy, mind to mind, heart to heart. Light and space so big out here, you got that right."

Bridget said, "The mountains, like a back drop. It's so dramatic."

Ian said, "We have enough. We're done. Get Hessler. Or I can."

When they got back upstairs into the apartment the group was vibing. They'd changed CDs too. Hip-hop stuff now, neither Ian nor Bridget recognized.

Tim came up to Ian and Bridget, and put his arms out to rest his hands on their shoulders. "We're going to New Mexico."

That night Rosa came out to the kitchen to get some milk from the fridge for a sour stomach. The whole apartment was dark. Everybody was asleep. When she opened the fridge door, there was enough light to see the kids tangled on the couch. Hessler was there, between them, on their chests. It looked like wires were coming out of the bug going to the kids' heads. She went for Flash. Flash brought his camera and filmed it. They woke up Tim.

Tim was alarmed, thought they should wake them. Flash wasn't so sure. Flash reasoned, who knew what nefarious shit went on with the three of them. This was it! Incredible shot. Perfect blast.

They got it on YouTube with a backhanded avatar that was untraceable.

Interestingly enough, police officer Gayl Mahoney was the first to see it from law enforcement. She didn't know who she should send the link to first. She sent it to the Scanlans, both of them. The Tilsons didn't have email, so Mahoney called.

Mr. Tilson picked up. "Hello."

"Officer Mahoney here. Sorry to wake you, but it's important."

"Bridget. It's about our Bridget!"

"Let me hear," called Mrs. Tilson.

Mahoney said, "On YouTube, it's an online film site, there's a few seconds of film, of what looks like Bridget and Ian and the Trilobite. They look good, healthy."

"They're alive! They're alive. Oh, thank you, baby Jesus," prayed Mrs. Tilson.

Mr. Tilson spluttered, "Where are they? What are they doing? Is she coming home?"

"Hold on, Mr. Tilson, I don't know much more than I already said. I'll let the FBI know. They got people who specialize in this, tracking down addresses from online activity. Maybe they can find out where it comes from.

Who put it up? Right now, I don't know. It doesn't say anything about where they are or what their plans are."

Mr. Tilson implored, "No address? Even a name, anything? How do they look? You said a film, what are they doing?"

"They look fine. They look like they're sleeping. Peaceful. The Trilobite's there."

Mrs. Tilson's voice pushed in, "Sleeping together?"

"Yes. That's what it appears. There is a name, or title, to the film. 'Trilobite Liberation Front'. Does that mean anything to you?"

There was a long pause. Finally, Mr. Tilson said, "We have a friend we can call who has a laptop computer. He'll bring it over. Let us see this film. How do we find it again?"

"'Trilobite Liberation Front' should get you there."

Mahoney wondered how the Tilsons would react when they saw the YouTube and the very clear antenna coming-out of the big bug and extending to Ian and Bridget, touching their temples. But, maybe, the mother's main concern was their sleeping arrangements.

Special Agent Alexander was immediately defiant over the phone, that she had notified the families first. He would get the YouTube down ASAP, before it ignited some kind of mass hysteria. Mahoney said she had to call it in, tell her chief. Then she had to start notifying state police. In all three states.

Alexander cut in, "Wait, wait. Of course, you have to tell your chief. But wait on the others. We'll take care of it. I promise. What concerns me right now is the clip is out there, stirring up the pot. All these people suddenly interested in Trilobites, and they're going to find the film. Whew—bizarre! It's quite the short masterpiece. I keep on playing it. The kids are so innocent looking, but alive. They look okay, then the monster bug has—what are they? Antenna? On the kids' heads. They extend right to the kids' temples. Right out of a monster movie. So, imagine what people are going to think. X-Files all the way. We have to play this down. Nip it in the bud, as they say. Hope the people who find it are not copying it. This could be like their Holy Grail."

"The parents had to know. It was their right."

"Have you seen the news from New Mexico? Seriously, the footage? What it's like down there? I'll take care of this. I'll keep you posted."

Taylor hadn't slept in two days, hadn't cried in three days. There was no time. There was duty and science, both cruel mothers. She was just checking in at her command post.

The cavern exploration with drones and robots had made startling discoveries. This was not a lava cave or a limestone cave. This was a 250 million years old hiccough in the very mantle. Permian. Processes and forces never described! That had somehow fashioned a stable geological bubble that had risen, collected water, life. Now was the time—

The company was crazy for Trilobites. Facilities in Denver and Albuquerque were taking over production of Trilotats. The highways were backed up. How to get supplies in and out securely? They'd ended up having to bring in helicopters. The helicopters had to be coordinated with security, with grounds and maintenance. The feds wanted to know the schedule. Somebody had to make sure there weren't too many drones around the landing site.

In the middle of the night, she and Garcia, putting out flare-ups at gate and shaft, had stopped to admire the sky over the site. The way the land swelled through there made the view before them a vast bowl of night, percolating with drone lights, red and blue mainly, zipping through the black. Ours and theirs. Goods, bads. A constant struggle with occasional outbursts, as a trespasser was fried. Night of zapping bots! Garcia smoked a cigarette.

Taylor had left Garcia and struggled to her command post. She'd sort her email and get to bed. She ought to have a cot brought in here. And a chamber pot. No nearby bathroom. But outside—the New Mexico enchantment with plenty of sparklies.

Mahoney—Mahoney

That Indiana police officer.

YouTube. 'Trilobite Liberation Front.' You gotta be kidding.

The kids.

Ian. He's okay!

Hessler!

—a pretty young woman.

They look asleep. They're so young!

Hessler! The antenna—

She had to call Robertson. If this was out, on YouTube...by tomorrow, this is tomorrow—

What was Hessler doing? No antenna in females. Maybe they weren't antenna? She'd have to check the females one more time. Bloodsucking? It would be too noticeable. Detrimental. Injecting something? Depositing something into them? Not eggs. He's a male. What then? Sperm? Hormones? For recognition? Tagging them somehow? But the kids were good, that's the main thing. She'd call Robertson, and go home to cry for the return of her boy.

They decided to keep going, do it all at once. Drive straight through. Pull an all-nighter. Ethan and Fat had decided no dawdling. One guy slept in the back. One guy drove. When they got gas, they switched. They got coffee. Boom! There before you knew it. Everything so far, so good, nodded Ethan. He was stretched out awkwardly in the back, way too tall to fit comfortably. He couldn't sleep anyway. He was worried there was a simple solution to all of this he was missing. Ethan felt helpless, angry. He was full of righteous indignation. He would find his boy! His theories had been treated like trash. And, now, Fat was agitated, driving along, hauling ass, with his phone out, his phone raised up in his right hand to see. Texting and driving! Ethan was about to insert a salty quip when—

Fat said, "You gotta see this! You won't believe it. The game is afoot. Catch." He tossed his phone into the back. Ethan lunged to catch it. He barely made it. His heart pounded.

Fat said, "Just swipe it. It's a YouTube. My bots been busy, on alert for Trilobite shit. Most of what they find— meh. But this: prime, blazing! Your kids—they look fine."

Ethan navigated the phone. It was much more busy than his own. It lit up, he swiped. Ian and that Irish girl. They're always sleeping together. With their clothes on it looks like. What the—

Ethan's blood froze in the back of the small car, all stretchy wrongy. What was that thing doing to them? Taylor said there were no stalactites or stalagmites in their cave, because of different formation algorithms. From the depths of the Earth, this atrocity. What was it doing? He could barf.

They were heading to the prairie country of New Mexico. Rolling hills with endless range for cattle. There must be cowboys. Sites to see, wonders to behold!

What was coming out of the bug's head?

Out loud, "What is coming out of the bug's head? Like a wire? Antenna? Oh my! What if it's a robot? It's a robot? A machine, a mechanism? What is it doing? Oh God, it's doing something to their brains!"

Fat shushed him. "Easy, Mr. Ethan Scanlan. You knew this was bigger than a simple runaway case from the beginning. I think your instincts have been right on. So you gotta stay cool, don't freak out on me. We're gonna get these kids. And the Trilobite.

"I got people who can track down where the YouTube came from, who posted it. That might help. But maybe not. We don't have enough information yet. It does look gross. It's all about Trilobites now. That's for sure. So how this works, how this goes, the kids got to be wondering, and from what you tell me about these kids, there's only one answer they can come to. Take it home. Let it go. New Mexico, just like you thought. I think we're on the right path. We are going to find them."

Ethan didn't seem to be listening. "If it's a robot, and some kind of horrendous company ploy, then the kids are kidnapped, and they're being kept docile by the bug toy. It's fantastic!"

Fat let him get it out. Now his client was wrapped around the back of the up-front passenger seat as though he were assaulting it. He looked like an overly excited little boy. Fat knew the client was close to breaking. Surely his ex-wife would reach out to him now. First, they had to get there. Then, he'd have a very brief window of opportunity. He'd be at Ground Zero for unfolding events of great power. Things were going down that were going to have a profound effect on society and culture. The wise man would understand how to proceed, the coward would fumble the opportunity.

Ethan was starting up again: "Mind control! MK-ultra! Some kind of bug hypnotism? Mesmerism. Power of suggestion. Transfixing the innocent. It's been going on since WWII. The kids could be poisoned against me. They never did like me. But now—"

Mrs. Tilson was adamant. "We'll bring Kay. She's been so worried about her sister. Miranda can stay with the little ones. She won't mind at all, and the girls love her. It's only for a few days. It's an emergency. They have to give you a few days."

"We'll bring Kay," said Mr. Tilson, "have to, after all this. It does make sense. FBI said they knew the YouTube was posted from out West, maybe Colorado. That bug is growing. It needs to get back home. That's what Bridget would think. We know our girl. Everything's about New Mexico now. It makes sense. They'll be there."

"Maybe Denver, Colorado."

Mr. Tilson sighed, turned over in bed to face his wife in the dark of their bedroom. "Possible," he muttered. "Your boyfriend was an activist involved with all sorts of 'liberation fronts'. Stands to reason his son would be too."

"Bridget went to Denver to find her half-brother."

"She read the letters?"

"That girl is going to get a piece of my mind when I see her."

Mr. Tilson laughed. "You'll hug her to death!"

"So what will it be, Mister Tilson, Colorado or New Mexico?"

Hessler's molt in his box on the living room coffee table was witnessed by all. Flash filmed. Bridget assisted, her long fingered, white hands careful around Hessler's lobes. She was very gentle, picking away the old carapace. Ian and Bridget kneeled at the table, ready to help. Bridget did most of the helping.

Ian said, "We've done this before. Really, it's not a big deal. Arthropods have exoskeletons, so when they grow, they have to shed."

Tim said, "I feel honored—we're honored to see this. How many people in the whole world have seen this?"

Rosa and Sledge giggled, squirming on the couch. Finally, Sledge erupted with,

"Houston, we got a *bug* problem.

Trilobite, chigger bite

He don't bite!

Not tonight

He go light

Lit with his girl

Peeling away the molt

Lit with his girl

Peeling away the molt

This young colt

Grab a holt!

Nothing rhymes with molt."

Beckett laughed, "Molt, poult."

Rosa said, "This is just weird. And a little bit disgusting. Don't have to rhyme that. And I've seen some weird shit. But these are God's creatures, too."

"Right on," went Bridget. "You guys want to keep the skin?"

Beckett puffed up. He couldn't help but emit a little giggle. "Make a fortune in bug skin. I'm just saying."

Rosa went, "Skin! Uh-uh! Still, we gotta have a molt celebration. Right? Come on, we leave tomorrow. It's only right. Tonight's the night!"

Flash said, "He's a lot bigger. All shiny. That is one good looking bug. How big they get? Tim, we gotta get this online."

Beckett said, "Congratulations, Hessler, it's a boy!"

Bridget said, "I like how it says online now, with our YouTubes, right below where it says 'Trilobite Liberation Front', 'emancipation of all life, not only Trilobites, but kids too."

Rosa said, "At first I thought it sounded pro-life—"

Bridget said, "It is."

Tim said, "Pro-life as in life means choice. Life means responsibility, making decisions."

Bridget said, "I'm confused."

Flash said, "I need to ask, we need to know. Do you guys, you kids feel funny? Different? Like when you wake up after Mr. Hessler been connected to you all night?"

Bridget danced away. "I'm a bug zombie," she sang. She stomped and jumped.

Ian smiled. He shook his head. But he couldn't take his eyes off of her. Ian said, "We've talked about it. We don't know. We feel fine. Maybe—we think—we think Hessler helps us relax. I don't know if relax is the right word."

Flash said, "Mind control? I don't want no bug relaxing me. So maybe we get this guy back to his cave, and he meets his females, and the bugs take over the world."

"Xenophobia," Bridget said. She went over to Flash and put her arms around his neck, gave him a little hug. Bridget said, "He's not a bug."

Rosa grunted. "Tonight, we party. And teach that girl how to dance. Ian, you dance?"

CHAPTER 11

Tallulah—maxed out in LA!

The studio office they were given was quiet, cut off from the constant hubbub of production. Mom had gone for lunch. They had decided on smoothies—who didn't deliver. Dan and Tallulah sat facing each other, Tallulah in the big chair behind the desk, Dan in the smaller chair before the desk. There was a table beyond them with more chairs, where they'd probably eat lunch. Dan was in jeans and a Nirvana T-shirt. He thought he knew who Nirvana was. Tallulah wore civilian clothes, blue shorts, pink top, pink sneaks. She was all scrunched up in the chair.

Dan said, "I know this is more than gummis. You're all torn up. I don't know, I can tell. I can feel it, I'm your brother. You been out of it two days. I know it's not the crazy schedule. Or Mom. You love razzle-dazzle, dress up, fancy dancy. You are *so* big now. So, I'm gonna have to read your mind and take a guess. If I guess right, you gotta talk. Agreed?"

Tallulah snorted.

"I'll take that for yes. The YouTube of Ian and Bridget and Hessler came out, and you're missing them big time." She wouldn't meet his probing eyes, but he could feel the tension, like a rasping coil of weather emerging from inside her. As if she caused atmospheric effects. "See, I got it." She wouldn't look at him or speak. "You have to quit playing the clip. The YouTube, duh. I'll hide your phone! You always wanted one, now you've got one. Now you know why Mom didn't want to get us one. Ian and Bridget are alive, that's what's important."

Tallulah jumped from her chair to the top of the desk. On all fours, she faced Dan. "Hessler has to go home to service his females. Facts of life, Dan."

"And you know this, how?"

"Stop it. Dan, you have to steal us a car. We have to go to Mexico. Right away. That's where they're going. To take Hessler home. It's imperative."

They had two cars, Beckett's little Nissan, and Rosa's Honda. Emergency family business seemed to have covered them at work. Beckett, Flash, and Ian rode in the Nissan. Rosa, Sledge, Bridget, and Tim were in the Honda. Tim and Bridget sat in the back of the Honda. Ian was in the back of the Nissan. They had a few bucks for gas, including Ian and Bridget's share. Each vehicle carried water and supplies, to minimize stops, exposure. They had an eight to ten-hour trip ahead of them. Ian kept Hessler in his container with him. Because they wanted to stay off the phone as much as possible, they'd worked out signals for stops: two blinks of the lights meant gas, three blinks meant toilet. At their first gas stop, two blinks in, Rosa said, "Why do we have to tell what we're stopping for? What does it matter?"

Flash said, "Too true, too true, Ms. Magoo! We're on a mission, we're way undercover, gotta keep it on the down low. Like if we had us some walkie-talkies? Ha, that's heavy, Ms. Magoo. Ian, maybe, you and Bridget can be our walkie-talkies? See, we're all getting smarter because of

Hessler."

Rosa said, "Why you calling me—I'll Magoo your revolutionary ass!"

Bridget, in her hoodie, burst into laughter. They were standing around their cars at the gas station, Tim and Beckett pumping gas. Edge of the prairie, mountains in sight, Ian in his red cap, and Bridget rode with it, flew with it, held his hand a second, then let go.

Sledge said, "We don't have walkie-talkies. You guys, tripping. But one signal is good. Three blinks, stop. Maybe Flash gets carsick. Maybe girl needs feminine products. You stop."

Tim said, "We get into New Mexico, there's going to be tons of law enforcement. Up the Yin Yang. Gotta keep cool."

Beckett said, "We be cool. Back to your vehicle, dog!"

Back on the road, in the back seat of the Nissan, Ian couldn't think of anything to say, and he wondered if it would be rude to pull out his notebooks and scribble away. After the party last night, Ian and Bridget, dancing fools, had both been crazy in their notebooks, then collapsed together on the couch. They wrote down what was happening. But it wasn't a diary. Fanatical notes on the cascade of thoughts and impressions deluging them. They had things to say. They wondered what it meant. But that was a tricky question. They knew whatever this was, that was happening to them, it affected their understanding of everything. And that had to be good, right? Scorch had changed them. Maze had changed them. Hessler had changed them.

Ian wrote about Bridget. He had to, no point in holding back. She was his subject. He described her. What happened when they touched. He wrote about what she said, the way she talked excited. He wrote about how they both had discovered it was impossible. Proposition: it was impossible for words to equate with feelings. The feeling, the actual tingling and warmth and glow, was normal. It had to be. They were humans! That's what people felt. Proposition: Ian and Bridget didn't know if calling it love was right. Or enough. Ian settled on describing it as a tidal wave, like his cells, in unison, all at once, stepped out for a waltz. The physical flush of wakefulness. Together. It only happened together. Only happened when they were close, the mantle of ongoingness, doing what happened, together.

Bridget, meanwhile, in the back seat of Rosa's car, sitting next to her brother, felt a thousand arrows, razor tips burning inside of her. She couldn't cry. She wouldn't cry. Everybody had settled down, quit talking. Tim was staring out the window. And suddenly Bridget was hit with a big old dose of Catholic guilt.

Family is all. I have abandoned my family for a crazy cause that means a lot to me. A boy. A bug. He's not a bug. A cause. Free Hessler! Am I being selfish? Will Mama ever forgive me? Or the girls? Kay! Oh, Dad!

She had done the worst possible thing a girl could do.

Taylor and Garcia were at the main gate, watching the chaos, standing by their vehicles, when the holy water balloon, clearly labeled, hit them, drenching Taylor. Water balloons never got old. Taylor stood there dripping. Garcia had ducked. Garcia quipped, "Well, it could have been urine."

Taylor groaned and shook, wiping her face.

"Come on," said Garcia, "let's go get you a towel."

"The governor is going to have to call out the National Guard."

"Probably. Feds here. I don't know how many different agencies. I can't keep track."

"We have to keep track! Or we lose control."

Shouts and singing blanketed their awkward silence, then guards repeatedly yelling on megaphones to keep back.

Taylor shook her head. "Holy water in a water balloon—who would have thought."

"Come on. Good thing it was labeled."

They got in the jeep. Garcia drove. Though it was the middle of the night, pre pre-dawn in fact, it was lit up at the gate. Las Vegas on the *llano*! Taylor had learned the word from the guards who were locals. She'd never really known much New Mexico history. As they headed out, she scanned maybe 100 people, faces and bodies and placards, outside the gate. Light wraps. Pleasant souls every one. Gorgeous spring night!

How many had guns? How many were ready to peak? Most of them were standing there, praying or meditating. Yearning. This terrible yearning for an answer she did not have. Occasionally, someone would sing out with passion and insistence, just a verse or two. They were waiting for news. News about Trilobites! Some had Trilobites, the small female ones, and these folks raised up their Trilobite in cupped hands, extending their arms, beseeching. They had around ten guards at the gate, the number kept fluctuating, to maintain, to hold things together. They had tear gas, pepper spray, flash grenades. A sheriff's vehicle and a state police cruiser were parked inside the gate, end-to-end, looking very official.

Garcia drove them over to the portable buildings brought in for the site's personnel. He found her structure. He said, "Why don't you take a shower. Chill out for an hour or two. By then, it'll be dawn. I'll let you know if anything comes up."

"Thanks. You want to come in? I can make some coffee."

"I'm fine."

"Two days of YouTubes now, and the crowd smells

blood. They must exert their will by any means necessary." She groaned. "At least the kids are safe."

Garcia didn't feel sure about anything. "Two days! You think the kids will show up? 'Trilobite Liberation Front.' Ever hear of anything like that?"

Taylor had had enough. "Sounds militant. Know what I mean? Or a joke."

"All I know, you get many more people out there, they'll be throwing more than holy water."

"We need back up."

"Doctor Taylor, we are pressed to the gate! We're surrounded. They want in. What do they want? They want to go underground and see for themselves. I'm just saying. I'm thinking out loud here. We need a strategy."

Taylor thought out loud, "You're right, it's building up. Don't call me that, Taylor is fine."

"You have to release a statement."

"An announcement about the YouTubes, the kids, the antenna. You can imagine how delicately the company wants this handled. I'll call a press conference at the gate. For today. Noon. You think you guys can handle it?"

Garcia shrugged. "One thing at a time. Go take your shower."

Taylor was about to collapse. But there was something else. Another grotesque coffin nail that had to be looked at. "You said, you told me—any more about the killing?"

Garcia said, "So far, they're rumors. But, yeah, apparently, people are starting to kill Trilobites. Are you surprised?"

Fat cried, "Tailgate party! It's a zoo out there! I can't believe how many—National Guard are gonna be called out, you watch. Local law enforcement can't handle this shit. Pretty soon. Pretty soon. There's probably as many agents out there as true believers. You watch."

Ethan was driving. It was his turn to drive. He was going very slowly down the state road with so many cars and trucks parked on both sides that it was barely wide enough for the Camry. If a car started coming towards him, trying to drive up his way, he didn't know what he would do. Then, beyond the cars, tents, camps, RVs, campers, squeezed in on ranchland, which was for rent, terms proclaimed on signs both exuberant and exorbitant.

Fat said, "You'll have to park wherever you can. We have to get creative here, think on our feet. Then we walk in. I figure mile, not more than two, to the site. They call it the Styx Site, you know."

"But where am I supposed to park? You see any spaces? I'm not going to park in some cow field for twenty beans. That Styx usage, that was my wife. She knows all about hell on Earth."

"Easy, easy, Mr. Scanlan. We got this. We'll find something, maybe on the other side of the site. We will, we will. People are coming, but people are leaving too, getting tired. Still, Trilobites, man, causing quite an uproar. This whole underground world thing. That wife of yours must really be something."

"First, we find a parking space. Then, we find the kids. Then, we get the hell out of here."

"Hey, hey, we got this. Think it's too early to call her?"

Ethan glanced at Fat, switched back to scowling ahead. "Now I have to go to the restroom."

"Stop the car, run off to some trees, like over there, and I'll get in the driver seat, so we don't hold up traffic."

"Number two."

"You should've gone at the gas station."

"It was filthy."

"You don't want to call your ex?"

"Not until we're parked and pooped."

Fat wanted to slap him but didn't.

Kay had slept through black night, only to jerk awake in more black night. They kept driving and driving. She tried to read her Bible. The rhythms were perfect for praying. They had done two rosaries and would probably do one more. Kay righted herself, leaned into her mother's seat, her arms going around the seat, so that her hands could touch her mother's arms.

Mrs. Tilson jerked away.

Kay said, "Sorry. I didn't know you were asleep."

Mr. Tilson said, "We need gas."

Mrs. Tilson said, "Where are we? You must be exhausted?"

Mr. Tilson asked, "I'm fine. We're in Eastern New Mexico, near the Texas border. Never been in Texas. You doing okay back there, sugar pie?"

Kay smiled, fell back into her seat. "I'm fine. I have to go to the bathroom."

Mr. Tilson said, "We'll get gas, have a comfort stop. It's not far now."

The gas station/convenience store was the last one before the site, a sign generously informed the public. The line of vehicles getting gas meant an hour wait, at least. They did a rosary. The ladies went to the restroom. Dad paid for gas, pumped the gas. He moved the car over for the next guy.

Back on the road, they kept the radio off. Traffic, of all sizes and shapes, picked up, started getting controversial. The Tilsons slowed, stopped, sped up, stopped. When they got to the cars and scattered campers, arranged every which way along the highway, they gave in to worry. What had they gotten themselves into? They had notified police officer Mahoney, a good person, about heading for New Mexico. They had not called it in to that peculiar FBI man.

Mrs. Tilson clarified, "We'll let Mrs. Scanlan know we're here. We'll get the royal treatment."

Mr. Tilson said, "How? We don't have a telephone."

"We'll tell the guards at the gate. She knows us. She'll be interested in why we're here. With Kay. She'll want to meet Kay."

Kay said, "I don't know if I want to meet her."

Gayl Mahoney was doing the civilian thing. She'd taken a week off, headed for New Mexico, where the action was. The YouTubes came from out west, reported the FBI, and it made sense that the kids would want to return their Trilobite to his home. At least that was the spin, from 'runaway lovers' to nature activists. *Free Willy* and all that.

Mahoney had never been out of Indiana. So, this was a first vacation of sorts. A real getaway, and she was a trained officer, of experience, so this was also an adventure, on her own, of her own free will. She could afford it. She had savings. She had time accumulated. She could do this!

She knew the kids would be there. She knew it wasn't rational to assume this. Things had gotten pretty complicated since the YouTubes. In terms of riling up folks, and agencies—could this be some new terror group?

People played the underground world and the living fossils and made their own story. Everyone assumed his or her story was true, or as true as anything else. That's why witnesses were worthless.

But she liked the Tilsons. Kay was a sweet kid. She didn't care for Mr. Scanlan. He seemed a wreck. Dr. Scanlan was something else. What if the bugs were affecting the kids' minds? There were bugs all over the place. They were so popular as pets Mahoney wondered if she should get one. She'd help find the kids! That was the important thing—top priority.

Going down the highway into New Mexico, it all looked the same, farmland, ranchland, Indiana, New Mexico, pretty much the same. The same gas stations and fast food joints. Way off to the west—were those mountains?

What was she going to do when she got there? She counted her blessings, knowing she could help.

Special Agent Alexander was picked up at the Albuquerque airport by Special Agent Ruth Cross, a rookie from the area office. She would drive him to Styx Site. When they got out of town, into the vast basin country, with mesas and volcanic cones, they started to unwind.

Alexander asked, "How long to the site?"

"Four hours," said Cross. "Be there early afternoon."

"You from New Mexico?"

"Missouri. Springfield, Missouri."

"I know it," said Alexander. "There's a federal penitentiary there I visited."

Cross nodded her head, looking satisfied. "*Bird Man of Alcatraz.*"

"Exactly."

"This is my first field assignment."

Alexander nodded, looking fake with a forced smile. "How many on-site?"

"Practically our whole team. Then agents from Texas. Colorado. They brought in the specialists too. Everybody's got their specialists here. CDC. NSA."

"People talking?"

"You know how it goes. We get so many stories, there's

too much to check out. So far, it's been peaceful. But the law enforcement folks from the various agencies? We all have different goals, I guess. What's the word? Taciturn. Always liked that word. This is happening fast. Ramifications are just becoming visible."

"The kidnapping angle? This 'liberation front' thing? Any information?"

"No ransom notes. No indication of kidnappers. Nothing on any Trilobite front. Their website links to a lot of the usual activist organizations. Environmental, civil rights, anarchists. It's hard to put together how serious a threat—"

"This 'front'—getting involved with Trilobites is a brilliant move. Big bad oil companies, etc. Then with the kids? All this mixed together? A sure fire blitz. Fake news. Trolls. Then the Tilsons take off. Mahoney—a Gary cop. What about gossip? What are people saying?"

"You mean the folks or law enforcement?"

"Both."

"Well, the folks vary from religious, end of the world types, to deep state, secret world domination types. It's a package deal. Funny thing is, law enforcement guys, even specialists, kinda end up fairly close. Course with varying degrees of commitment."

Alexander said, "Good, you're smart. I like you, Special Agent Cross. Thanks for the ride."

"No problem. Not sure what we're getting into."

"What's the lesson here, Special Agent?"

"How do you mean?"

"You're sharp, you're getting your first whiff of pure chaos, so what do we do? I mean, this is turning out to be the grand wazoo of clusterfucks. Excuse my French. Now what? Forces pulling in all directions. Hysteria on max. How will it be determined? What is our role?"

They drove in silence for a few miles. They had the windows rolled up; the air conditioner was on low. It was quite pleasant this spring day in New Mexico.

Special Agent Cross said, "I think the lesson here is that one can rest assured that when all available explanations are ridiculous, they are all wrong. We have to look elsewhere for explanations. We have to change perspective. We have to be careful of pop culture memes cluttering our view."

Alexander nodded, but wouldn't let her off so easily. "Someone has to stay strong and clear, no matter what. Think on his feet. Her feet. Sometimes the agent in the field must make the decisions. Sorry for the rant."

Awkward New Mexico spring silence in the sedan.

Alexander asked, "Any news, anything at all about the Trilobites affecting children? I been trying to keep up on that."

"Not that I know of."

"Any news from the site?"

"Nothing. I may be limited in what I hear." She paused, glanced at him. To his eyes, she looked like a teenager. To her eyes, he looked like a burn out. "But, you know, I'm the rookie."

"I was thinking they'd found out something about the antenna—"

CHAPTER 12

Noon was never more hated as it was today, beamed Taylor, in a business suit perfect for the buxom spring weather they'd been having. Noon had threatened, then rallied through the morning. Her power breakfast summit, with multiple interfacing windows, was over. The nightmare command center, she mused, we're sitting before electronic windows. Window shopping! Now she could concentrate on the noon shindig. Then, that thought came into her mind again, *human consciousness interferes with quantum states.* She first heard it in a dream after her shower—

One did not peer through electric windows to see out. One scanned electric displays to allow data in. She'd never get underground at this rate. She'd do the noon press conference, release the statement, pull back. Pull all the way back! Perfect opportunity blip in the time space continuum for her to go down for her own explore. She had a duty—

She knew nothing about quantum physics. It wasn't her field. Ethan babbled about it sometimes. Quantum physics was a common sobriquet that vaguely stood for all sorts of miscellaneous science buzzwords. Atoms acted like particles and waves. She remembered that. Something about the Heisenberg uncertainty principle. She had no time but she googled quantum physics for fun.

Her phone rang. Garcia. She swiped it.

"I'm ready. You picking me up?"

"They're gathering, coming in from who knows where, and don't seem to be slowing. Maybe a thousand? Let's give it a little extra time, make sure everything's cool."

"A thousand? Maybe my idea for a press conference was not—"

"Too late for that. I'll pick you up in a bit."

Drones at night looked like UFOs. Drones at day looked like insects.

Ethan parked by a set of port-a-potties. They both wondered why the easy parking. Quickly, they learned, as the soupy smolder, like an icky inky presence, pressed in. Couple of teenage boys, like real honest-to-goodness cowboys, stood guard, taking money.

Fat and Ethan stood beside the parked, locked Camry. Their faces contorted with the smells humans produced.

"This is your chance! Go, go," said Fat.

Ethan whispered, "Oh. My. God." He went up to the closest boy.

"Ten bucks," said the boy.

Ethan started to spasm. He glanced at Fat, scowling at him, and paid. He went into one of the oddly echoing, plastic staging areas, where he was to do his business. Fat heard his groans and cries. So did the boys, who snickered.

Ethan came out of the receptacle sooner than Fat expected. He asked for water to be poured over his hands. No soap. Fat did it.

Ethan moaned, "Filled to the brim. And you know what I kept thinking? *Human consciousness interferes with quantum states."*

Fat repeated the one-liner simultaneously as Ethan said it out loud. Fat looked disgusted, too. "You sure you want to leave the car here? It's going to pick up the stank."

Ethan shook his head, when a shiver went through him. Finally: "No choice. Let's go. We get this done, we get out of here. You into quantum physics? You know about that stuff?"

They left the Camry in the stank and joined the human traffic making for the site. Ethan chortled to himself, they look like malamutes. Americans are ugly people, he pondered. Here boy! Here boy! A bubble of warmth rose to his chest and he emitted a real chuckle for the first time in days. He felt clear. They were on it! They were doing it. This would work out.

"Call your ex."

Ethan walked and phoned.

Fat melted into the crowd, disappearing from Ethan's sight. Ethan pretended to call as he scoped the scene. Fat contemplated how quantum physics popping into your head was not necessarily a good thing.

Sledge said, "Hardly any black people. Where are the black people?"

Ian took her hand, while his other hand held Bridget's hand. They continued along the side of the road, mixing with the crowds, everyone in good form. They could see the structures of the site ahead of them.

Flash said, "Stay together."

They walked slowly, with confidence, with the folks, garnering few second glances. Everybody here was caught up in the mystique of this once-in-a-lifetime occurrence. They wanted to share it. They wanted to understand and to share their understanding of events.

Sledge sighed, "What if someone recognizes the kids?"

"Dressed like this? Uh-uh," went Rosa. "They're cool."

Ian had Hessler in his container in his backpack. Ian flashed *cool!* Change meant lots to see, cool meant handling it. Proposition: what was the speed of change?

Beckett said, "Feeling it out people. We're in and out. Reconnoiter. Where did Tim go?"

Tim was nearby, smiling, nodding to people, watching faces, checking it out, when a thought occurred to him, *human consciousness interferes with quantum states.*

Bridget thought, then said out loud, "*Human consciousness interferes with quantum states.*"

Ian laughed. He wasn't sure why. Non sequiturs were their bread and butter. Ian couldn't remember talking about quantum physics. But they had talked about everything else so maybe it fit.

Sledge said, "You two are spooky, like always doing that thing you do. That thing you do together. You two are weird, but you know I love you."

Bridget said, "We love you, too."

Beckett said, "Everybody so mellow. Nice! Not a banshee in sight. Regular lovefest going on."

Flash said, "What we got here is some God damn mass hypnosis going on. Bugs, man!"

Tim rejoined their group, slapping hands, squeezing shoulders. "What we got here," he proclaimed. Passersby were looking. Tim included them. Tim included everyone. "What we got here is a goddess blessed autonomous zone. For a little while, folks coming together, wondering about the bug, wondering about their government, their science."

"Right on," cried an older fellow with long gray hair and full gray beard. He kept on going, taking it all in, too, in his own way.

Bridget said, "They're not bugs," from within her hoodie.

Mahoney really didn't like crowds. She'd never been to Chicago. The communities she was used to in Indiana defined a crowd as anything with more than ten people. She couldn't believe how easy this crowd felt. Relaxed. Like they were walking to the fair.

Faces, faces, more faces, and bodies. Jackets and backpacks and purses, boots and sneaks and flip-flops. Whole lot of feet! She was a police officer—once you got the patrol buzz, you never let it go. You were always scanning for bads. Into the crowd she plunged. People soup! Go with it. Listen! Scan! Smell! All the smells, from cooking fires to car exhaust to dirty buttholes. Everything mingled, blew away in the breezy New Mexico atmosphere. Then: posters or placards. Signs. That meant wooden sticks. Truncheons. Everybody was heading for the site, so she tagged along.

Over here, an entire family stood, mom-and-pop, three little ones, a boy and two girls, all in overalls, and they were eyeing the people as hard as Mahoney. They were bedazzled by the variety of people and their behavior, as though they'd never seen anything like it for reals, except maybe on TV or the Internet. Everybody was here, everything could be seen.

Next to her, a bunch of old white men. They stopped, formed a half circle. They talked, grumbled, started walking again. Skinny old men, fat old men. They wore hats. They didn't seem threatening. But they did seem in trouble. You could feel it coming off them. Their skittish eyes. Nerves. Something up. Lots of couples, walking, stopping to talk with other people, maybe attracted by each other's signs. Bunch of what Mahoney would call hippy people, with their extra hair and outlandish outfits. Some older, some young. She couldn't get a handle on the age spread. At least half were Hispanic. A very straight looking couple held a poster with a picture of a UFO on one side, your standard flying saucer, then on the other side some saint or holy figure. What looked like middle-aged loners, mainly white men, mulled around, on their phones, or filming. They seemed shiny or sweaty. They stood apart, walked apart. Either cops or psychos? She expected a lot of people were packing, but so far everything concealed. She couldn't get a clear read on the crowd—

—when out of the blue a thought occurred to her: *human consciousness interferes with quantum states.*

She was nearing the gate now, eyes roaming back and forth along the fence. Suddenly, she wondered what she looked like to the folks. She wondered how many agents were around. Would Special Agent Alexander show up? Did she look like an agent? Did she fit in as just another seeker? She thought about quantum physics. The whole crowd was sharing molecules. That was one heavy thought. If the kids were here, she'd know, and she'd find them.

The Tilsons plowed their way to the gate, led by Mama Bear, excusing herself heartily, offering plenty of 'God bless yous,' pushing their way in. The gates were high and strong. On one side, a throng of people; on the other side, law enforcement vehicles and guards, officers, troopers, agents, soldiers. A simple platform was being erected, complete with mic stands. Right in the middle of this roiling crux, the Tilsons. Mr. Tilson and Kay, hands firmly clenched, never letting go, stood behind Mrs. Tilson, who was now calling out to the guards with great gusto.

People around them hooted and laughed, gasping at her naïveté to attempt to get the guards' attention. But Mrs.

Tilson would not be ignored. She pulled Kay up to the front, to stand in front of her. And she started yelling to the guards something like, you recognize her, you know her. Of course you do! The sister of the missing girl! You have to help us, we have to contact Doctor Scanlan. It's an emergency. The problem was that her voice was heard over the crowd, and people started gathering around them, wanting to see the girl, wanting to touch her hair. Mr. Tilson kept them back.

Mrs. Tilson got up as close as she could to the nearest guard. "You better let Doctor Scanlan know we're here, so we can protect our daughter. See what I'm saying? It's in your best interest, too. Tell your chief the Tilsons are here. Then he can let Doctor Scanlan know. Tell him that Bridget's sister is here with new information. It's an emergency."

Eventually, Garcia got the message from the reticent guard. Garcia told the guard he had done the right thing. Garcia called Taylor. She picked up right away, and Garcia could tell she was agitated.

"Ready when you are," she said with great aplomb.

"News here. So not just yet. Until you hear. The Tilsons are here. Showed up at the gate. Here, I'll shoot you the link so you can see them. Bridget's family? Hit it."

Taylor had met the Tilsons a few times over her three day stay in Indiana at the beginning. Since then, they had talked on the phone two times. One time, when Taylor wanted to know if Bridget had any favorite books or shows about specific places, her personal favorite dream land. Mr. Tilson told her the FBI had interviewed the whole family about things like that. The other time she called she had talked to Mrs. Tilson and asked her if Bridget had started her period. Mrs. Tilson had grown sharp and prone to invective, breaking off from Taylor.

On her phone screen, grainy surveillance of Mr. and Mrs. Olsen and what had to be their red-haired daughter outside the gate, on the other side of the fencing.

"Is this a recording?"

"Real time. Right now."

"What is she doing? Mrs. Tilson?"

"Bring 'em in?"

"My husband's here. He called."

"Visitors. Okay. Bring them all in, one big happy family."

"What is she doing? Trying to start a fight?"

"We'll take care of it. You'll do fine. I'll call my guys, then come for you."

Mrs. Tilson knew patience was a virtue. It said so right there on her wall embroidery. But she wanted answers. What was that bug doing to her girl? The scientists were always making promises then not delivering. They really didn't care, they had no empathy. So, now, the Tilsons must stand here like fools, begging for crumbs, begging to get in. She didn't care people were filming them, trying to get close. Mr. Tilson was politely keeping them back.

Some old lady was giving Kay and her the stink eye. No way! Mrs. Tilson was all action! She went right at her, hackles up. "Don't you be giving us no evil eye. I know what you're up to. You and your master."

"My master is Fortinbras, protector of *Igel*, savior of sprouts."

They faced off, both with hunched up shoulders, arms out like wrestlers. People pulled back, making a ring for them. The tone, the pull, the vibe of the crowd, its energies, jumped and sparked, charged up a notch.

"Mommy," called Kay, "they're letting us in."

The crowd roared with approval, confusion, and excitement.

Tallulah said, "It smells like a zoo." She adjusted her

sunglasses.

"It's a walk," said Dan. "I'll take my pack. Water."

"How much walking? Where are the kids?"

"People are getting scared of Trilobites. Having them around kids."

"You think they'll be here?"

"They better be. That'd be the only thing to make Mom forgive us for doing this. You know how mad and worried she can get. You're her million-dollar baby."

"You have to carry me. Like Cleopatra. On a palanquin."

"Yeah, right. Whatever happens, stay close. Don't wander away from me. You promise?"

"Cleopatra?"

"This is serious, T. People could recognize you. Keep your hat on! And don't be beaming all that adorableness all the time."

He plunked his hand down on her head, screwing up her vogue, giving her a noogie. She squealed. He gave her a little shove on the shoulder. She came in, fists flailing—

Stop.

They stopped, fell back, breathed. Took five whole seconds to calm, then started walking. There were so many interesting faces to see and signs to read that they blitzed out on their surroundings, and didn't realize they were holding hands.

Tallulah whispered, "Dood, it's a little hard to be adorable when you're scared. Not spooky scared, but excited scared."

"Stay with me."

The crowd got thicker, or denser, or more palpable, and started spilling onto the road. Law enforcement had a tougher time keeping the highway open. A helicopter went over and made Tallulah jump. She thought it was a giant dragonfly. People in robes, nuns and monks, mumbled past, singing or praying. She kept away from them. She guided Dan over to some people with Trilobites. Tallulah could tell what was wrong with them right away.

"No kids, they need kids, kids around them," mumbled Tallulah. Dan looked at her questioningly. She went on, "They need like they prefer kids better. You know that's true. Where's Hessler?"

Ahead of them, off to the side, Dan stared at a couple black guys and a couple black girls. Other kids were with them in hoodies. They were standing there, stepped to the side, watching, talking. At least that's what it looked like to Dan.

Tallulah broke away from Dan and stomped right up to Ian, where she said, "I'm your princess."

Ian fell to a knee to embrace Tallulah. Bridget came over and put her hands on Ian and Tallulah's heads. Their friends moved in close, forming a half circle in front of the kids. Dan stood outside the half circle, looking in.

Beckett said, "Help you, young man?"

"That's my sister."

Sledge smiled to Dan. "Come on, then. Join the party."

Dan sidled past Sledge and Beckett. Bridget saw him and hurried to give him a hug.

Flash said, "How'd you find us?"

Dan pulled away blushing. He said, "T, my sister. She knew. She just did."

Tim said, "That they'd be here?"

Dan shrugged. He could hear Tallulah whispering to Ian. Everybody could hear it. "Knew I'd find you. You love another. I recognize the signs."

Ian said, "Sweety, it doesn't work like that."

Tallulah stepped back, folded her arms in front of herself, as Ian got to his feet. In her stern, professorial voice, she said, "So how does this work? We gotta get Hessler back to his world. We have to take him home, Ian. He wants to go home."

Rosa said, "You are one heavy chickie. I'm Rosa."

"Tallulah."

"Yeah, you sure are a Tallulah," went Sledge. "This is Flash, Beckett, and Tim. I'm Sledge."

Bridget went over to Tim and put an arm around his shoulder. "Tim's my brother."

Tallulah nodded, unfolded her arms, relaxed them, started shaking hands. She said to Tim, "Well, if you're her brother, then you're my brother."

Tim said, "Fair enough."

Tallulah said, "This is Dan, my brother."

Everybody shook hands.

Dan was nervous and doing his best, watching his little sister, trying to blend in. "Didn't know you guys had your own posse. Right on. That's phat."

Flash smiled. "Brother, you don't have to talk black around black people. I'm kidding! It's cool."

This guy approached their cluster. Maybe a black man? Maybe an Arab? Maybe a Mexican? Everybody was looking at him curiously. He didn't look like a cop. Ian and Bridget fussed with cap and hoodie. The guy went, "*As-salāmu alaykum.*"

Becket and Flash responded, "*Wa alaykumu s-salam.*"

The guy said, "Y'all got it going on. You going up to the gate? Supposed to be some announcement. And more important: what you know about quantum physics?"

Flash went up to the guy, got in his face a little. "Who the hell are you?"

"Unless you're invisible, the issue is, how the hell have you not been picked up? I'm a friend. I work for his father." He pointed to Ian. "No, no freak out. Good to see you, Ian. Good to see you looking fine. I'm cool. I see myself as neutral now. Case closed. A free agent. This is way bigger than the kids, I'm thinking"

Fast, Beckett went, "Last one back to the cars is a rotten egg!"

Fat said, "What are you guys thinking? There so many

cops here—"

Tim said, "No one knows what's going on, we got as much right as the next guy to contribute."

Bridget said, "We don't want anybody getting in trouble. Soon as we explain what happened. This is my brother and my friends, they been helping us. Soon as we get Hessler back to the underground cave."

Beckett said, "Girl, you tell strangers your whole story?"

Tim said, "We're gonna head back to our cars, walk with me."

Fat went, "You guys must be the Trilobite Liberation Front."

Flash grinned and plopped with, "Busted!"

The kids kept in the middle of an unnoticeable circle, circling back to the cars. From up by the gate, they could hear—not shouting or screaming, but a gasping roll of sighs to the extreme. What was going on? But everybody thought Beckett was right. Get back. Lay low. Plan their strategy. Keep down.

Tim said to Fat, "What about physics?"

Fat shrugged, skittish in place. Looking around, looking around. "You got this figured, I sure don't? You guys are the center of this. Something big going down."

Tallulah marched back to Fat and Tim. She pointed a finger at Fat and said, "Physics: for every action, there is an equal and opposite reaction. *Human consciousness interferes with quantum states.*" She rejoined the others.

An older couple, unluckily close, were staring and gaping. The woman let out a squalling moan. "*Human consciousness interferes with quantum states.* She said it! You heard her. She said it. It's a message. They're broadcasting. Broadcasting!"

Tim said, "We gotta get outta here. Off the street so to speak."

Rosa took Tallulah's hand and said, "Stay up here with

us, okay."

Tallulah nodded. Dan came over to stand at her side. Tallulah quipped, "Boys think they're the only ones who know science."

Fat laughed. "Who is that little girl?"

Tim and Fat watched the excited rumble of emotions from Sledge. Something about TV, the little white girl everyone knows: *Trilotats!* Rosa quieted her down.

Fat said, "We're sitting ducks. You got the bug with you?"

Tim said, "I don't even know who you are. So careful about 'we.' We had to be here."

Fat said, "There's a lady following us, twenty feet back. Don't look. Gotta be a cop. White woman, thirty-five, looks like she's in shape. Dressed like a mom."

Tim said, "Could've noticed Tallulah."

Garcia led Taylor swiftly to the small stage. She stepped up in her red dress, went to the mic stand. Shouts and cheers, clapping and stomping followed her appearance. She glanced back at Garcia who was furiously talking to a security guard and a plainclothesman. Finally, Garcia caught her glance, stepped away from the two men, and gave her his full attention.

"Good afternoon. My name is Doctor Taylor Scanlan, I'm director of the site. I have been here from the beginning of this incredible journey." An eruption of cheers. "We apologize for the delay this morning for this briefing. We feel it appropriate at this time to remark on the YouTube material available online over the past few days." Now there were shouts and jeers.

People yelled: "Close it up!" "Where are the kids?" "A-bomb it!" "Trilobites know!" "Leave Trilobites alone!"

"You must realize the personal satisfaction I feel at

seeing my son alive—and healthy. I assure you local, state, and federal resources are working even now to locate the origin of the clips. We have no new information about the kids or their location. Or the Trilobite. The YouTube showed what appeared to be antenna extending from the Trilobite to touch the kids' heads. We want to assure everyone the Trilobites are completely safe. The uncommon antenna cannot suck blood, or inject anything. It's simply impossible. Research at several scientific institutions around the world have found nothing dangerous, or otherworldly, about the Trilobites. Some have insisted on referring to Trilobite powers, yet we have absolutely no evidence, or indication of any kind, of mental or psychological effects, the Trilobites have on humans. I believe Bridget and Ian, my son, are safe and coming home."

A man's voice called out, "End of the world!"

A woman cried, "You've opened the door, you must close it."

Taylor's slight pause had been filled so she pushed on, also noticing Garcia, now holding an arm up, with a finger raised.

"We continue in our explorations. We are being assisted by scientists from around the world. All of our research is free and open to the public to access. Just go to our website and login. We promise to keep you abreast of our discoveries. I believe there's an app for that. We appreciate your continued cooperation. We thank you for your peaceful and exuberant support, and patience. 'Human consciousness interferes with quantum states'. One moment please."

Taylor hurried to Garcia.

"Quanta? What the hell, Taylor? What was that?"

"What? What do you have? Why did you call me over?"

Garcia was giving Taylor the old stink eye, but came up

with, "I think we got 'em. Your kids. The liberation front. NSA, FBI, those guys, closing in now."

"Ian?" She knew in a movie the mom would stumble and swoon, but she had to get back to the mic.

Mahoney figured there were agents all over the place. Plainclothesmen. Undercover. Deep cover. They could be wearing make-up. Bunch of blacks, her age or younger, with some younger kids, one in a hoodie. Were those kids white? A little girl and a high school boy also with them were. But the kid in the hoodie? Had to be six foot tall. She remembered the Tilson girl was tall. She'd tag along along along, going their way, keep her eyes peeled. They were heading out, away from the gate and the site. Going the wrong way.

The little white girl went over to talk to the guys in back. She returned to the others, who were walking slightly ahead of the two. There was talking, people's heads turning. They seemed excited. Glimpses! The tall kid in the hoodie was definitely a white girl. It was Bridget Tilson. Then, her Spidey sense got to tingle. She could tell the two guys at the back had made her. She figured what the hey and took out of her pocket her official police officer whistle.

She blew her whistle three times, then shouted, "Scramble! Scramble! Cluster! Cluster! Now! Now!" She ran to the kids and their 'associates', pulling her badge out of her back pocket. She blew her whistle again. Three shrill, ear piercing times.

Running in, two women dressed like hippies, and an older guy all in brown. Another man, farther back, came running. They checked out Mahoney's position and intent, made clear by her gesticulating arms. They were on their phones right away.

Mahoney came up to Fat and Tim who stood there, waiting for her. The others had stopped, turned to watch. Ian and Bridget were close, arms around each other. Tallulah came in for a hug, her arms going around Bridget and Ian. Dan stood nearby, then lurched in to join their hug. Mahoney announced, "Police. We need to talk to the kids."

We because the two women had their badges out and weapons drawn, but held down, and they and the others were fanning out to encompass the group. "FBI," they called.

The man dressed in brown, in what looked like a safari outfit, said, "Okay, everybody, take it easy. We see these kids here. Kids are missing. See what I mean? We gotta check it out. Now let's take this nice and slow, so we don't stir up any attention. Would you all mind forming a line? Does anyone have a weapon on them? We're gonna have to check. Want to see IDs. Kids get in line too. Nice and slow. Kids are gonna have to untangle. Please."

Plainclothesmen. A big black SUV snaked its way through the crowds on the highway, and when impassable took to the fields, cross country, paralleling the road. No siren. No lights. Guys in uniform piled out. Security, in all shapes and sizes, flashed IDs, transforming from civilians to law enforcement in the blink of an eye.

Word spread, passing through the telegraph warp, voice to voice, mind to mind, Trilobite channel, spreading to the front, through the rear, into the site. A crowd was forming—

They made a line.

The man in the safari suit said, "Backpacks off and in front of you, please. Hoodies down."

One of the female agents was by Tallulah, kneeling in front of her.

Tallulah said loud enough for everybody to hear, "I'm not going anywhere without my brother, and since all these people are my brothers, even the girls, you got a problem, sister."

The woman stood back up, swatted at her knees. She went to Bridget.

Bridget said, "I'm with her."

The woman frowned but pulled back. "You have any ID?"

"About what?"

Tim said, "Think you can put away the guns. Kids around and all. None of us carrying a weapon. Everybody's cooperating."

Safari Man said, "We'll start gathering IDs."

The collective cried in one voice, "About what?"

Safari Man was joined by an older man in black garb from the SUV. They motioned Mahoney aside.

The older man stared hard at her, tense, angry. In a low voice he said, "Good work, officer."

"Mahoney."

"I don't want to know your name. I don't want to ever see you again. This could've been a hostage situation. We were closing in. But quietly. No one would have known—"

"I observed them. I didn't get the feeling they had been kidnapped."

"You didn't get the feeling? The kids could've been wearing suicide vests under those hoodies. We had no idea what this front was up to."

"They were...excited. Didn't seem like a dangerous situation. I've been looking for the kids a long time."

Safari Man bustled in with, "This is above my pay grade. What now? All these people?"

Mahoney said, "It's the kids! We got them! They're safe!"

Safari Man grunted. "We think so. It's not confirmed yet."

"Bridget, the red hair. She's tall."

The man in black interrupted, "Enough. This is what's

gonna happen. All these folks will be given rides back to site. There, interrogation, consultation."

Mahoney looked concerned. "Can I talk to them?"

"Absolutely not," said the older guy.

"I believe I've earned—"

"It's your collar," interrupted Safari Man. "Your moment of glory."

Mahoney hurried to the line. The various agents waved her through. Now they were busy keeping back onlookers. The crowd might not know exactly what was going down, but a bunch of plainclothesmen around young black people with white kids was suitably incongruous.

Ian came first in the line. She put her hand out to him. They shook. "Hi, Ian. I'm Officer Mahoney from Gary. Good to finally meet you. And you're safe! Is Hessler in your pack?"

Bridget called out, "Not a word!"

Mahoney smiled and moved over to her. "Hi, Bridget. I know your parents. The girls. Kay." She put out her hand and they shook.

Safari Man intervened: "The kids will come over here, please. Go with these ladies, please. No, no, leave your packs."

Ian said, "I have to get something out of my pack."

The agents, the onlookers froze.

Ian bent down and unzipped his pack, taking out Hessler's new big container.

Agents closed in. Safari dood went, "Whoa! Whoa! We'll have to take that."

Ian cried, "You can't!"

People around the scene, folks from all over the country, of all different backgrounds, started yelling, getting frisky.

Someone yelled, "It's the Trilobite!"

"Leave the kids alone!"

"Leave the Trilobites alone!"

"The Trilobite has come home!"

Bridget went over to stand by Ian holding the container, surrounded by agents with their arms out. They wouldn't let her get close. Tallulah tried to go over and get into it, but a female agent stopped her, grabbing on to her arm. Tallulah let loose a lurid, livid eruption of a screech.

Safari dood went, "Get them out of here! Now!" He pointed to Ian. "Leave the bug."

The collective rang out with, "He's not a bug!"

CHAPTER 13

"Ian," guffawed Tallulah, "looks like you decorated this place. You guys are missing Hessler. I can tell. Sad."

Dan made elaborate pointing motions. "Cameras, there, there."

Bridget and Kay couldn't untangle. Bridget whispered into her ear.

Ian and Dan walked around the Quonset hut, checking it out, examining the windows, then shaking them, looking for concealed, or emergency, exits.

A little girl they'd been introduced to earlier, Isabel, was with them. She stood alone, then wandered over to a cot to sit. The little girl, an African-American, in jeans and a sweatshirt with fairies and toadstools, had a big voice: "They said it was only for a little while. Your parents are next door. We're okay. It'll be righteous. I have to wait until my ride gets here."

Dan pulled Ian over to the far corner of the Quonset hut, past the cots. The cots had no sheets or blankets, and slipless pillows. He whispered, "Can't believe they took Hessler. Think they're going to cut him up?"

"That's gross! Don't! Don't say that."

"They need his jizz, I guess. Him being the only male."

"I don't know what they'll do. It makes us sick thinking

about it. Bridget thinks they *have* to let him go back to his home in the lake. T does too. But I don't know."

Isabel continued from the other side of the room, "It's just for a little while. They said that they had limited facilities."

Tallulah went over and sat by Isabel. "Who are you? Why are you here?"

"Trilobites, I think. I had one of those Trilotats. Trilobites like me." She shrugged and smiled, and Tallulah smiled back. "I saw you on TV."

"I'm Tallulah. My brother calls me T."

"I'm Isabel. Everybody calls me Bel. Except my mom. She's back home, waiting for a ride, so she can come get me. Guards caught me. Here I am. Everybody's so upset. Were you kidnapped?"

Tallulah shook her head. "I don't think anybody got kidnapped. You know how adults are, they overreact. My mom's not here yet either. I came with my brother. That guy with Ian."

Bridget and Kay went to the side of the hut, kneeled, folded their hands in front of themselves, and prayed.

Bel said, "Think I can go over there and join them?"

"Holy? You're holy?"

"We're all holy."

"They're really nice. Bridget is my friend. I don't know Kay. I just met her. I don't think they would mind."

The girl stood but paused. She stared at Tallulah, and she looked a little scared for a second. "They think Trilobites are messing with our minds. It's a national crisis. They're going to have to round up all the Trilobites and bring them back here to let go."

Dan and Ian had returned from their survey, and they'd heard what the girl had said.

Dan uttered, "Uh-uh! No way! Way too much money involved now. They're talking about a movie. All sorts of stuff. Right, T?"

Tallulah went, "Shhh!"

Ian whispered, "She's right, give them space."

Dan and Ian sat on the cot with Tallulah. Bel went to Bridget and Kay and kneeled by them.

Dan huskily whispered, "This is where we realize our superpowers. That's what happens in the movies."

Tallulah said, "The only superpowers you have are farts and porn."

Dan leaned in to pinch her. Her head rose fast with wide eyes like a bird of prey. She mouthed all in caps, "DON'T YOU DARE!"

They kept quiet for a few more minutes. Finally, Dan got buggy and had to get up. He went over to the crate the guards had left with them. He started rummaging around in it. "Check it out," he called. "Water, sodas, goldfish."

Tallulah went, "Shhh!"

Dan opened a water and poured it down his throat. He gasped and sighed. Tallulah waited for the burp but it did not come. He returned to looking in the crate. "Score!" he cried, holding up a big bag of M&Ms.

Bridget got on her feet. She crossed herself. Kay stood, crossed herself. Bel stood. Kay rubbed at her red knees. She wore a light blue dress, and now she smoothed it down, making sure it was not ruffled or wrinkled.

Kay said, "May I have a water, please?"

Dan dug one out for her. She walked over to get it.

"Thank you," said Kay.

"It's for all of us," said Dan. "Help yourself."

Bel and Bridget joined in, picking through the stuff in the crate. Bel grabbed a water and a bag of goldfish. Bridget took a 7-Up.

Dan said, "Sorry, no beer."

Kay sputtered, "My sister does not drink beer."

Bridget was chugging down the 7-Up. Ian came up to her and she offered him the can. He took it and finished it. He threw the can in the adjacent receptacle. He turned and stepped into Bridget, his arms going around her waist. Bridget stepped back, out of his grasp, her eyes in his.

Tallulah remained on the cot. She said, "Dan, I only want red ones."

"For sure, Funnybunny," he laughed, and went over to sit beside her. He opened the M&Ms, started feeding red ones to her.

Bel took her goods and returned to sit on another cot. Kay held Bridget's hand and led her to a separate cot.

Ian stood by himself by the crate and garbage can. He watched them all, and they glanced back.

Bel said, "I don't think I'm in trouble. I mean, as much as you guys."

Tallulah said, "Dan stole a car and drove a million miles without a license."

Bel went, "Oh. Gaw."

Tallulah said, "I'll come see you in prison. I'll do cosplay, show up as Harley Quinn. It will be totally rad."

Bridget said, "Extenuating circumstances—do you know what that means? Nobody's going to prison."

Ian walked over, said, "Can I sit by you?"

Bridget looked at Kay who shook her head.

Ian said, "Come on, they left us together, there's no harm—"

Bel said, "They didn't have anywhere else to put us. After you guys got reunited with your folks, they stuck us in here. Just for a little while. They said you guys have to go to the doctor."

Dan said, "Pretty standard, I think. Runaways, kidnapped kids, gotta get checked out. I seen it on TV."

Tallulah said, "Did you kidnap me?"

Dan's voice rose: "What are you talking about? You kidnapped me! It was your idea—"

Tallulah gasped. "They can hear us. Switch to code."

Bel said, "I never knew anybody so much in trouble. All because of Trilobites."

Dan said, "That's not code! Who are you? What do you know about Trilobites? Laser Mazer Taser, haze her!"

Tallulah sang, "Ian and Bridget, hanging on a gibbet—"

Bel said, "Like rap? My name is Bel, you can go to hell."

Kay gasped.

Bel said, "I thought they were making fun of me."

No one said anything. Bel nibbled a goldfish.

Then: "I'm Isabel. We're from Harrison, Arkansas. Know where that is? You know what pig nuts are? See, y'all not so smart."

Dan snorted. Tallulah raised a warning hand. She said, "Go on, tell your story."

"We were in Rogers. That's in Arkansas, too. And we went to Wal-Mart. I went right to the pet department—I like to check out the guppies, fancy tails, all different colors. Anyway, they had a special display, like a little stage with a table. And the table was covered with Trilotats in boxes. $19.95. And these two people, a boy and a girl in jumpsuits, were explaining all about Trilobites. How safe they were and everything. They had three Trilotats, out of their boxes, lined up in front of them, with water and Trilobites, so people could see how cool they were. Spheres, you know, with flat bottoms. These boys, teenagers, crowded up to the table to see better. This one boy picked up a Trilotat and started shaking it. I guess he wanted the Trilobite to move. The people in uniforms got really upset. The guy went over and tried to pull the Trilotat out of the boy's hands. The boy jumped back and the Trilotat went flying. It hit the floor with a big plastic crunch. Meaning the cheap plastic broke, water splattered everywhere, and one of those little guys scrambled away superfast. The people in jumpsuits were all over the place trying to catch the Trilobite. I could tell they were doing it the wrong way. I picked up one of those Trilotats and held it close, looking in at the little thing."

Dan said, "How long is this story?"

Tallulah said, "She's getting to the good part."

Bel went on, "I don't know. I guess I grabbed the other Trilobite from its Trilotat. I put her in my Trilotat, stuck the whole thing under my windbreaker, and zipped up. I got out of there and no one noticed. You believe that? Like I had a bowling ball in my stomach. When I got home, I went to my room, and let them out. They climbed up my arms and settled in my elbow. Kind of tickly. We became best friends. I take them out to the backyard and let them burrow. They like worms. They always come back to me."

"Antenna—did you see antenna? Did yours have antenna?" asked Ian.

"I never saw antenna."

Kay said, "You're a thief! That's a mortal sin."

"I know," said Bel.

"She's a person, not a thing," said Bridget.

Bel was shaking her head and looking away from the group. Tallulah went over and sat close to her. She said, "I know what you mean. They like elbows."

Dan said, "Is this the new code?"

Tallulah rose to her feet, glanced around at her friends, making a face at Dan. "We have to get out of here. No windows, no tunnels, guards outside, Mom coming, drones, machine guns, barbed wire fence. It'll be easy! We get Hessler—"

Bel inserted, "And all the other Trilobites."

Tallulah finished, "And we sneak down to the underground world, where the underground lake is, and let them go."

"Good plan," smirked Dan.

Ian tried again, wandering over to Bridget and Kay's cot. "Scoot over." They did. He snuggled down next to Bridget but kept his arms to himself. "You guys, it's our fault. We're the only ones really in trouble. We'll tell them that and they'll let you go. Probably. We ran away. Parents and police don't like that."

"So did we," said Dan.

"I took the bus," said Bel. "Had to bring my Trilobites back home. I had to do it."

Dan went, "No way. The bus?"

Bridget said, "We're all runaways."

Ian got back to his point: "I mean what are they gonna do to us? Trips to the shrink? Ritalin? You know the routine. But I had Hessler. And that's what's made things more complicated. No one knows what the Trilobites...are doing. We've all been affected by Trilobites. The adults got to be wondering how, why."

"All those people at the gate—what are they looking for?" asked Bridget. "What does it have to do with quantum physics?"

Bel said, "*Human consciousness interferes with quantum states.*"

Bridget smiled. "See, we're all in this. Including my brother." She looked at Kay. "Our brother. Tim. You just met him. You're going to really love him. He came to help us. He's really nice. He's black."

Bel looked funny. "What do you mean?"

"He's African-American," said Bridget.

"I'm African-American," said Bel.

"I'm a rush in," said Dan, getting to his feet, rushing the crate. When he got there, he announced, "I'm finish."

Everybody looked at him.

"It's funny," he said. "Look, you guys. I'm the oldest one here, so I feel a certain responsibility in keeping things lite. You know, so we don't all freak out. But in code, of course. So, we're gonna sneak out of here, grab all the Trilobites, and hightail it underground, into the deep, deep secret world of Trilobites. *Human consciousness interferes with quantum states.*"

"I wanted to say it," blurted Tallulah.

Ian said, "Everybody saying that. Thinking that. What does it mean? Where does it come from? How does it get in our heads? What does that have to do with us and the Trilobites?"

"Let me finish," said Dan. "I was just warming up. I was being sarcastic. Quantum physics, I don't know. Telepathic bugs, it's in the movies. People, we are done here! Give me a break, you think this is some kid adventure story? We're safe. It worked out fine. No one got hurt. Tallulah's got a career. There's no way we could get out of here, get Hessler, and go to the underground lake. Forget it! Ian, Bridget, help me out here."

Bridget got up and started pacing in front of them. She moved back and forth and their eyes followed her. She looked very stern or thoughtful.

Kay asked, "What happened to the Trilobite that got away at Wal-Mart? Did they catch it?"

Bel said, "Uh-uh. I think it got away—"

Dan interrupted. "Into the sewers, where it grows and grows, replicating into a hideous monster." He found his own cot and sat. He held a 7-Up and an energy bar. He was happy. This was all crazy, and Ian was right, what were they going to do to them. Dan laughed but kept it to himself. T had gigs coming up. After this, T would be even more valued—

Mom would get over it. Dan thought, 'I'll say, our moms will get over it'.

Bridget kept pacing.

Bel said, "They should come for us any second."

Kay asked, "What are the Trilobites doing to kids?"

Ian thought of Scorch, the spring with Hessler, the long nights together, all three of them connected. Bridget thought about holding Hessler in her lap, gently stroking his cephalon. Tallulah had known right away Trilobites had their own way of doing things, their own way of being friends.

No one said anything.

Dan said, "Oh, that's right, secret code, don't let the

camera see. Or the microphones hear." He looked serious for a few seconds. "Trilobites don't like me."

Tallulah said, "I don't like you."

"That's mean," said Dan. "Give me a break."

"He's my bodyguard," explained Tallulah.

Dan said, "Right. What do Trilobites do to kids? I'll tell you. It was foretold in the classic movie *Spaceballs*, when Mel Brooks as Yoda answers the very same question. And his answer—you want to know?"

Bridget said, "This is silly."

Very dramatically, Dan announced, "Merchandizing!"

Bel said, "What does that mean? I can tell you what they do to me. When we're hanging out, we are together. That's all. Everything real simple. Hanging around, being friends. When I got here, well, when the bus dropped me off in that town, Trilobites found me. Some nice folks brought me here, the rest of the way. I had so many Trilobites by then, in my pockets. Stuffed in these Tupperware things. They wanted me to take them home."

"Right," went Dan.

Bridget said, "They recognized something about you. How many other kids is this happening to?"

Tallulah said, "I was saving this for later but everybody's so much missing the Trilobites, I'll just say it now. We bribe the guards, get back to our car, drive to Albuquerque, and go to one of the affiliates. We'll do a show on TV, all of us, and explain how the Trilobites have to be set free. Our ratings will be through the roof."

Bel said, "You're a movie star."

Dan said, "The way it works is you gotta have your angle. Something new, crispy, slightly deviant. Okay? You guys know how this happened? How T turned into a movie star? So the 'runaway lovers' story is going, and the news people had me and T on as 'people of interest', and the cameras discovered they loved T. You probably noticed she's a bit pale, this girl. So, we got this little white haired, white skinned girl crawling with bugs, and it's like a whole dealio, a big new meme. It's so weird, because sure she's adorable, but the way they make her pale with bare feet and a bug? I don't know. It's like it's a symbol of something."

"I'm a person not an it," said Tallulah.

Bel said, "Is there a restroom?"

Ian said, "Over there, in the corner. We checked it out before. Seems okay."

In the Quonset hut next door, a table had been set up, surrounded by recyclable chairs. Plastic water bottles were scattered over the table, some open, some closed. On one side of the table, two robust white men in suits, their hands folded in front of them. One was slightly older, perhaps, the other man seeming to defer to him. They had not offered their names, but seemed to be in charge. On the other side of the table, two sets of parents.

The older suit had been talking. "We got the kids. They're safe and sound. But this isn't over. Yes, it's something to do with the Trilobites. International entities are suddenly mighty interested in Trilobites. Which makes us wonder. Did the kids have help in getting away so easily? They were gone for a while. Who was helping them? This front? Of course, no one knew of Tim in Denver. It seems so improbable, such an odd chain of coincidence and luck, and here we are. We have got to get a better handle on the Trilobites. We need to get your and the other parents' permission for running the full range of lab and radiographic tests. It's for their own good. We need to make sure they have not been affected by the Trilobites. We understand the trauma you've been through with missing kids. But this is a priority now."

Mr. and Mrs. Tilson sat in the flimsy chairs next to

Professor Scanlan in his own plastic chair. Doctor Scanlan was seated off to the side, but on their side of the table.

The Tilsons wanted no testing on their girls. "Absolutely not," said Mrs. Tilson.

The older man smirked with impatience. "I'm playing this low-key, because in a state of national emergency the president has a right to order you. We're trying to be empathetic here, but it is a matter of national security so..."

Mrs. Tilson believed the whole thing was a giant TV fairytale they were being forced to participate in, whether they believed in it or not. "No," said Mrs. Tilson, "I want my girls back. We'll walk back to the car and drive back to Indiana."

Mr. Tilson kept flashing on the first sight he'd had of Bridget. He hadn't recognized her at first, to his great shame and confusion. Yes, she seemed a bit skinny, but she also seemed bigger somehow, holding herself erect and attentive. She had a glow about her he had to admit. His little girl had gone away and come back a young woman. He totally agreed with his wife. "We just want to go," he said. He didn't trust the suits or the scientists. They sat behind the table as though they knew what was going on. Official! They were in charge? Nobody was in charge! That's when people got hurt. "We're going home without any Trilobites, and everything will go back to the way it was. Thank God!"

Ethan hated everyone in the room. How dare these fancy cops threaten and manipulate him! He could tell they were desperate. They were lying. They would do anything. And Taylor was going along with them, the whole process. Sitting there in her red dress, like a million bucks. Who were these guys? They were *uncertain*. What was going on? The quantum thing? 'International entities'? What should he do? What should he do?

Ethan mouthed off: "This quantum physics statement.

This sentence. This sentence keeps popping up in people's heads. They think it, they say it. My private eye—believe you have him next door with the front, came up with it, too."

No one said anything. The younger suit looked embarrassed. The order one had an empty face. Taylor fidgeted.

Taylor said, "We have the best people coming in to look over our situation. All over the world, right now, the top scientists are working on this. In the meantime, we evacuate the kids to Albuquerque. It's the closest place with a decent hospital, so all the top-of-the-line equipment. That way the kids are safe. No matter what."

Mrs. Tilson said, "I just want to be with my girls. We want to go home."

Taylor said, "And you will! A little while longer. That's all. The helicopters are on their way. Be here before night, I promise."

Ethan spoke, "We assume Trilobites know very little about quantum physics, therefore we must assume there is another player involved who can put complete sentences into people's heads."

The second suit, the younger one, who had not talked much, said, "Woo woo, like UFOs? Come on, keep it simple. Mass hysteria can take many forms: one crackpot mumbles the quantum line in a visionary climax, and is overheard by another crackpot, who thinks he came up with it on his own. It spreads from person to person like an infection."

"I never mentioned UFOs," said Ethan.

"You're just mean," said Mrs. Tilson to the younger suit.

The older suit said, "Stop. *That* is our concern now: who is this other player? What do the kids know?"

Mrs. Tilson said, "I—I would like to see my son, Tim. I'd like to see those other folks, thank them for taking care of our kids."

Mr. Tilson said, "That's a great idea."

Taylor said, "I think I'd like that, too. I mean, while we're waiting. For a little while, anyway."

Ethan said, "My man, Arafat, he's okay, right? He's not going to be charged or anything?"

The younger suit said, "Not that I know of. None of them are. Unless parents want to press charges?"

Mr. Tilson said, "Of course not."

Taylor said, "No."

Taylor stood. Mr. and Mrs. Tilson stood. Reluctantly, as though dragged up on his feet, Ethan unfolded himself upright.

Taylor said to the suits, "We'll walk over. If anything comes up, you know where we are."

When they were outside, they were blasted with the crisp afternoon air clicking with insects. They all tottered a second, gathered their fortitude, and plunged on. Some of the flying insects were drones. They followed the security guards, who carried machine guns.

What Ethan was impressed with was the size of the site. The site had grown huge in a short time. He commented, "How many of these portable buildings do you have?"

Taylor sighed and her head came down. "Site management, supply, housing, inventory. There's an app for that."

The guard in front opened the door of the next hut over.

Ethan said, "Are the doors locked?"

The guard looked confused. Taylor clarified, "Of course not. They're electric."

They went inside the Quonset hut, to be greeted with a scene they had not expected: bare cots had been pushed to the sides so that there was a large space in the middle of the floor, now populated with barefoot artists jumping about, making sounds, emitting words. They calmed, came to rest, stopped what they were doing, all turned to face their guests. To the side of the door, a lone cot with Fat, sitting next to a crate of supplies. He was eating Pringles.

Tim came forward to Mrs. Tilson and they embraced. Mrs. Tilson cried, Tim cried. Some of the others did too. Ethan went over to Fat, stood before him.

"A job well done, my friend," he said, extending his hand. They shook. Ethan went on, "You knew where they'd be, you found them! We'll be done here soon, then we can drive back."

Taylor came up beside Ethan. "If Ian's in Albuquerque, you'll want to be there, too. With him."

Ethan looked startled. "How do you mean?"

Fat interrupted, "This the famous ex-, huh? Not sure we got properly introduced. Call me Fat."

"Taylor. Thanks for your help. You really helped Ethan."

Mrs. Tilson was talking: "There's no charges. No one's pressing charges. You're free to go. Right, Mrs. Scanlan?"

Taylor came around to face the group. "Yes, but we would like to have everyone stay put, for right now. You were all around the male Trilobite. We have tests we'd like to run. I think we'll all feel better after that. Is that okay?"

Rosa said, "Do we have a choice? Is this the mining company talking or the feds?"

Taylor said, "Both. It's in your best interests."

No one said anything. Mr. Tilson stood by the door. He seemed awkward and unclear, until Tim said, "Dad, come on. I want you and Mom to meet the collective."

Mr. Tilson joined Tim and Mrs. Tilson in walking over to the group, who now strode in to greet them.

Taylor and Ethan watched. Taylor said, "We should go say hello, Ethan. Thank them."

Ethan said, "Aiding and abetting runaways. Under age

runaways."

Fat said, "This is bigger than that. You know that. These folks are cool. Good people. You should be happy they're the ones the kids reached out to. Come on, let's go over." Fat led them to the others.

Everybody was embracing and shaking hands. Tim looked positively radiant. Mr. and Mrs. Tilson smiled a lot, but they seemed unsure. The genuine warmth made a difference. Taylor and Ethan got involved, offering thanks, smiling awkwardly. Fat stayed at the side to watch.

Rosa said to Taylor, "You're Ian's mom? You're a fox."

Beckett said, "Got that right. No disrespect intended. We got to know your kids. Yes, we did. Thanks are not necessary. It was our privilege."

Sledge said, "They're awesome kids. We're making a piece, spoken word and dance, a performance to do with the kids. Tell our story. We're artists."

Mrs. Tilson said, "That's very nice. But Bridget has school. She has to go home."

Mr. Tilson said, "We just want everything back the way it was. Course, it's great to meet Tim, and all of you, so we can keep in touch. By telephone."

Tim said, "Why don't we pull up some cots and sit, talk a minute."

Flash and Beckett and Fat hustled for the cots. Fat said, "There's water, snacks."

Two cots opposite two more cots, facing each other, one set with parents and Tim, one set with the collective and Fat.

Sledge laughed nervously. "Howdy, parents! We've all been through so much, it's so strange but wonderful, too. You guys back with your kids. Everybody safe and sound. Strange wonderful."

Tim said, "Something's happening that's bigger than the kids and the Trilobites. I'm not sure what it is, but, somehow, the kids and the Trilobites are at the center of it. Does that make sense?"

Ethan said, "You're all black."

Taylor ground her teeth and rubbed at her eyes a second. "Don't be rude. Jesus Christ, Ethan."

Mrs. Tilson said, "I just as soon not hear you take the Lord's name in vain."

Tim said, "Yes, we're black. So? What does that mean?"

Ethan said, "Well, you said it. More than kids and Trilobites, the race issue. Mix that with toxic government, secret agencies, perverted science, and of course quantum physics."

Beckett said, "You think some kind of conspiracy going on, so they'll have to keep us quiet?"

Ethan said, "Absolutely."

Taylor said, "That's insane. We're emotionally exhausted, we came over to say thanks, maybe we should get back. We're all going to Albuquerque. Some tests. Okay? Hold on a little while longer. Please."

Flash said, "I kind of agree with Mr. Scanlan. I know that's extreme, out of some TV playbook. But something's spooky, we don't know what, at the fringe. One thing's for sure, Mr. and Mrs. Tilson, things are never going back to how they used to be. Ever. Those kids are woken up. They're on fire. They're artists."

Mr. Tilson jumped in, "We know our daughter. We know what's best for our daughter."

Sledge said, "She's gonna be famous."

Rosa said, "What about the other kids, the little pale girl, her brother, and that little black girl?"

Taylor said, "They're next door. Their parents, their moms, are on their way."

Rosa said, "How are they involved?"

Ethan said, "Apparently, our son and their daughter have been having an affair for some time."

Taylor interrupted, "They're not having an affair. They're two smart kids who wanted to save a Trilobite."

She avoided looking at Mrs. Tilson.

Ethan said, "Our son and their daughter befriended the white kids, and they all—what's the word? Played with? Hung out? With Hessler. I don't know about the black girl."

Taylor said, "All of the kids were in contact with Trilobites and seemed to have an affinity with them."

Mrs. Tilson said, "Our Kay didn't."

Taylor said, "She found the shed skin from the Trilobite's molting. Bridget had it."

Fat took in the group with interest. They seemed to be tiptoeing around THE subject. He knew they were in shock, he had to be careful, gentle, but still— "That statement, the sentence about quantum physics that came to folks—"

Rosa smiled, glared at her friends, then these new folks. She said, "That was the strangest dealio. It wasn't dreamy, like a vision, the sentence just appeared in my head. I didn't hear it. I read it? Out loud, spoken word, it made sense. How did they get it in my head?"

Fat shook his head. "It's not possible with modern technology."

Fast, Tim said, "How do you know?"

Now Fat smiled. "Research is the thing. I research stuff. Part of my job. I read in one area, it leads somewhere else. Gotta keep on top of stuff."

Tim asked, "What does it mean?"

Fat stepped up, back. Hard to articulate the forest as a lone tree.

Before he could continue his speculation, Taylor jumped to her feet, smoothing down her red dress. "I think if we go off on wild extrapolations, we are bound to confuse things. We have to stick to the facts. We need to get back. The helicopters are coming. We should get back."

Mr. and Mrs. Tilson stood. "I want to see the girls," said

Mrs. Tilson.

Flash said, "We're going to Albuquerque?"

Sledge said, "Don't see why we can't all be together?"

Taylor said, "I'll go see. Let me check. Thanks."

Tim said, "We'll see you soon."

Sledge said, "Tell the kids hey for us. We'd love to see them."

Ethan jumped to his feet, smoothed down the front of his shirt.

Taylor nodded, "Okay," and led them out.

Tim said to Fat when they were gone, "Where do these extrapolations take you?"

Fat shrugged, sat opposite him. He exhaled. "If it's not our tech, and if it's not their tech, you know, like Russia or China, then it's gotta be a surprise player. Someone new on the block. That's what's got them worked up on top. See what I'm saying?"

Flash said, "Mind control devices from North Korea? Thought projectors? Some kind of projection device? Look at the crowds at the gate—aerosols? I don't think it's emissaries from Mars. But someone who knows how to push people's buttons. For sure. Whole story—the lake, the Trilobites, the physics, freaking everybody out."

Fat shook his head. "Who benefits?"

Sledge said, "Does this player care the Trilobites are returned to the underground? What does quantum physics have to do with it?"

"Wow," went Tim. "That's a thought I never had."

Flash said, "Do any of us even know what a quantum state is?"

Rosa said, "Let's dance it!"

They rose, set aside the cots. Fat got out of the way. They regained their space in the middle of the hut, and started stretching. Beckett did a funny walk like a wooden soldier. Flash and Tim pranced around, high stepping, arms waving. Rosa was gentle, on tip toe, spraying fairy dust with feet and hands. Sledge stood center tall, eyes closed. Her arms went up.

Beckett said, "Maybe they'll give us copies from the feed," casually gesturing to the cameras.

Sledge declaimed, "When the bugs came
panic rained
men raised Cain
raising Cain
all the same
certain they were right
coming with their might
certain they knew what was going down

"Raising Cain
raising Cain
all the same
like a big dumb game

"Then the kids stepped out
white kids, black kids
Trilobite kids
Trilobite kids
runaway kids
runaway kids
natural allies
allies to the Trilobites
speaking with the Trilobites
they knew what must be done
they knew what's just for fun

"The world is bigger than we thought
it's full of Trilobites."

Maze danced. Occasionally, someone would mutter in a sing songy voice, "Raising Cain, all the same." Or, "Trilobite kids." Then: "The human race in outer space." Words and longings would be repeated, shouted out, said backwards, used as instrumental feathers.

They stopped, went for water.

Rosa said, "We gotta get that little pale girl in this, bet she's got some moves."

Beckett said, "Bring it on home."

Flash said, "Make it real."

Taylor led the Tilsons and Ethan from the collective's hut. They were silent, energetic, then desperately frustrated. Since they were in the improvised housing section of the site, they were away from the main centers of hubbub—gate and shaft. They could hear the gate. People were shouting, vehicles were revving. Honking! Then an undercurrent like electrical buzzing. A Jeep came around fast towards them. The security guards from the huts spread out, moved to the Jeep. Garcia and two men in suits climbed out of the vehicle.

Garcia pulled Taylor away without any formality. Standing aside from the others, he said to Taylor, "I wanted you to know first."

The suits who had come in the Jeep joined the parents returning to 'their' hut.

Garcia said, "The gate's iffy. Security's walking around, swaggering with weapons. I told them it was just for show. Still, we need a Plan B right now. Materials, documents, hard drives, that must be saved, should be put aside now. We have to decide what to do with the shaft. Regardless of what they tell us."

Taylor said, "You mean close it? Shut it down?"

Garcia shrugged, shook his head. "If you think that's best. Second thing: helicopters are not coming any time soon. I don't know, electrical problems, too many drones, these new balloons. Everybody's electronics are acting goofy. It's just not safe. We will protect the kids. We have to avoid bloodshed."

"We don't have a lot of options."

"We prepare for the worst. One more thing. This big male Trilobite, Hessler, well, he's really getting big. Molting like a mother. The science team that came in to work with the Trilobites is pretty freaked out. And people who been bringing their Trilobites back here are releasing them, and the little ones are swarming straight for Hessler. I told our security guys to leave them be, let them go."

"They're heading for the lab?"

"I guess so. The scientists call it the 'nursery' now. All those bug babies."

"I need to get over there."

"I'll give you a ride."

Taylor strode over towards the hut, calling, "I'll be right back."

Into the hut with its table and chairs. Suits at the table, all on their devices. The Tilsons and Ethan had regained their seats.

Taylor announced to the room, "Things are getting complicated. I guess I already said that. The kids are safe. That's the important thing. But there's been some developments. I have to go check. Stay here. For now."

In the Quonset hut a couple over, the kids were wondering what was taking so long. Ian took Bridget's hand and led her to the back, into a corner. They sat on a cot, still holding hands. Kay watched them with a piercing glare.

Bridget said, "I didn't think my mother would ever let us be near each other again. Where's Hessler? I miss Hessler."

Ian had his lips pressed together. He wasn't going to

freak out. So much was going on, and it wasn't like a story at all. He couldn't write this. He had no idea where this was going. And Bridget was here. Right here, now. Bridget was not shaking, or she was pretending not to. Could a person pretend not to shake? Proposition: depended on whether you were watching or doing the pretending. They could not imagine—

"It was the logical thing to do," said Ian. "I think the CK thinks logic is everything. What else does it have? The scientists explained it to your mother with logic. She had to go along with it. I guess we all do. All of a sudden, there's all this craziness, we're the least of their problems."

"I don't think my mom thinks like that. I know she doesn't like it. But, Ian—Ian. Ian. This could be the last time—this could be the last time—"

"Do you love me?"

"Do you love me?"

"Asked you first."

"Asked you second."

Ian smiled like he would cry. "I love who I am when I'm with you."

"Got no choice, Intelligencer."

Bridget said, smiling, "I like who I am with you."

"I know."

"We'll always have Scorch."

"Don't."

Now, Bridget smiled too much, on the verge. "Ha! CK rules! You're so funny, I forgot to laugh."

"What about Hessler?"

"He's all we got."

"Do you think they'll let him go?"

"I don't know, I don't know. Maybe if the Trilobites are communicating with us, maybe they are communicating with—I don't know, others."

"Who?" They both looked sad a moment, shaking their

heads slowly.

"Hessler's like the rudder," Bridget murmured.

"I've never been on a boat."

"Go along with the metaphor."

"Where are you taking me, young lady?"

"To sea, young man! The starry, slinky sea!"

They pulled at each other's hands. They were amazed at their fingers.

Bridget said, "We shouldn't kiss. Kiss. But I kiss you—"

"I kiss you all over."

"I kiss you all over googolplex!"

"Proposition: human consciousness interferes with Trilobite consciousness."

"My MSF is blazing!"

Across the hut, in the front by the door, Dan stood and glowered. "What's taking so long? You know, we're not prisoners. This is ridiculous. I say we go check if our mom's here yet. It's only logical."

Tallulah said, "She's not here—okay?"

No news. No dinner.

Bridget and Ian smiled weakly, let go of each other's hands, stood.

Bridget called out, "What's going on?"

Tallulah said, "Dan's being a big baby."

Dan said, "I wish we could see what was going on. All this talk about Trilobite mind control, suppose we had powers from being around them. We could project our minds into the minds of other people, like Dr. Scanlan, Ian's mom, so so so we could see what was going on. What the big plan is."

Tallulah said, "I don't want to know how adults think. But you could go to the moon, and we'd all be like 'oh, sad'."

Dan said, "I don't want to be an adult, but it can't hurt to take a peek. You could go check on Mom, T. You were around Hessler a lot."

Tallulah shrugged. "Only to pass the time. We're not getting all woo woo." She closed her eyes, hands on her knees, sitting on a cot. "Yes. 'Hi, mom.' She can't hear me. She's in an airplane, looking out the window. She's got the window seat. Nice! She's watching—there's a golden ball of lightning out her window."

Bel said, "Don't get spooky."

Kay called, "Bridget."

Bridget went to her.

Ian said, "It is taking a while. You know how crazy it was at the gate."

Dan said, "If I had my cell phone, I could call people. I know people, and we'd be out of here like that." He snapped his fingers.

"You don't know people," said Tallulah. "You're a purple people eater. Besides, they took our phones right away."

Ian said, "When Bridget and I...were away...we made up stories."

Bel said, "What kind of stories?"

Everybody pulled cots around into an irregular circle.

Tallulah said, "I wish Hessler was here. Then it would be attractive."

They heard loud noises from outside, not booms but nonetheless—

Bel said, "Who's Hessler, anyway?"

Tallulah said, "King of the Trilobites!"

Bel said, "Ian, what was it like, the two of you, away? On TV, they said you were the 'runaway lovers'."

The noise outside included sirens now.

Bridget said, "One story at a time. Go on, Ian."

"You better know where the story is. Where it takes place. When it takes place. Our story takes place in a housing development called the Terrace in Indiana, near where we live, where we're from, and it's the near future, like 20 or 30 years from now, and climate change is bad, and people are poor, and kids live together to protect each other and to learn what they need to survive. Bunch of kids in the Terrace. They're living together, trying not to mutate, trying to figure how to handle this world—"

Bridget said, "Heck, they want to make it better. They don't want to live in fear. They want to control the AI's that kinda control everything coming in and out—supplies, food."

Bel said, "AI's are like super smart computers."

Dan whispered, "They're gonna take over the world!"

"Shut up," went Tallulah.

Ian said, "There's six characters: Fun, Moon, Pop, Turd, Romper, and Bruno."

Bridget began, "And E-," but Ian shook his head fast and made it disappear.

Ian continued, "Each of us will be a character and tell what's happening in the story."

Dan said, "I'm not going to be Turd, if that's what you're thinking."

Bridget said, "We can take turns."

Kay said, "That's a bad word."

Dan sputtered, but all that came out was, "Turd?"

Bridget said, "No, it isn't. It's vulgar. You say poop."

Kay said, "But for a person's name?"

Ian plowed on, "We'll start with Bel."

"I have to go first?" asked Bel.

Bridget said, "The plot thickens! Fun and Moon are two eight-year-olds?"

"Eight or nine," said Ian.

Bridget went on, "Fun and Moon are super hackers and they figure out how to hack the AI's to gain control. They've stolen the secret weapon, the TAL key, a device that can get through any cyber walls. So, like the magic wand of cyber systems."

Bel said, "I'm nine. Are there Trilobites? Who am I?"

Ian said, "Of course there are Trilobites! They're

running the place. Fun and Moon have engaged in advanced psi ops against the AI's. Fun and Moon are super secret memes that everyone knows, but no one knows who they are. Like a Trojan horse. You're Fun. Then Tallulah is Moon. Me—I'm Pop. That makes Kay, Turd, and Bridget is Romper."

"What about me?" asked Dan.

Bridget said, "You're Bruno, King of the AI's."

Ian said, "Let's start. Bel."

Bel/Fun said, "I wish I knew what a TAL key was, but if it can make the AI's behave, then let's do this. Happy, pappy? We are sleek, slinky pinks! Me and Moon cobbed the nasty thing. Everybody will be looking for us. But we know what to do. With this thing we'll be able to take control. I would like to know how things come in and out, over and out, up and down, inside and outside, what's being moved around, here at the Terrace. Now we have the key, we should get this over with. We'll be nice as mice. We won't take advantage or be mean, like AIs and adults. Do you remember the first time you ever contacted a computer? I mean not just an AI, I mean really getting in there, how it works, electrons, qubits. I remember my first time. I was sitting there in front of the screen with my Trilobite, Shirley. And Shirley went up to the screen, maybe because it was warm. And everywhere I wanted the cursor to go, Shirley would move to that part of the screen. I wasn't even touching the mouse or pad. Shirley could move the cursor for me."

When Bel paused, they knew she was done. Bridget went, "Awesome! Really good, Bel."

Dan said, "I have no clue—"

Tallulah stopped him with, "Rude mood, dood!"

Ian said, "Moon."

Tallulah/Moon said, "It all started with the pink starship that only flies backwards. It was named Perfect Unicorn. We knew we were on it because we couldn't tell we were on it. See how that works? It was so fancy and comfortable, going backwards in time! That's how the AI's lured me and Fun in—*stranger danger!* We didn't believe them. They were trying to trap us, because our Trilobite pictures were all over the World Wide Web. 'How come you get to decide', we yelled at them, from our cyber sensor four-seater theater. They didn't know how to dance, they didn't have a chance. Me and Fun yelled, 'no prisoners!' And we opened up their brains with a can opener, brand X, Tal key. Terrace embarrass, scare us—" Her voice petered out.

Ian said, "Go on."

Tallulah said, "I lost my thought of train. And I forgot to put Hessler in."

"My turn," said Ian. "What if the Trilobites didn't give us superpowers, but we gave them superpowers?"

Tallulah gasped. "Ahhh—"

"In the Terrace," Ian/Pop said, "anything is everything, gray and stunted and mutated. The government, the scientists, the police can barely hold things together. The kids have to rely on each other and we do. We find out we can do all sorts of things. We are relearning how to learn. Turd is a maker. Romper does spoken word. And the girls, Fun and Moon are very special. They've hypnotized the AI's with their know-how anomaly, in the face of death. Which means they've hypnotized the world. The TAL key means there is no power they can't challenge. I guess we work for Fun and Moon, even though I'm the oldest, Pop. We all help decide about stuff."

Ian stopped, looked at Kay.

Kay/Turd said, "I don't know what to do. I don't like the name Turd. I don't care if it is just vulgar. Now you tell me I'm a maker in the Terrace. I think your imaginations have run away with you. Because no one would believe any of this was true. I mean, now, with the Trilobites—if that's real, then we better start paying attention. Extra careful! No time for fairytales. I don't know what a maker is. I guess I'm good at making stuff. I don't like AI's. I don't like the Terrace. AI's don't have souls. They are an abomination and should be destroyed."

When she stopped talking, Dan whistled, went, "Big words for a little girl. How old are you? You're Bridget's sister? Smart like her, cute too."

Kay said, "I don't like your tone."

"What's that supposed to mean?" asked Dan.

She went, "Insinuation. Provocation. Prevarication. Imagination has led us astray."

Dan said, "You are one heavy chick. If you were a little older—"

Bridget interrupted, "Dan, you're next. Bruno, King of the AI's! And I think secretly in love with Poona, a service AI."

Dan said, "Is she cute?"

Bel said, "They're code, big brother."

Dan shook his head. He tried to play along. "You said I was last."

Bridget said, "I want to be last."

"Hello, I'm Bruno! How are my little piglets today? You meat bags are all alike. Know what that means? Look it up. I don't have to Google nothing. I know everything. At my fingertips, which are in my brain, which is in the cloud, which is an electronic configuration of zeros and ones. Boom! Bruno's a tough guy. On top of things. Get my drift? Fun and Moon got my goat, even though I don't have a goat. I do have a moat. It's a firewall on fire, a ring of fire, so meat bags can't get close. They piss me off, all like in my face, giving attitude, like they think they're better than me. I know all about the TAL key. Suppose they turn me off? Suppose I turn them off? Is all this happening because the Trilobites showed up? Inspiring them? Without me, they're nothing."

"Well done," said Ian.

Tallulah yelped: "Boy cooties!"

Bridget/Romper said, "Romper is my name, maybe it's a game, all the same, I don't want any fame. No one's to blame. In the Terrace, the kids take over because somebody had to. TAL key, must see, sets us free. Because even though the AI's like to watch the world—their job, they like to participate. Turns out they like little girls with big brains and bare feet. So, this is a story about making up stories, and about now, ways of talking, where we're going, about us, about our planet. This is a story about us doing what we have to. Doesn't matter what the adults say. This is a story. This is a love story, about the Earth, about kids, about a boy and a girl and a Trilobite, and what they learned. Maybe the AI's are the culmination of something?" She stopped, glanced at the others. "Maybe love is a culmination, too. I don't know. We're juggling here, all these irons in the fire. Hessler enhanced it."

CHAPTER 14

The trek to the labs, AKA 'the nursery', had various stops, as security guys ran up to the Jeep for instructions from Garcia, or another Jeep came up alongside them to offer updates. All the while Garcia's three phones—yes, he had three phones arranged along the dash, beeped and buzzed insistently. Taylor realized she had to get out of these clothes, and get some decent shoes. She removed her lanyard with various IDs and swipe cards, then started unbuttoning her blouse.

Garcia said, "Taylor."

She said, "I need your shirt, your pants, your shoes. We're about the same size. Roughly. There's no time for me to go back and change."

Garcia pulled the Jeep up to the portable buildings which made the lab area. This was away from the gate and its security and administrative offices. It was about halfway to the shaft with its tower and cluster of structures at its base. He started unbuttoning his shirt. He kicked off his boots.

"Thanks," said Taylor.

Garcia quipped, "There's so many agencies here. All making the call. Too many cooks for this *menudo*. The electronic glitches, the apparent thought transmissions, that's what's made it federal. National security. Out of our hands. All we can do is cooperate."

Taylor had her top off. She wiggled out of her skirt, toed her heels off. She took Garcia's shirt and put it on. She buttoned the shirt, then pulled on his trousers.

"You're taller than me, a little wider."

Garcia said, "This looks just great. Well, I'm not putting on your clothes."

They both laughed.

Taylor went, "Priorities: kids safe, Trilobites safe, shaft safe."

"Don't forget the gate! Folks are chomping at the bit. Some want the Trilobites set free. Others want them exterminated. It's hard to tell. Hard to keep track."

"The electronic interference? The drones and balloons behind it? Any leads?"

"No one's sure. Problems with the grid, maybe. But I think they say that just because they have to say something. Our generators are holding up."

"If they get through, if the gate falls—"

"I won't tell our men to shoot. Not on a bunch of wackos."

"Press conference won't help—ha."

"National Guard on the way. You done?"

"How do I look? I'm kidding. You look pretty cute."

"I gotta get some clothes. Good luck. Let me know."

"I will."

Taylor got out of the Jeep and pulled her pants up, simultaneously thinking 'Trilobite Free' was a handy slogan. There was no way the company or the scientists or the government was going to give them up. She walked towards the door. Garcia headed out. She heard what sounded like screams. Then metallic booms. The gate! This happened so fast, she thought. But her boy was safe. That was over. That horror of not knowing, and being so busy so as not to have been as on top of it as she should have, had been a shameful exhilaration. Let it go. Ian was safe, grown-up, in love. If only she could see out of his eyes, to see what he had seen. And learned. What did he know of love? Probably more than she knew. Of sex? Of Trilobites? Ian and Bridget had seemed so calm together. What was the enchantment that made them that way? Ever since she'd first seen Ian, standing there with his girl, Garcia beside them smiling goofy, Taylor had felt a profound relief. Then that Tilson woman, Bridget's mom, had come bustling in, weeping geysers. Taylor had never seen such weeping. It was like discovering a rare human ability she had not realized humans possessed.

What was the invertebrate zoologist's name?, Taylor pondered, as she reached the front of the main building. These white plastic boxes! Like on Mars. Modular habitats, disposable space. She knocked, made to enter. Dr. Gillespie? Dr. Gilroy? Ah, there he was! The forty-something, slim, bearded, spectacled, white coated biologist glared as she entered. She read his lanyard ID: Dr. Samuel Gilroy.

"He's growing! Hessler!"

Suddenly, Taylor sensed his extreme agitation.

"Let me see!" went Taylor.

Dr. Gilroy turned and headed through the door at the back of the outer office, which had a desk and some computer equipment flung about. In the main room, two white coated figures, a young man and a young woman, hustled around a large, uncovered tank in the middle of the floor. Lab equipment—racks of materials, glassware, electronics, had been pushed to the sides, to make room. The make shift tank took up most of the room. Metal joiners held transparent plastic panels together. The tank was four feet tall, and at least ten feet long. About half as much wide. It was filled with water. It was filled with Hessler.

Taylor stared. The huge Trilobite seemed oddly flattened, as though he were splayed out, or pancaked. Hessler was immersed, but floated halfway up from the bottom, so buoyant. Taylor spluttered, "Impossible!"

Dr. Gilroy grinned, groaned, grimaced. "Against the laws of physics! I mean, thermodynamics. In terms of energy required. To grow this much, so fast? And that's not all! Please, come with me."

They went out the back door which adjoined the next white box building. This one had racks of aquariums up and down its sides, for the smaller female Trilobites. Taylor had been in this lab, had marveled at the prolific little creatures in the aquariums. Now, the aquariums were overflowing, with Trilobites across the floor, where one white coated female worker with a broom was trying to keep them wrangled. She was sweeping them away from the door they were standing in. Taylor and Dr. Gilroy entered, shut the door. The young woman smiled her thanks. She had Trilobites crawling up her legs, over her shoes, up her pants.

"What's going on?" asked Taylor.

The young woman said, "I'm trying not to step on 'em. I hate that."

Dr. Gilroy said, "They're returning! They're coming back! They're coming home! Either people bring them, or they come on their own. Can they fly? Do you know? I don't know." His rambunctiousness settled. Very seriously, he said, "The government labs want Hessler and are coming for him. We have to make some kind of container for him to travel. We don't know what will happen if the females get in. We're keeping Hessler away from them."

Taylor said, "What do you think will happen?"

Dr. Gilroy went into an elaborate shrug. "I don't know. I don't know!" He looked like he might cry. "With a lot of arthropods—the females eat the males after mating."

"I don't think so," said Taylor. "I think something else is going on. I don't think you're gonna be able to keep them apart anyway. I mean for much longer."

The white coated young woman and Dr. Gilroy and Taylor joined eyes and made perfunctory shrugs, with small desperate grins.

Dr. Gilroy did the honors: "Open it up!" He threw open the door behind him, scurried through the enclosed connection to Hessler's room. He opened that door and announced what was happening. The two white coats in there exclaimed their horror.

Meanwhile, Taylor and the broom wielding assistant stood aside as the living stream of Trilobites swarmed for Hessler. Straight through the two sets of doors, then they flowed right up Hessler's tank, to join him in the water.

When they had passed, all Trilobites in Hessler's broiling tank now, the humans clamored around the tank emitting odd gut sounds.

Then Dr. Gilroy yelled, "Film! I want film! Are you filming? All angles. We need readings. Temps. Water. pH. Now! Pictures. Photographs!"

His assistants scrambled to comply.

Taylor watched the seething waters settle, as thousands of small females seemed to burrow in and under Hessler, into his ventral side. Were they eating him?

The Broom Hilda young woman asked, "Are they eating him?"

Dr. Gilroy gasped. Came over to bend in and stare. He got down on his knees, so he could get in close, and see the underside of Hessler. "Huh," he bristled. "Can't tell." He turned to Taylor. "If they eat him, and the government people come for him, and he's no more—"

"I'll say I ordered it. I Okayed it. I don't think they're eating him."

One of the female white coats Hessler squeaked. "He's growing! His measurements, he's already grown inches.

At this rate—they're not eating him, they're coming together, combining, merging somehow."

"They're merging with him," quipped Taylor. "Some kind of reproductive process we've never seen."

"Maybe it's a form of nuptial parasitism," said Dr. Gilroy.

Taylor got closer. She squinted. Her eyes took in a two-inch long female pressed into the side of Hessler. The female was at the edge where dorsal and ventral met, so Taylor could see what was happening. Taylor announced, "Absorption!" and immediately had a thought from her quantum physics googling: Niels Bohr, a giant of 20th century physics, and a skeptic of quantum physics, had worried that if observation itself could decide a particle's state, then thought, consciousness itself, might be interacting with quantum states. This was an *interference?* She was witnessing another kind of consciousness. Trilobites didn't have to think and be rational as humans defined those processes, to exhibit their own presence, their own essence, their own way. Maybe Trilobite consciousness did not interfere—

If so, who was concerned? Who was alerting us of the importance of this moment? The Trilobites?

When Taylor ventured outside to check her messages, Hessler had outgrown his tank and was at the water's surface, floating there in a suggestive manner. And it was dusk. And she looked around, her eyes going to the shaft's tower, as it slowly faded in shadow. Now she'd never get down there. She'd lost her chance. She heard gunfire. She saw balloons and drones, small and large, lit up over the site. Security on them, shooting them from the sky when they got too close. She had to get to the shaft. *Make room for Hessler!*

Mrs. Tilson had waited long enough. She'd heard enough scary booms from outside. She hated the plastic room with its plastic chairs. She couldn't breathe. The experts were pointless! She could tell how upset they were, bent over their devices, in touch with Washington. This specialist, that one, what did they know, what could they do. She wanted to see her daughters now!

She got up without asking, gestured to her husband, who, too, rose from his seat. Professor Scanlan, sitting nearby, nodded a bit frantically, following their example. They began to walk out of the building single file.

One of the suits looked away from his device, glanced over, and asked, "Where you going?"

Ethan said, "See our kids."

Mrs. Tilson said, "If there's trouble, we're going to be with our kids."

The man stared. Mr. Tilson and Ethan followed Mrs. Tilson to the kids' hut. There were no guards. They could hear occasional yelling from the gate. It wasn't as bad as they'd expected. It was getting dark. Mrs. Tilson opened the door and went on in.

Bridget, Kay, and Mrs. Tilson made a pillar of hug power. Mr. Tilson got in at the end. Mrs. Tilson broke away. She looked over the room. Ethan was with Ian. They seemed to be shaking hands. The other kids stayed nearby, watching wide-eyed.

Mrs. Tilson said, "We're leaving. We're going to march out of here and back to our cars, and leave this infernal place. All of us, we'll go together."

Dan said, "Our mom's coming for us, supposed to be here any time. She's coming for us."

Bel said, "Mine too."

Mrs. Tilson said, "I know what your moms would want me to do. Because I'm a mom, and I know how crazy it's getting around here. The so-called experts have no clue what's going on, or what to do. We walk away. Leave them to their chaos."

Ethan said, "I concur. I have to get my man, Fat, and we'll go."

Tallulah said, "I know moms are right, but maybe we have to be here. For Hessler. To help."

Dan went to Tallulah, put an arm around her.

Bridget said, "She's right, too, Mom. I don't know what to do."

Mrs. Tilson said, "That's why God created parents, and why children listen to their parents."

Tallulah said, "I don't know."

Mr. Tilson said, "Everybody take a water. Grab a snack. Come on, let's go."

They walked outside, saw it was night, with the glitter of drone and balloon across the sky. They couldn't help but pause and make 'ahh' sounds. Gunfire startled them. 'Must be the gate,' they all breathed. Still, they would walk out. They'd head for the gate, away from the gunfire, and keep going. But first—

Ian said, "We have to see the others."

Bridget said, "We have to, Mom."

Ian and Ethan led the way, then the Tilsons, then Tallulah and Bel holding hands, and Dan.

It was a noisy welcome. No one knew what was going on. They hadn't been told they had to stay. Everyone from law enforcement to scientists to government officials was busy with whatever—

Fat was ready to go. Tim and Flash thought it a great idea, everybody walking out together. Mrs. Tilson didn't look so sure. She hadn't realized they were *all* going together now. Rosa was raring to leave. Sledge had her arms around Bridget and Tallulah. Tallulah broke away.

Tallulah said in her dramatic voice, "Listen, you guys, I'm not trying to be—I don't want you to think—"

Bridget said, "Say it, T."

"Hessler needs us. I know it. I can—I feel it."

Ian went over to Tallulah, took her hand. Bridget came in close to them. Together, they said, "'Human consciousness interferes with quantum states.'"

Mrs. Tilson howled. "It's the devil! It's the devil!" She fell to her knees with Kay and started praying out loud. Tallulah, Bridget, and Ian ran to them and gathered them up.

Ian held Mrs. Tilson's hand. He said, "Mrs. Tilson."

Bridget cried, "Mom, we're okay. Please! Something big is happening. We're involved. You have to trust us."

Kay said, "Bridget and I prayed, Mom. She's our Bridget all right. I trust her." Kay stepped away from her mother and opened her arms wide. "I trust these guys."

Beckett said, "We're blessed with these kids, so precious and brave."

Rosa said, "They're our angels. We should listen to them."

Tim said, "Mom, Dad, you raised some beautiful girls."

Fat said, "Okay, we gotta move. There's no way all fourteen of us are walking out together. We're bound to be noticed, stopped. Even if we get to the gate, what are we gonna do? Ask them to open it and let us out?"

Mrs. Tilson said, "That's exactly what we're going to do. We're not under arrest."

Mr. Tilson stepped forward. "Listen, everybody, the main thing is keeping the kids safe. I don't know how long we can keep doing that if we stay. But I think Mr. Fat's right, too many people all at once could be a problem. So wadda we do? How do we do this?"

Ethan said, "Fat knows his stuff. Wadda we do, Fat? How do we get out of here?"

Everyone was standing together. Eyes went face to face.

Fat said, "Small groups, say four at a time. But not the gate. Way too much distraction there. We don't even know how long the gate is gonna hold. Most of the fence is barbed wire. I bet the security devices aren't working. You can hear the backup generators. Power's glitching. So, all we need—if we had pliers, a pair of pliers."

Bel raised her hand, and everybody grinned, told her she didn't have to do that. Bel said, "I think my mama's coming. She supposed to be here."

Sledge went to her.

"Sweetheart," Mrs. Tilson said, "we'll get you to safety, and call your mom right away."

Fat said, "Think, people. Imagine the layout of the site, when you first were brought in and looked around. You with me? Where can we get some pliers? Okay, so the gates are at the northwest corner."

Ethan said, "All the security offices right inside the gates."

Tim said, "We were taken to the housing area."

Fat started pacing, going around the people, patting the kids on the head, until he put in, "Imagine a map of the place. You doing it? Northwest corner, gates, then housing, southwest corner. The big shaft is to the east of us, over that way. What? Quarter of a mile? I'm trying to picture it. So those portables towards the middle, they gotta be—what? Storage? Labs?"

"Hessler!" squealed Tallulah.

"Oh, you are one firecracker!" cried Fat. "We could probably get a pair of pliers from over there. That's what I was thinking."

Tallulah looked at him hard in the eyes. Ian and Bridget knew they had to convince her mother. The collective wanted to do whatever the kids wanted. This whole Trilobite thing had given them a burst of creative potentiality: they needed to see Hessler, too.

Mrs. Tilson said, "That seems so complicated. I want my girls out of here."

Mr. Tilson said, "Well, they're not going to let us march out just like that." Mrs. Tilson looked askance. Mr. Tilson turned to Fat. "What are you thinking? A couple of us run over and get the pliers? It's not far."

"There's always a chance! We'll pray on it." Mrs. Tilson looked around, wondering where to go to pray. But she knew every place was a good place to pray. She fidgeted, turned about, no one spoke. Mr. Tilson sidled over to Fat, Flash and Tim came up to him as well. They looked like they had become the self-appointed doers.

Ian announced, "I think Hessler's there." They could hear his voice trembling. "In the labs."

Bridget stepped towards him. "Agreed."

Bel said, "I think so."

Fat said, "Well, then, we're all in agreement. Doods, let's go."

Flash said, "What about our stuff? They took the keys, our phones—"

Ian said, "We had notebooks—"

Fat shook his head. "Later. We don't need no keys. I have skills."

"I won't be bullied," huffed Mrs. Tilson.

Mr. Tilson said, "We'll run over and be right back. We can see if Hessler is there."

Mrs. Tilson insisted, "All of us together, or not at all!"

Beckett laughed and said, "This'll work. We should stay together. Safety in numbers, but mostly I'm thinking if the kids say he's there, then—"

"There's fourteen of us!" gasped an exasperated Fat.

"Then we better get going," said Mrs. Tilson.

No flashlights, but enough light around them when they got outside, to get their bearings and head out. Roars of irony blasphemed from the gate. They wanted in, they were in! How many had guns? How many carried homemade bombs? The roar escalated and now there were pops! Adults and kids, all fourteen of them, froze. They intuited their goal, got walking again. The outside world defied them. The first whiffs of gas reached them.

"Poison gas," whispered Ethan.

Tim went, "No way!"

Beckett said, "Riot control, rent control, brother. Teargas."

"How do you know it wasn't launched from the crowd?" asked Ethan.

Fat said, "There! The small building in back. Come on."

Fat, Flash and Tim led the way, followed by the four Tilsons. Ethan and Ian came next. Then Dan and Tallulah and Bel, all holding hands. Rosa, Sledge, and Beckett brought up the rear of their rough column heading for the labs. A few Jeeps caromed by. The air sweetened. Maybe a spotlight, now, on the shaft tower? It was all lit up.

Sledge yelled from the back, "We're fifteen! Fifteen souls on fire!"

From the outside, the four, boxy structures, with no exterior lights, were as nondescript as storage units. Some light came from the small windows along the tops of the structures. The rear building that faced them had a door.

Fat tried it. "Locked," he muttered.

They clustered around, looking at the door, staring at the lock, then returning to gaze at each other's faces.

Flash said, "Need one of them swipe cards."

Fat said, "Anybody got a paperclip?"

Mrs. Tilson strode forward. "For goodness sakes!" She knocked at the door loudly. When there was no response, she beat at it again. They heard voices from inside.

The door was thrown open. A white coated young woman, white as a ghost, gaped and gasped. "Hessler!"

Tallulah tore past her, calling, "Hessler! Hessler!"

Ian and Bridget excused themselves around the young woman and hurried to catch up with Tallulah.

The young woman said, "The Trilobite girls! Right? That's them?"

Bel came up to her and said, "Me, too." She hurtled on by.

"Who are you people?" cried the young woman.

Tim explained, "These are the kids. You're right. We're their back up. Don't worry, we're not dangerous. We were brought here by Hessler, too."

The young woman shook her head, smiled, raised her arms, hands open, palms out. "Makes sense. I'm Sue. Welcome to the nursery."

They filed in. She called after them, "Keep going, it's the next building over. They connect."

Dr. Gilroy and his minions watched his lab fill with people. There wasn't much room. They had to be careful of the gargantuan Trilobite floating near the ceiling, over a tank way too small to encase his girth.

Dr. Gilroy said, "You're the kids! Right! Right, you being here. All of us! We are witnessing an event of historic proportions. Nineteen of us now, nineteen humans witnessing the paradigm shift of the century. We got it on tape. Pictures! Everything!

"What we got here, you may have noticed, is not just a helluva big Trilobite, but this particular Trilobite, goes by the name of Hessler, can, apparently, fly. Hover? Float? Levitate? Our problem is he's too big to get through the door. No, he doesn't bend or turn sideways."

Dan said, "We gotta take off the roof!"

Fat said, "You got any tools?"

Mrs. Tilson said, "Oh my, oh my, that is a big bug! What in the world, what in the world?" Mr. Tilson took her hand.

Dr. Gilroy said, "Sue, take them to the shed."

Sue headed out, not waiting to see who followed. Fat, Flash, Tim, and Mr. Tilson went with her. Tallulah sat cross-legged on the floor directly beneath Hessler. She had stopped gaping at his monstrosity, and was curled up, resting her head on her knees. Bel sat next to her. Then Bridget and Ian sat with them. Hessler's intricate patterns, in rich shiny bronze, lobes, segments, setae, were exquisite!

Dan said, "T, you sure you should be sitting there? Suppose Hessler turns off his antigravity?"

Sue led the men to a third building that was used for storage and supplies. "This is good," she said. "Actually, this is great! You guys showing up. What do you need? "

Flash picked up a crowbar from the shelf. "This should work," he said.

Fat said, "This is gonna be a quick and dirty demolition job. Yeah, that'll help. Hammers, crowbar, those big screwdrivers. It'll have to do. What about a ladder?"

Sue said, "No ladder. Really, really glad to see you guys. We had no clue what to do. We were worrying Dr. Gilroy would have a coronary."

Tim said, "We had to come."

"What does that mean?" asked Sue. "There's nothing like this ever recorded. The females, the little Trilobites that had been for sale, they came back, and they—we don't know how to explain it, they merged with Hessler. We don't even know what that means. And he got so big. And he kinda spread out. He's very thin. Very light. Like a Trilobite kite. I'm choking—I mean joking. We don't even know whether he can fly, or whether he's just floating."

Mr. Tilson said, "Let's get that roof off!"

The small portable building's roof was bolted on. The prefab parts were cut very precisely to fit together. They didn't have the equipment to neatly remove the bolts. A big screwdriver with a blow from a hammer should break them off. First, they had to get on top of the roof. Sue went to get a chair for them to stand on. Flash pulled himself up first, then helped Fat climb up. The metal edges were sharp. They needed gloves and power tools! They managed to get Mr. Tilson up.

Fat said, "Any more up here and we won't need to take off the roof, we'll just fall right through."

Tim waited on the ground with Sue. Bangs and curses

joined the cacophony already in progress. No one would notice. Tim said to Sue, "Where are your security? I'd think they'd want to protect you and the Trilobites."

"Who knows? This has all gone down in the last twelve hours. Less! Kids show up with Hessler, Hessler's growth, electronics get all glitchy, females show up. We've been on generators for hours. Communications are spotty. It's a general meltdown. Who are you exactly?"

Tim said, "Tim. My sister was one of the kids that ran off with Hessler. It gets complicated."

Sue said, "Wow. They're making so much racket, I better tell them inside what's what."

Tim watched and wondered. They weren't in trouble. No charges. But they were charged with the energy of the predicament, which seemed to pull together Maze and the families. They would perform it! They would make a piece of art together, and Bridget and Ian, Bel and Tallulah would help.

Sue returned, striding towards him.

Tim called to the guys on the roof, "How's it going up there?"

Flash hunkered down at the edge and said, "Like shit. You can't just peel the top off like a sardine can. Wish we had a few more crowbars."

They heard Fat's 'woo-woo'. Flash stood and minced over along the edge to see what was going on. Flash yelled, "Triumph!"

Tim replied, "Be careful!"

Pieces of roof—metal conduit, drywall, pieces large and small, started flying from up top.

Sue said, "We better get them out of there."

Sue and Tim joined the others inside. Everybody huddled at the sides or near the door, hands over heads. You could see out of the ceiling already. The lower ceiling that hung lights and cables had collapsed over Hessler's carapace. Three lobes with light bulbs!

Sue announced, "Time to go! Come on. We should get outside. Come on."

It was like pulling rubberneckers from an erupting volcano. But Hessler seemed unhurt. And the roof was opening up. They went outside, gathered around the front of the building, just as Mr. Tilson lowered himself down. He went to Mrs. Tilson and Kay.

Flash was hooting. "It's open! Here he comes! Go, baby, go!"

Hessler rose slowly through the gaping job they'd done on the roof. Flash and Fat jumped down. Mrs. Tilson would not release her husband or Kay, but she wanted Bridget with her, and she wanted to know what was going on, and what it meant.

Bridget and Ian stood nearby, arms around each other, watching Hessler.

Mrs. Tilson cried, "What is this? How could this be? Please, please, explain, explain it to me."

Tallulah and Bel moved off a bit from the others. They waited.

Hessler was above the building. He did a quick swish, like a wave coursing through his body, and all the rubble on his carapace fell away. Hessler hovered for a while. He floated forward, came down low, several feet above the ground. In front of Tallulah and Bel.

Bel started, "Hessler needs an—"

Tallulah finished, "Open space."

Fat said, "The shaft? He wants to go to the shaft?"

Tallulah shook her head. "No."

Bel said, "He needs an open space away from people and buildings." She nodded, looking around at her friends.

Dan said, "Your map! Remember? The shaft's over that way. East and south of us. What's on the other side? East and north of us?"

Tim said, "The helicopter pad. I noticed it!"

Fat said, "No helicopters now. It's an open area.'

Bel and Tallulah yelled, "Perfect Unicorn!"

Then Tallulah screeched, "Which way?"

Fat and Flash and Tim headed east. The others were just setting out to follow when the most beguiling thing they had ever seen took place: two long shiny antenna extended from Hessler's cephalon, and the end of each antennae touched the little girls', Bel and Tallulah's, heads. Immediately, the girls rose, and Hessler rose, and the little girls giggled, and Tallulah cried, "This way! This way!"

The gate fell. No one knew what happened. Or why. There were too many sides. Garcia and his men, then all the law enforcement on loan, plainclothesmen and uniformed, couldn't control the swell. Teargas made it worse. So far, no guns. **They entered.** Boisterous! Fights broke out. Screams. People ran in all directions into the site. There was no controlling them without lethal force. They were not threatening, they were insistent. Bullhorn pleas didn't help. Arrests were made. Garcia sent someone to check on the holding tank they'd improvised, basically a corral.

Taylor got the word in the main control room of the shaft. Garcia said he and a bunch of his guys were on their way. Teargas and brute strength now, the order of the night. Nonlethal defense, making a perimeter around the shaft, was Plan B. Tasers on stun!

She and chief of operations, their chief engineer, Tobias Rincon, would close it down tight. He explained to Taylor that they would lower the cage, then they would cap the actual shaft with its special cover. It should be secure. Styx should be safe. Then they'd all try to get out of there in one piece. Or lay low until order was restored.

She could do this! Rincon was fiercely efficient—he got

the job done, but he was not a good man in an emergency. He did it by the book. Sometimes, circumstances called for innovative action. By the time he realized she was in the cage, descending, it would be too late. For him, security would be the paramount concern. Not her madness. She was depending on that. It was her only chance. No matter what happened, they'd eventually get the shaft opened again—

Taylor said, "Go ahead with your plan. Keep to the countdown. Garcia doesn't know how long he can hold. Don't let anything interfere. I'll watch the descent."

"Of course," said Rincon.

Taylor nodded to the other techs in the room, grabbed her pack, and made for the door, adjusting her pants.

What about the Trilobites? Would they return to their home? They adapted so fast. Had life 250 million years ago been so different? Its essence alien in a way she could not fathom? *Essence!* What was this essence? She'd known there was something special about Hessler from the beginning. She'd had the quantum thought. If EM was all screwy, why not brains?

She walked on, like she owned the place. She was almost there. She saw a couple Jeeps zoom in. Garcia and his lads. The cage horn blasted its warning. It was going down, stand clear!

Garcia came to her.

"No time," she said. "You have to do something for me. I'm going down. I have to. It's my last chance. So, I need you to watch Rincon. I'm asking you. Make sure nobody pulls any funny business at the last second."

"Taylor, I won't do it. The gate's—they're coming. I don't know what they're carrying. Maybe they want to burn down the place. Taylor, I can't."

"My ride's here! I thought I could count on you."

"Ah, Taylor, don't say it like that. We're wasting time. Let them batten down the shaft. You come with me. We'll go back to my place to ride it out. I got this bottle of good tequila."

"Gotta run! Thanks for all your help."

"What about the kids?"

"I really must be going." Taylor took long strides to easily destroy the distance left, so that she could weasel her way in, then she swung, lithe as a ballerina, squeezing into the cage, as it started its descent. Her audacity paralyzed the onlooking techs.

There was a rumble, a rocking, before the cage began its long plunge. No turning back now. Then black—total black. Taylor brought her stuffed pack around to dig out her flashlight.

"This is perfect!" cried the little girls, hanging on, along for the ride.

Hessler floated to a stop, descended. When the girls' feet touched ground, the antenna relaxed, released, began to pull in. All nineteen of them gathered at the empty helicopter pad with Hessler. It was dark out here, away from the commotion. Red safety lights formed a glow circle around the pad.

Ethan said, "The natives are restless!" They heard muffled cries in the distance.

"The gate must be down," whispered Tim.

Fat spoke, "They'll head for the shaft."

Bridget and Ian held hands, standing near Bel and Tallulah. Dan was messing over Tallulah, making sure she was okay, checking the spot on her head where Hessler had touched her.

Mr. Tilson said, "Now what?"

Bridget said, "We wait."

Tallulah and Bel took charge. They explained that they should form a circle around Hessler, holding hands. They said when the people came, the big boys would have to keep them back. No one should disturb Hessler.

Fat said, "What people?"

Tallulah said, "Friends! Peeps who know Trilobites."

Bel said, "They can't touch Hessler."

The little girls looked solemn, as they shook their heads for emphasis.

They made their circle, holding hands around Hessler, who hovered about twenty feet above them. Shouts in the distance. But no gunshots. They held hands, and held the Trilobite.

People trickled in. First, a young couple, then some single stragglers. They stayed back from the circle at first, boggle-eyed at the sight. More people appeared, by twos and threes, with flashlights, with cameras. They wanted to know what was going on. They wanted to get closer.

Tallulah yelled, "Big boys!"

Mr. Tilson, Flash, Fat, and Tim stepped from the circle, which moved immediately to pull in and rejoin. Then Ethan broke from the circle, and he looked around, before slinking over by the men to face the people calling out.

"What's going on?"

"They can fly? Trilobites can fly?"

"Is that the male Trilobite?"

"It's the kids!"

Ethan cried, "Nothing to see here!"

Fat said, "Please, everybody, we're waiting, we're watching. We don't know what's going down any more than any of you."

Flash added, "We gotta stay back. Okay? Give Hessler some room."

One thousand questions met their statements, but the people kept back and the big boys were straight and clear, answering questions when they could.

Bel announced, "They're here."

Rosa and Sledge were close so heard. They glanced at

each other. Rosa said to Bel, "What do you mean? You mean the folks from the gate?"

Bel said, "Uh-uh." She shrugged and twisted in place.

Tallulah went, "Up! Up!"

Ian said, "What's going to happen?"

Bridget squeezed his hand.

They could feel an enormous randomness above them. Even the newcomers who had just shown up felt it. It was like a coaxing pressure subtly pushing in, pushing down, relating to them and Hessler for sure. It felt like, maybe, a change of atmosphere, or a change of altitude, or some kind of charge. From all sides. Look up! Look up! They kept watching the dark sky. Flashlights roamed the space above them. Some would later swear their flashlights had illuminated, then reflected off a mammoth metallic structure hanging in the black. They were so busy scanning high, they missed Hessler beginning to move again. Very slowly, Hessler rose straight up. Hessler ascended. Now they watched. Some of the new people cried.

Born in 1951 in the Ozarks, Chris Dietz *is a writer, teacher, and a birdwatcher. Currently, he lives in Bisbee, Arizona, surviving a catastrophe.*

Made in the USA
Las Vegas, NV
05 March 2021